U.S.
Marshals

U.S. Marshals

by Max Allan Collins

Based upon the motion picture
written by John Pogue and on
characters created by
Roy Huggins

BOULEVARD BOOKS, NEW YORK

U.S. MARSHALS

A Berkley Boulevard Book/published by arrangement with
Warner Bros.

PRINTING HISTORY
Berkley Boulevard edition/March 1998

The Penguin Putnam Inc. World Wide Web site address is
http://www.penguinputnam.com

ISBN: 0-425-16438-1

BERKLEY BOULEVARD
Berkley Boulevard Books are published by The Berkley Publishing Group,
a member of Penguin Putnam Inc.,
200 Madison Avenue, New York, New York 10016.
BERKLEY BOULEVARD and its logo are trademarks belonging to
Berkley Publishing Corporation.

PRINTED IN THE UNITED STATES OF AMERICA

10 9 8 7 6 5 4 3 2 1

For Greg Ballard—
sound man

"At the heart of *The Fugitive* is the preoccupation with guilt and salvation which has been called the Great American Theme."

—ROY HUGGINS

U.S.
Marshals

One

For a fugitive, the best place to hide is often in the open. On this mildly overcast fall afternoon in Chicago, Illinois, the towers of the city looming in all their geometric glory, the man behind the wheel of a Powkowski Towing truck, hauling a crushed Ford station wagon from a southside accident to a northside garage, was hiding among millions of people. A good number of them were black, as was he— just another working stiff among countless working stiffs, driving along scenic Lake Shore Drive among thousands of drivers, one more grain of sand on the nearby beach, just another ant among an anthill army, carting his bread crumb to its destination.

He was also hiding behind a name, which was partly his own—Mark, consistent with the patch of his work shirt, was indeed his first name, the very one provided by his late, devoutly Baptist mother (just ask his older brother, Matthew, or younger brother, Luke—there had been no John). But Warren was not his surname; Sheridan was. He couldn't use Sheridan, because Mark Sheridan had killed two men.

Actually, he had killed more than two men, in his time, but these two particular killings (not, in his view, murders) were the reason he had become Mark Warren, why he had constructed a life to become invisible within, while he decided what to do about what had been done to him.

"Headin' back to base," he reported into his CB mike. "Driver walked away, but his wheels need a priest, not a mechanic."

He had not expected to become quite so comfortable in this temporary life; he'd always been mechanically adept and had already received two raises at Powkowski's. He had not been a fugitive long enough to know how dangerous it was for him to feel this comfortable, to be able to get lost (as he was now) in the sound of Otis Redding's voice on that oldies station, paying more attention to whistling along with "Dock of the Bay" than the police scanner he also had going.

Sheridan even had a lady in his life, which was not unusual, considering his lean, sinewy frame, and his well-chiseled features. And, of course, he had not counted on falling in love. But who does?

Nor had he counted on Craig Opelt, vice president of marketing for Computer Software Services International, to be tearing his assistant a new asshole, right then; the assistant had forgotten to remind Opelt about an important mid-afternoon appointment with a client in Bollingbrook. None of this would have mattered to the fugitive, except Opelt was in his sandstone Toyota Land Cruiser at the time, swerving around slow traffic while fumbling to brush cigar ash from his lap even as he yelled into his cell phone at his assistant ("... if you want to *keep* your goddamned job ...") until his face turned red, which was also the color of the light he inadvertently ran.

2

Sheridan was entering the middle of the intersection, a perfect target for the Toyota, which was roaring up Jackson to where it intersected Lake Shore; and while Sheridan was a careful driver, and beyond that, a man whose senses were finely honed due to the nature of his dangerous job (his real job, not this tow-driver side route), he happened to be glancing to his right, at the joggers, the bikers, and the vast sparkling expanse of blue water beyond them, when the Land Cruiser crossed the path of his vehicle.

The fugitive's eyes turned from the tranquil blue of Lake Michigan, filled suddenly with the blur of the Land Cruiser, and he yanked his wheel to the left, ramming into road repair equipment, workers scattering from harm's way like human bowling pins. Sheridan was unaware of the station wagon whipcording around to slam into the Land Cruiser—whose driver had finally hit his brakes—and the crash turned the tow truck onto its side, sending it sliding into more traffic; at the instant of bone-crunching, muscle-jolting impact, the thunderous cacophony—the clangor of the crash, metal collapsing and entwining, tires screeching, glass cracking, shattering, spiderwebbing—barely registered in his ears before unconsciousness came.

Sheridan slept through the billowing smoke, the flames shooting to the sky; was unaware of other drivers, shaken in the pileup, abandoning their cars in terror; missed entirely the dying screams of Craig Opelt.

Piercing pain jolted him awake, a pain in his arm, his elbow, sharp as a blade—he'd broken this elbow before, had he broken it again?—and the acrid stench of smoke flared his nostrils, stung his eyes; he tried to move, but he could not.

He was trapped within the cab of the truck, it had collapsed around him like a paper cup under a boot heel, but somehow it had twisted in a fashion that had not mangled him, providing him rather with an unwanted cocoon of

3

steel. The crackle of fire in his ears and heat on his face told him he was seconds away from his fugitive status becoming meaningless; the dead no longer had to run, or hide.

But he struggled against his crumpled metal sarcophagus; it was not his way to give up. He had a life to live, a woman he loved, and he would not let them win, he would not give them the satisfaction of knowing that fate had rid them of the Mark Sheridan problem. . . .

His struggling did nothing but exacerbate the sharp pain in his elbow, but he did not give up, and the approaching shriek of emergency vehicles, cutting through the snapping flames, strengthened his resolve. That was when he passed out again.

A voice joined the pain to shake him awake: "You alive in there?"

Sheridan blinked at the smoke and swallowed, the acrid taste almost choking him, and said, "Get me the hell outa here, man!"

A young white cop was leaning toward him. "We got the Jaws of Life comin', pal. Just hang in there. Don't move!"

"There's another option?"

Yellow-garbed firemen and blue-shirted paramedics were swarming the scene; a hose was working at the flames, mist meeting smoke even as the can opener–like Jaws of Life cut through the crunched cab, metal petals spreading.

A helmeted fireman was trying to lift him from the caved-in cab, and Sheridan said, "Easy! My legs!"

Another fireman moved in, said, "He's caught under the steering column," and reached down under and somehow freed Sheridan's legs, and they lifted him like a bride over the threshold into the loving arms of the Emergency Medical Services team, who placed him on a gurney, wheeled him to a nearby ambulance, and shut him within, medical aid descending as consciousness again left him.

The young uniformed cop, Officer James Doherty, plucked a wallet from the pavement—dropped from the victim's pocket as he was lifted out of the wreckage—and then took a quiet moment, surveying the snarl of surly backed-up traffic this pileup had turned Lake Shore Drive into; rush hour coming, what a bastard this would be. He was about to climb in on the rider's side of his black-and-white—his partner, Officer Jane Keenan, was behind the wheel, and as they had been the first on the scene, policy was they had to follow the ambulance to the hospital—when the fireman who had pried the tow-truck driver from under the steering column called him back over to the wrecked truck.

The fireman nodded toward the collapsed cab, gestured under the dashboard. " 'Fore you go runnin' off, check this out."

"I don't see anything."

"Way under."

The young cop bent down, got halfway inside the wreckage, craning his neck around. Under the dashboard, a .32 automatic was Velcroed alongside two ammunition clips.

"I know these tow-truck guys pack protection," the fireman said, "but what's he plannin' for, a war?"

Officer Doherty said nothing. "Have another officer take a Polaroid of that," he told the fireman, "and bag it as possible evidence."

"It isn't a crime to get hit by a Toyota."

"No, but a lot of fugitives get nailed in these kinds of half-ass circumstances."

Then the young cop bolted to his black-and-white. The ambulance had long since peeled out, and his partner had to use the siren to catch up with it.

Doherty sat going through the wallet, as his partner smiled over at him, saying, "Buckin' for detective again?"

He had found a driver's license and a firearm owner's

5

I.D. card in the wallet, and was checking them against the computer. "Mark Warren—no priors, wants or warrants. Very clean."

He reached for the hand mike and radioed in: "Twelve-twelve," he said. "We're ten-nineteen on the way to Chicago Memorial, tow-truck accident on Lake Shore near Jackson."

Mike still in his hand, Doherty said thoughtfully to his partner, "You know, just for the hell of it, I'm gonna check the registration on his gun."

"Aw, give the guy a break, already," his partner said. "That accident was the fault of that crispy critter in the Land Cruiser."

But Officer Doherty was back on the radio, saying, "Call up DMV info, Mark Henry Warren. Fax his firearms owner status and Soundex photos over to Chicago Memorial, ASAP."

Officer Keenan, amused, casual at the wheel considering that her siren was screaming, said, "Aren't you a suspicious son of a bitch."

"That's Detective Suspicious Son of a Bitch, thank you," he said. Then to himself, "Funny how he had that piece Velcroed under there. Two extra ammo clips."

"Sounds like he was expecting trouble."

"Yeah. But I guess he just wasn't expecting it to come up Jackson Boulevard."

They had caught up to the ambulance.

And Sheridan.

TWO

On the same mildly cool afternoon when the fugitive named Sheridan was blindsided by fate, a manhunter who did not believe in fate stood on a busy commercial stretch of Sheridan Road, dressed head-to-clawed-toes in a yellow, feathery chicken costume in front of the Chic-o-Rama restaurant, halfheartedly handing out chicken nugget morsels to passersby. With an occasional homeless exception, this neighborhood, Uptown, with its peculiar mix of gentrification and lower middle-class, wasn't evincing much interest in his fowl samples; but United States Deputy Marshal Samuel Philip Gerard did not care. Feeding the masses was not his business.

Yesterday, on this same street corner, he had worn the navy blue uniform of a Salvation Army volunteer, seeking donations, but Gerard wasn't interested in salvation, either, or redemption; not even justice.

His team, the warrants squad, went to work after justice (or anyway the system that bore that name) had done its work—they sought escapees, like the bad-ass Conroy brothers, who had slain two bank guards in a Memphis bank robbery, and whose mother lived across the street.

Gerard was not a big man, though he gave an impression of size greater than his sturdy five ten; beneath the chicken mask, his pale pockmarked features had a somber blank beauty, an unlikely melding of innocence and worldliness, his eyes hard and dark and bright, partly hooded, almost sleepy—and yet they rarely blinked. Sam Gerard could not afford to blink—he might miss something.

Like the shiny new red-sparkle Buick sedan that had lucked upon a parking spot across the way. From the back-seat emerged two young ladies, a blonde and a brunette, their lean bodies boasting improbably large busts; their heads were apparently where Farrah Fawcett's 1970s hair-style had gone to die.

"Betty and Veronica," Gerard said to himself, as a young housewife sampled a nugget.

"Delicious," she said.

"Even better with honey mustard," the manhunter in the chicken suit said without enthusiasm. His eyes were fixed upon the Buick and its emerging occupants.

Betty wore a black halter top and yellow spandex skirt, and a squalling baby was in her arms, swaddled in a little yellow blanket. Veronica, whose thin arms clutched a cou-ple brimming bags of groceries, wore a blue midriff-baring T-shirt and a leopard miniskirt, and had biker tattoos around her trim ankles.

The Conroys really knew how to keep a low profile.

Last of the thousand clowns to emerge from the backseat was Mildred Conroy, the boys' heavyset momma, pushing fifty, adorable in black stretch pants in which she seemed to be smuggling doorknobs, and, housing mammoth mam-maries, a short-sleeve sweatshirt with a kitty whose appli-qué eyes glittered with sunlight.

Betty was checking out the street and her eyes barely

landed on the chicken man giving out samples; then she came around and rapped on the driver's-side window.

Greg Conroy got out from behind the wheel, with no thought for traffic, giving the finger to the car that almost clipped him.

"Bingo," Gerard said silently.

A human bull, Greg sported a Harley Davidson T-shirt and frayed jeans and well-worn boots; his dark stringy hair brushed his shoulders and his Zapata mustache rode a concave face that looked like a catcher's mitt with eyes. His brother Mike, just as big and hairy and nasty-looking, his ugly face lost in a snarled bird's nest of beard, got out of the front seat, rider's side; he wore similar attire, but with a black leather vest over his T-shirt, which advertised a local strip club, Big Al's.

Momma got two more grocery bags out of the trunk, though the boys didn't help either their mom or their ladies, with the exception of Mike lugging several six-packs of Budweiser. Then the Conroy clan trudged toward a brownstone apartment house on the corner.

Gerard withdrew a small walkie-talkie from under his feathers. "Headed your way, Cosmo," he said. "Make yourself inconspicuous."

Moments later, the Conroy family unit disappeared inside, menfolk first, women fending for themselves despite their armloads of groceries and child.

Just down from where the chicken man was hawking samples, a street crew, in their gray coveralls, hard hats and fluorescent orange jackets, was filling potholes; one of the workers, a tall, shovel-jawed, mustached brute, his pale skin tone not in keeping with the tanned, leathery look of his coworkers, leaned on his shovel and his eyes met Gerard's.

Robert Biggs, deputy U.S. marshal, watched as Gerard moved into the street, kicking off his chicken feet as he went, picking his way through traffic, crossing Sheridan Road.

Biggs dropped his shovel, trotted into the street and fell in beside his boss.

"Why did the chicken cross the road?" Biggs asked.

"To bag the asses of some low-life white-trash dipshits on the other side," Gerard said, whipping off his chicken head and flinging it aside.

Each man reached to the back of the other and yanked down hidden-away black identifying strips that said: "U.S. MARSHALS."

Cosmo Renfro met them at the locked lobby door, letting them in—earlier, they had secured entry with a warrant. Renfro's eyes were alert in his spade-shaped face, a smile always ready in the neatly trimmed beard; he was the smallest of Gerard's crew, and at thirty-eight, the oldest next to his boss. His styled brown hair was perfect all over, and he looked typically dapper—light gray Arrow shirt with rolled-up sleeves, darker gray Hugo Boss trousers and black Italian loafers.

"What's this, the Village People meet *Sesame Street*?" Renfro smirked as the street worker and the chicken man strode into the shallow lobby with its cream-color cracked-plaster walls and dark wood moldings. He spoke softly, almost a whisper.

"You'll have to trade your suspenders in for an Indian headdress, then, Cosmo," Gerard said, taking Renfro's cue, keeping it hushed. "Glimpse our happy family?"

Renfro smirked. "Took a peek from behind the paper I was readin'. It's always touching when the cast of *Deliverance* has a reunion."

Biggs was kneeling over by the modest waiting area where a supermarket tabloid lay on the coffee table by the chair where Renfro had been hanging out.

"Keepin' up with current events, Cosmo?" Biggs asked,

nodding toward the tabloid as he withdrew a cardbox box from under the coffee table—it might have contained flowers, but it didn't.

"Trying to fit in," Renfro said with a shrug. "Turns out they found that 'vampire bat boy'—he was in a cave in Kentucky. But the government's hushing it up."

"Noah," Gerard whispered into his walkie-talkie. "You and the little lady in position?"

"Roger that," Noah Newman said.

Newman, at twenty-eight still the new kid of the crew even after four years on the job, and Savannah Cooper, black, compact, tough, definitely one of the boys, were keeping company with a Dumpster in the alley at the rear of the Conroys' first-floor apartment.

Biggs, who had deposited his hard hat on the coffee table, had the tubular thirty-five-pound, one-person-operation battering ram out of its box; he was holding it by one of its two handles, loose at his side, as if it were a flashlight.

"Since we're speaking softly," Biggs said.

"Why not carry a big stick?" Renfro finished, handing Gerard a nine-millimeter Glock.

The manhunter in the chicken suit chambered a round and lifted an eyebrow at his boys. Renfro was slipping his U.S. marshal I.D. badge on its neck chain over his head so that it rested on his Nicole Miller tie; then he reached behind him for his .38 Smith and Wesson, two-inch barrel, where it had been holstered out of sight.

They moved down the first-floor hallway in pyramid formation, with Gerard at the point. Near the end of the hall, Gerard positioned himself to the left of the door—number 7—while Renfro took the right, both men with handguns at the ready, barrels up. Biggs clutched the battering ram by its two side-by-side handles, ready to swing; the ram would deliver 14,000 pounds of kinetic force.

Whispering, Gerard spoke into his walkie-talkie: "Newman—just so you know . . . we're about to knock.''

Biggs swung the ram and punched a hole in the door, splintering the wood, and as Biggs stepped back, getting himself and the battering ram out of the way, Gerard in his chicken suit shouldered forward, exploding through what remained of the door, thundering inside the modest apartment with Renfro right behind him.

The place didn't betray a woman's touch: it was a dumpy furnished apartment, mostly decorated by spent beer cans, unemptied ashtrays and out-of-date *TV Guides*. A television—a thirty-five-inch job that hadn't come with the apartment—was blaring a wrestling match.

''U.S. marshals!'' Gerard yelled. ''On the floor, now!''

''Get down!'' Renfro shouted.

Three of them were in the kitchenette area, at left, putting groceries away, Momma and the brunette and Mike, who was helpfully stowing the beer in the fridge, except for a six-pack he'd set over by his easy chair facing the big TV. The trio—faced with raiders whose leader was wearing a headless chicken suit—froze in deer-in-headlights fashion, for an instant, but soon Mike's eyes were on the .357 Colt Python that was serving as the kitchen table's centerpiece.

Biggs had dispensed with his battering ram and entered with both hands free, and took it upon himself to pounce on Mike, yelling, ''Gun!'', even as Renfro snatched that .357 from Mike's fingers.

''You lousy sons of bitches!'' Momma shouted, grabbing a butcher knife from the counter. ''You mangy good-for-nothing cocksuckers!''

She was coming at Biggs, who was on top of her boy on the kitchen floor, where they were going at it as if the All-Star Wrestling play-by-play on the tube was referring to them; Momma had her butcher knife raised high, in true psycho-mom fashion, the fat wattles under her arms swinging like fleshy pendulums.

Gerard stepped around Biggs and Mike and plucked the knife from Momma's fingers like a flower, then dragged away the squirming wild-eyed woman, who was still shouting quaint motherly sentiments—"Fuckin' pigs, goddamn fuckin' pigs!"—not quite worthy of sewing on a sampler. Renfro passed handcuffs to Gerard which he snapped on Momma's right wrist and the brunette's left wrist so fast neither woman knew it was happening till it was over.

Gerard stuck a finger in the foul-mouthed broad's ugly puss. "Be good," he said sternly.

The brunette was sneering at him; she had druggy eyes and the kind of hard features that encourage strip club owners to keep the lights dim.

During these frenzied seconds, Greg Conroy had fled to the back bedroom where his blonde babe and his blonde's baby were, and had snatched a Cobra eleven-millimeter machine pistol from atop a dresser. The baby, a boy, was shrieking in his bassinet, frightened by the commotion. His father could have gone out into the other room to fight for the honor of his family; instead Greg Conroy moved past his blonde to a door that led to the alley, kept locked by the management but nonetheless a suitable emergency exit—once Greg's foot had reasoned with it.

With the door kicked open, however, Greg found himself in the alley, facing a redheaded kid in a ponytail and a short black woman, both in black body armor vests, marshal badges on neck chains, both pointing handguns right at him.

"Put it down!" Deputy Marshal Cooper ordered.

"Now!" Deputy Marshal Newman added. "Do it!"

But Greg still seemed to be thinking about it, when Cooper said curtly, "You're hurtin' my feelings. Maybe you don't think a sweet thing like me would shoot you through your motherfuckin' eyes."

"Okay, all right, okay!" Greg said, kneeling, placing the

gun on the cement. "There's a kid in here, okay?"

And the stringy-haired bank robber began backing into the bedroom, hands up.

"Freeze it up!" Newman yelled.

But Greg Conroy had already ducked back inside.

The two deputy marshals, Cooper in the lead, followed, fast.

"You're scarin' my kid!" Conroy was saying, sidling toward the bassinet, where the baby was screaming bloody murder.

The blonde in the yellow spandex skirt was moving away from her man, her eyes full of fear. "Stay away from my baby!" she yelled; it was unclear whether she meant the child or Conroy.

Cooper skirted the bed and cuffed the blonde's hands behind her and dragged her ass out of the bedroom, as the baby—seeming to know its mother had gone—began to wail even louder.

"Don't you hurt my kid," Conroy was saying, edging near the bassinet.

"Get away from that crib," Newman advised.

"Have a heart, man—he's cryin' his eyes out, he needs his daddy!"

And the child's father lunged toward the bassinet.

Gerard stepped into the room just as Deputy Marshal Noah Newman squeezed off a round that caught Greg Conroy in the shoulder, blossoming blood, dropping the bank robber to his knees.

Now it wasn't just the baby screaming, but the blonde, out in the other room, and Conroy, rolling on the floor howling, clutching his bloody ruined shoulder and occasionally spewing epithets he had apparently learned from his mother.

In fact, the baby in the bassinet had gone silent.

Newman turned milky pale, swallowed and moved to the

bassinet; so did Gerard, who flipped aside the baby's yellow blanket to reveal a sawed-off Remington shotgun.

Lifting the shotgun from the bassinet, Gerard smiled down at the baby, who was gurgling, even beginning to laugh.

"Good boy," he told the child.

He popped the shells from the shotgun, then looked at Newman. "Good boy," he repeated.

Sounds of scuffling in the other room drew Gerard back, empty sawed-off in hand, with Newman on his heels.

Unbelievably, Mike Conroy had squirmed, like a stung rhino, out from under Biggs, who had been struggling to cuff the son of a bitch. Renfro dove on top of Mike, who tossed him off and onto a coffee table that broke with a nasty crunch of glass.

"Don't give up, son!" Momma was shouting. "Don't take no shit!"

Scrambling, not quite on his feet, Mike Conroy grabbed that six-pack off the table by his easy chair, and was hefting it, ready to slam the thing into Renfro's head, when Gerard spoke from across the room.

"We can keep dancing, Michael," Gerard said, "if you like—but I'm having this vision of your future where you went for my gun and got killed."

Gerard smiled at him, just a little, but his unblinking stare was enough to give Mike pause.

And that was enough time for Gerard to slap the six-pack from Mike's hand, and Biggs to finally jerk the big bastard's arms behind him and lock on the cuffs.

"Fuck!" Mike shouted, straightening, and a growl of animal rage rumbled up out of him, as he reached his head around and bit Biggs on the arm, clamping down hard. Biggs yelped and pulled away and Mike roared with laughter, at least until Gerard whapped the top of Mike's head with the butt of the sawed-off and shut him up.

And sent him down, whamming to the floor like a felled tree.

"Boy needed professional help," Gerard commented.

Standing in the midst of the now-upended apartment, Gerard surveyed the scene. Cooper had rounded up the women in the kitchenette by the half-put-away groceries; the Conroy women stood silently now, even Momma, heads hanging. Through the open doorway, the slumped form of Greg could be viewed—he was unconscious, and bleeding some.

"Well, all right," Gerard sighed. "Let's get that baby's daddy a doctor. Take care of that, would you, Noah?"

Newman nodded, and got on his cell phone.

"Look at me," Renfro was saying, shaking his head, his expensive clothes mussed and torn. "Why do I dress like this on a frickin' raid?"

"Because you're an idiot?" Biggs offered innocently, holding his arm where Mike had bitten it.

"Hope you had your shots," Renfro said.

"Cosmo," Gerard said irritably, "quit pissing and moaning and help me get out of this damn chicken suit."

Renfro smirked at his boss. "Doesn't take much to ruffle your feathers today, does it?"

The whole squad laughed at that—including Gerard.

The Conroy clan, however, seemed unamused.

Three

The woman digging into her purse at the emergency admissions counter of Chicago Memorial Hospital did not know that the man she loved was a fugitive. That he was black and she was white—dark tousle of curls, slender, strikingly pretty even in her work clothes (Joe's Java T-shirt with its distinctive coffee cup logo)—was not daring in a city this size, in this day and age. Marie Bineaux was, after all, an artist, or anyway an art student, and the crowd she ran with wouldn't blink about her boyfriend's ethnic heritage. Mom and Dad back in Toronto, well that might be another matter. . . .

The hospital cashier, a heavyset Hispanic woman, seemed mildly irritated at getting paid in cash, particularly in small bills and change.

"The taxes you Americans pay," Marie muttered, "and no health care?"

"Get your man to start believing in Blue Cross, honey," the cashier said, "and maybe it won't come out of *your* pocket, next time."

Marie was coughing up the final $38.50 from a wad of crumpled bills and loose coins in her purse—tip money—when an Italian-looking male orderly pushed a wheelchair bearing Mark Sheridan (Warren, to Marie) into the waiting area from the adjacent corridor. Mark was wearing the blue T-shirt and jeans she had brought him—they weren't living together, but he kept a few changes of clothes at her place, as she did at his—and a neck brace; his right elbow was in a plaster cast.

Trailing behind the orderly pushing Mark into view were two uniformed police officers, a man and a woman, both rather young for cops.

"Marie," Sheridan said, and his heart leapt when he saw the look of devotion on her face as she rushed to him; she really loved him—the seriousness of that encouraged, and dismayed, him.

"Thank God you're all right," she breathed. "You could have been killed! Can you walk?"

"I'm okay," he said. "The legs work fine, baby. . . ."

He did a little dance with them in the air.

A slender woman in whites approached, clipboard in hand; her name tag said "DR. PAMELA CLEMENS," and she was perhaps forty-five, little makeup, dishwater blonde tucked back in a no-nonsense bun, but her eyes were light blue and kind in the professional mask of her face.

"That neck brace is only a precaution," the doctor said. "If you're comfortable without it, by all means leave it off. . . . Those things are a nuisance, anyway. You're in remarkable physical condition, Mr. Warren, which explains your resiliency. Are you, or were you, an athlete?"

"High school," he admitted. His physical condition had more do with his job, and the training it had required, however, than any childhood ability in sports.

"Well, for what you've been through," the doctor said, "you came out relatively unscathed. The elbow isn't broken, but obviously you did break it before. . . ."

"Still got a pin in it," he explained to Marie.

The doctor continued: "You can see your own physician about that cast, which can come off fairly soon, at his or her discretion . . . or make an appointment here if you like."

"Thank you, Doctor."

Then she was gone, and Sheridan was turning an embarrassed gaze upon Marie. "I'm sorry about this," he said.

"About what, silly?"

"Asking you to come down . . ."

He didn't want to say any more, particularly not within earshot of the two looming uniformed cops. He didn't want them to be thinking about why he didn't have any credit cards much less medical insurance, about why he'd had to ask his girlfriend to bring him clothes and enough cash to get his bill quickly taken care of.

At the admissions window, the cashier was leaning out. She called, "Are you Officer Doherty?"

The young cop said, "Yes, ma'am."

"Something just came in for you."

"Excuse me," Doherty said to Sheridan.

"Thanks for helping me out, Officer," Sheridan said, smiling a little. "Appreciate it."

"No problem," Doherty said, smiling back, heading for the counter.

The female cop handed Sheridan a clipboard, saying, "If you can just read over your statement, Mr. Warren, and sign it, that should just about do it for now."

Sheridan signed without reading, handing the clipboard to the woman. "Appreciate it."

He began to rise, but the orderly said, "Sorry, Mr. Warren—gotta wheel you over to the exit . . . it's the rules."

"Okay," Sheridan said, with another nervous smile, as the orderly did that, Marie walking along at his side, holding his hand, Sheridan sneaking a look back at Officer Doherty, who was being handed something at the cashier's window. *Probably nothing,* Sheridan thought. *Don't be so fucking paranoid. . . .*

But Mark Sheridan should have known, after six months on the run, that fugitives do not experience paranoia: for the fugitive, the notion that people are out to get him is not a fantasy, but an unending reality.

Near the exit, the orderly held the wheelchair in place as Marie gently helped Sheridan to his feet; he felt wobbly, woozy—they had given him painkillers. Sheridan nodded his thanks to the orderly, who nodded back and wheeled the empty chair away.

"I'm sorry about sticking you with the bill," he said, as they paused by the exit.

"Don't be silly," she said.

"I have cash at my place. . . ."

She looped her arm in his; she smelled so very good— it was that Bijan perfume she always wore. "Well that can wait," she said, "because you're going to my place. Let me spoil you rotten for a few days."

"I could live with that."

Shaking her head, she looked him over. "That doctor was right—getting hit broadside that way, coming out in one piece. You were lucky."

"You have no idea," Sheridan said, with the barest glance back at the two cops, who were standing together near the admissions counter, looking at a sheet of paper, casually, no urgency in their manner whatsoever.

Marie hugged his arm, whispered in his ear: "She was right about your body, too."

He grinned at her, kissed her on the nose. "I am lucky."

"Mr. Warren!" a voice called.

Sheridan turned. The two cops were approaching. He was too unsteady to run—and maybe they didn't want anything special, maybe there was just another form to sign. . . .

"You're under arrest, sir," Officer Doherty said.

"If you could just come with us," Officer Keenan said.

"What?" Marie asked, eyes wide with alarm, flashing from the cops to her boyfriend. "What's this about?"

"Must be a screwup," he said to her weakly. "Go on home . . . I'll catch up."

"The hell you will!" she said to him, then to the cops she demanded, "Where are you taking him?"

Within an hour, Sheridan found himself seated in an interview room at the First Central District station on State Street. Fairly large, with a banquet-style table that could accommodate a suspect and multiple interrogators, the room was various shades of institutional green adorned with memo-choked bulletin boards. They had complied with his request to remove the neck-brace collar. He sat alone in this room for forty-seven minutes. Sat with his hands folded and his face impassive, though the skin under the elbow cast was itching like a bastard. A large mirror on one wall was undoubtedly two-way glass, and he didn't feel like giving them anything to see.

Three men entered, plainclothes detectives, obviously. Two were in shirtsleeves, a dumpy fiftyish cop with a fringe of mustache and glasses, and a black guy in his thirties with sad eyes that told Sheridan the man's presence was to keep a racial balance. The guy in the lead was the boss, clearly—a blandly good-looking six-footer, brown hair graying at the temples, trimly fit, forty-something, Brooks Brothers suit, Christian Dior tie.

Just the kind of detective the Chicago PD liked to use for its nightly news sound bites.

"I'm Lieutenant Caldwell," the dapper detective said, not bothering to identify the other two. "And your name is Mark Warren . . . or is it?"

21

He held up a palm and the dumpy dick filled it with a file. Then, with melodrama that Sheridan would have found funny if his life weren't at stake, Caldwell slapped the file on the table and opened it to reveal Mark Warren's concealed weapons permit.

The photo of Mark Warren showed him to be a bearded, overweight white male.

"Let me clear this up for you," Sheridan said. "That's not me."

"We caught that little detail, Mark."

"Hey, you guys ever try to tow a car on the Dan Ryan at three in the morning, without some life insurance?"

"Your falsified firearms permit is only one of several discrepancies, Mark, that we'd like to help you clear up."

Caldwell lifted a hard-shell glasses case from his jacket pocket and withdrew gold wire-frame reading glasses—Armani.

He put them on, lifted another facedown sheet from the file and examined it as he said, "Your driver's license has your name on it, but your social security number belongs to this same Caucasian individual, who died almost five years ago, incidentally. Natural causes. Of course, that's more than can be said for Sam Harmon and Neil Kasinski."

Sheridan said nothing.

Caldwell smiled blandly; his voice was cordial, as if they were discussing the weather. "You want to tell us about East Forty-second and First Avenue in New York City, Mark?"

"What about it?"

"That's the United Nations building, isn't it, Mark?"

"I wouldn't know. I'm a Midwest kid."

"Ever been to New York City?"

"No."

"Not even on vacation?"

"No."

"Never?"

"That's right, never."

"Not even to murder and rob two people in a parking garage? The United Nations parking garage?"

Sheridan forced a laugh. "Are you guys serious? Fellas, this is about a tow-truck driver protecting himself from carjackers. What's this United Nations shit?"

With more melodrama, Caldwell flipped over another sheet in the file to reveal the State Department warrant for the arrest of Mark Roberts.

"My name is Warren," Sheridan said.

"Right. And you're white, and you died of a coronary in 1993. In the meantime, see if any of these faces look familiar. . . ."

And Caldwell turned over the next item in the file: a color crime-scene photo, and another, and another, various angles of two men sprawled on the pavement of a parking garage, the neck of one obviously broken, the clothes of the other splotched red, both with open-eyed faces empty with their deaths.

"See what I mean, Mark?" Caldwell asked pleasantly. "About these not being natural causes."

Sheridan shook his head, no—it made his neck hurt to do it, but he did it just the same. "You got the wrong guy . . . I drive a tow truck. Talk to my boss."

"I know. He's already vouched for you. You're a hell of a worker. You've been there six months. These murders happened six months and two weeks ago, Mark. By the way, the fingerprints we took of you, when you got here? They flagged that warrant. Matched prints found in that parking garage."

"That's impossible . . ."

Caldwell raised a hand for him to stop. The detective removed his Armani wire-frames, tossed the gold glasses atop the crime-scene photos and rubbed his eyes.

"I thought maybe you'd like to get this off your chest, Mark," he said, wearily disappointed.

You wanted a piece of the nightly news, Sheridan thought.

"This is bullshit, fellas. I'd like an attorney. Now."

Caldwell said, "You'll get one over at Criminal Courts, at your extradition hearing—which is in about half an hour. You'll be glad to know that here in Chicago we can move an individual through the court system quickly, when necessary. Unlike, say, New York—which is where you're going back to."

"Back? I told you, I never been there in my life!" Sheridan, cool within, exuded rage as he jumped to his feet and screamed, "This is a frame! It's not right, I wasn't there!"

"You'll have plenty of time to explain that in New York."

Sheridan reached across the table and grabbed its edge, turning it over on its side, the crime-scene photos, the file folder, even Caldwell's glasses sliding to the floor; the fugitive began windmilling the air, freaking out, or seeming to, inviting the attention of Caldwell's backup dicks, who shoved him to the document-strewn floor. Soon they had wrestled him down, and had him handcuffed, hands behind him.

His expression one of faint disgust, Caldwell retrieved his expensive glasses from the floor and returned them to their hard case and back to his jacket pocket.

Within half an hour, Marie Bineaux, in the police station lobby where she'd been inquiring of the desk sergeant about what was taking so long, suddenly saw her Mark Warren, and the cops' Mark Roberts, in chains, getting hustled down a hallway toward an exit. She tried to follow but a uniformed officer held her back, traffic-cop style.

"Mark!" she yelled. "What is *happening*?"

As they dragged him down the hall, he called back to

24

her, "Some bullshit mistaken identity, baby! I'm gonna straighten it all out!"

"I don't understand . . ."

"Be cool! It's gonna be fine. . . ."

"Where are they *taking* you?"

His eyes sent her his regret, and he mouthed, *I love you*, and then he was hauled through double doors.

No longer a fugitive.

Four

Many people who work together choose not to socialize, but the manhunter, the police officer, leads a life that only others of his (or her) ilk can understand and, in some cases, tolerate. Like a fugitive, a manhunter lives apart from society, even as he inhabits it. So in every major city, and many smaller ones, there are police haunts, "cop bars." Emitt's, on Chicago's Rush Street, was one of them.

Late afternoon, in the dark, masculine catacomb, with its framed photos of sports figures and actors and deceased cops, a big-screen television normally devoted to the Bears or the Cubs was filled with the painfully pretty visage of Stacia Vela, local news superstar.

Dark-eyed, dark-haired Stacia was positioned outside the brownstone apartment house on Sheridan Road where the Conroy bust had gone down, earlier that day.

"Convicted murderers Mike and Greg Conroy escaped en route to federal prison last month," Stacia was saying.

Now the screen was filled with the image of U.S. Deputy Marshal Sam Gerard and his team members hauling the disheveled Conroy brothers toward the entry of the Everett McKinley Dirksen Building that housed both the federal courts and the offices of the U.S. Marshals Service.

"Chicago's own U.S. Marshals Warrants Squad," Stacia continued in voice-over, "the so-called 'fugitive squad' who were instrumental in capturing and clearing accused wife-murderer Dr. Richard Kimble, arrested the brothers today in a daring Uptown raid . . ."

The table of U.S. marshals listening to this erupted in cheers and hoots, drowning out the specifics of their own derring-do, as other off-duty coppers at the bar and in booths applauded and gave thumbs-ups and "Way to go"'s.

Gerard's face suddenly filled the screen.

"Who is that guy?" Gerard said of himself. "That's not me. That's some ugly asshole."

"On a good day," Renfro said, mildly pouty about being on the tube in torn, mussed clothing.

"You look sexy, Sam," Cooper was saying, swirling her glass of beer. "You got character, like Al Pacino."

On screen, Mike Conroy was sticking his face into a camera lens, lowering his head to point at the stitches there, even as he nodded at Gerard hauling him along, ranting, "Lookit what that scumbag done to me! It's police brutality! It's abuse!"

The TV camera had caught Gerard's response, as well: "Mr. Conroy, kindly shut your mouth and move your ass."

Laughter and applause erupted from the table.

Stacia continued in voice-over as the image of Gerard dragged Mike Conroy inside the high-rise: ". . . warrants squad leader Sam Gerard achieved national prominence, and some criticism, for his zealous pursuit of the now-cleared fugitive Dr. Kimble, a case which attracted nationwide attention second only to the O.J. Simpson—"

"Still talkin' about that damn Kimble case," Gerard

muttered. He yelled at the screen: "Old news, Stacia! Old news!"

"Barkeep," Biggs yelled, "turn that thing down. The Big Dog's gettin' testy!"

The sound lowered and the table erupted in more applause, as Newman, his natural shyness overcome by several beers, half-rose to raise his glass. "Here's to the Big Dog!"

"The Big Dog!" Cooper yelled, and Biggs and Renfro went, "Woof! Woof!" The U.S. Marshals Warrants Squad included no brain surgeons.

"Speech!" they called. "Speech!"

"All right, all right," Gerard said, standing, lifting his Diet Coke; he hadn't touched alcohol since the Army. "Since I'm the nationally prominent one, I'll make the damn toast. To my pups!"

More woofing filled the air as the warrants squad raised their beer glasses.

"Cosmo Renfro," Gerard said, "you are a clotheshorse, a two-bit comedian and a royal pain in the ass, and why the Justice Department would arm such a person is anyone's guess."

That made Renfro smile, and everyone else howl with laughter.

"Biggs, there's a lot I could say about you, but it would require the use of words far too large for you to comprehend."

Biggs chuckled and the rest hooted and hollered.

"Savannah Cooper, you could probably outrun my grandmother, but I wouldn't want to bet good money on it. . . . And Newman. I have ties older than you, Noah."

"We know, we know," Renfro said, rolling his eyes.

"Also, Newman," Gerard continued, "I have every confidence that someday you will be fit to make my coffee."

"Thank you, thank you all," Newman said, taking a little bow.

"All in all," Gerard said, "you are the most pitiful excuse for a warrants squad it's ever been my misfortune to have to put up with."

This elicited cheers and mildly drunken applause, which Gerard quieted with an upheld palm.

"But nobody got hurt today, except a couple crawling pieces of shit called Conroy . . . ," his voice was quiet now, and he allowed a rare tenderness to creep into his tone, ". . . and that is important, yes it is. So here's to the goddamn fugitive squad . . . you stayed close on the Big Dog and he loves you for it."

He raised his Diet Coke to them and they quietly did the same with their beer glasses to him.

"Now, drink up," he said, sitting back down. "As designated driver, I got to drop this pitiful excuse for law enforcement personnel off at your respective abodes and subway stops . . . and I got somewhere important to go, and much more important people to see tonight than this sorry-ass bunch of civil servants."

"What would that be?" Renfro asked. "Is the Grand Ole Opry in town?"

"It's a very sophisticated event," Gerard said. "The mayor's fundraiser for sick kids or somethin'."

"Sounds rockin'," Newman said with a smirk.

"How did you land a chair at that affair?" Cooper wondered.

"Pay attention," Renfro said, pointing toward the big-screen TV. "The Big Dog has media contacts, remember."

"Ah," Cooper said, nodding, with a cat-that-ate-the-canary smile.

The others were smiling and nodding and laughing, and Gerard said, "Hey hey hey! Let's not overstep, children."

The whole crew was well aware that Gerard had been

dating the very woman they'd been watching: Stacia Vela. And he was well aware of the irony of the situation: a young local celebrity like Stacia would not likely have been within his range of social contacts if she and others like her had not turned Gerard into a local media star, himself.

And several hours later, climbing the stairs to the hallway that led to the main ballroom at the Drake Hotel, Gerard walked arm-in-arm with that same newswoman. He edged a finger down into his too-tight collar, seeking comfort, succeeding only in making his black tie more crooked.

"It's not too late to catch a cab over to the Berghoff," he told her.

"It'll be a lovely buffet," Stacia said, as if calming a child. She looked beautiful in her costly green gown, though no designer could compete with those big brown long-lashed eyes. "Besides, you know I've been looking forward to this. Didn't you say some of your coworkers would be here?"

"My bosses."

"Well, then, I can finally meet some of these people you're always talking about."

They were at the top of the stairs, and began making their way toward the registration table, moving gingerly through a crowd of well-to-do's, tuxedos and ball gowns, enough jewelry in sight to open a Tiffany's.

His mouth twitched in a humorless smirk. "I don't like these social functions. People always want to talk about the damn Kimble case."

She hugged his arm. "I already apologized to you about that, Sam. It was a cheap shot, mentioning that today. But it's something everyone can identify with."

"I just hope he isn't here tonight."

"Kimble? I don't think he likes getting out in public any more than you do. Now, behave."

"Hello, Deputy," a throaty female voice said, almost into his ear.

He turned, and just behind them stood a rather tall, attractive woman in her forties, in a stunningly elegant dark blue gown, a brunette whose physical beauty was offset by her poise and professional mien.

"Surprised to see you here," Catherine Walsh said, joining them, positioning herself between Gerard and his date, "considering the day you've had."

"Catherine," Gerard said, working his voice above the noise of the hallway crowd, "this is Stacia Vela."

The woman smiled at Stacia. "Of course it is—Channel Four News."

"Stacia, this is Catherine Anne Walsh, United States marshal of the Fifth District. . . . My boss."

But Catherine Walsh—ex–federal prosecutor whose hard-bitten professionalism had allowed her to rise in the man's world of the Justice Department—was more than just Gerard's boss. At least, she had been once.

"I recognize you, of course," Stacia said, "and I've always wanted to interview you."

Catherine kiddingly said, "I leave the television cameras to Sam. . . . He likes the bright lights."

"Stop it," Gerard said, wincing.

"I've heard so much about you, from Sam," Stacia said.

An eyebrow arched. "Really? Well, I watch you on television, all the time. You're really quite lovely in person."

Gerard hoped Stacia wasn't picking up on the cattiness underlying Walsh's cordial tone.

"Th-thanks," Stacia said.

Inwardly, Gerard groaned.

"Ms. Vela," Catherine said regally, touching the young woman's arm lightly, "could I borrow your date for a moment?"

"Of course." Stacia's practiced smile betrayed just a hint

of uneasiness. "Sam, I'll go on in and get us a drink."

"Good idea," he said, and as Stacia moved away, he asked his boss, "All right—what did I do?"

Catherine arched an eyebrow as she watched an admiring crowd part for the shapely newscaster. "Little young, isn't she?"

"She's legal."

"They're legal at thirteen, where you come from."

"What did I do, Catherine?"

"Maybe when you two go your separate ways, you could give me her number for my nephew, who just graduated law school."

"This is about the prisoner I hit, isn't it?"

She turned to him and her smile was brittle; so was her voice: "He had his handcuffs on when you struck him. We'll be lucky if he doesn't sue."

"Tell him to take a number."

"Oh, be sure to share that one with your little friend. That'll play swell on the nightly news."

"The son of a bitch was a biter, Catherine, he bit one of my kids! So he got smacked in the noggin. So what?"

"Twenty-seven stitches worth of 'smacked in the noggin,' Sam."

"The boy needed a smack on the noggin. I was around to give it to him. I don't see the problem."

Her eyes narrowed more in concern than criticism. "Sam . . . with the kind of media attention you attract—and I don't just mean that sweet young thing in there—you can't be going off half-cocked like this."

"I'm always fully cocked, Catherine."

Her smile tightened. "You have to take the edge off of the Conroy bust. D.C. wants to take full advantage of this high-profile collar, and they want you to help with spin control."

"How the hell am I supposed to do that?"

"By taking a little vacation. You've been running in high gear too long, Sam—you need to take it easy."

"Where do you have in mind for this getaway?"

Her faint smile stopped just short of openly mocking him. "You're going to personally escort these clowns back to the federal pen at Memphis, and if you have the opportunity along the way to give the occasional little speech to the press, the powers that be will be grateful."

"I should thank *them,* for givin' me this chance to take it easy."

The smile softened. "When you get back, I really do want you to take a vacation, go the hell fishing or something. Enough of this hyperactive bullshit for a while."

"Oh hell, Memphis here I come. . . . When?"

"Tomorrow morning."

He frowned. "Christ, Catherine, I got plans; this is gonna be a late night for me . . ."

"Not that late. When I say tomorrow, I mean one A.M. tonight."

"Oh, now, Catherine, you can't be serious . . ."

"Catherine!" It was Ken Levin, that handsome Yuppie S.O.B. from the State Prosecutor's Office. He had a martini in either hand. "Let's go! We're at the mayor's table."

Catherine took the drink and, granting Gerard the barest nod, headed inside on Levin's arm, pausing only to whisper, "Be on that plane, Sam."

Then she was gone, passing Stacia, who was on her way with her own stinger and Gerard's Diet Coke.

Catherine had screwed him again, he thought, remembering a time when that had been a more pleasant prospect.

Five

A fugitive on his way to prison is a man in transition, mentally as well as literally—in custody, clearly a prisoner, he retains the fugitive's mind-set; until those prison cell doors slam shut on him, until those gray bars and thick walls become his world, he thinks like a fugitive. He plans for a future of freedom.

He looks for a way out.

Mark Sheridan, stepping from the Bureau of Prisons bus in the nighttime glare of runway lights at sprawling Chicago O'Hare airport, had not given up hope, despite his cuffed hands and shackled legs. The bus's escort of police cars and United States Marshals Service sedans formed a phalanx around the orange-jumpsuited passengers as they exited the bus into a circle of unfriendly light. Just one of a dozen hardened prisoners—the bank-robbing, murdering Conroy brothers among them—Sheridan was under the watchful gaze of half a dozen Federal Prisoner Transportation Service deputies.

Each prisoner was thoroughly searched and examined by

the deputies, and Sheridan's neck brace was removed for examination.

As a solemn black deputy in his thirties began to take the brace apart, Sheridan said, "Don't bother, bro . . . I don't need it."

The brace was passed along to another deputy for disposal, while the black deputy ran a metal-detecting wand up and down the fugitive's body. The wand beeped at his elbow, and the deputy's sad hooded eyes opened wide.

"Got a pin in it," Sheridan explained.

A bulldogish deputy with a name tag reading "HOL-LANDER" stepped forward, clipboard in hand, thumbing through paperwork until he came to an X ray, yanked it loose and held it up to the lights.

"He's not lyin' about that pin," Hollander said, and moments later the bulldog deputy—who was apparently a medical officer of some kind—handed Sheridan a paper cup of water, which the prisoner clasped in his cuffed hands.

"You're gonna be the envy of the other girls on this field trip," Hollander said, patting Sheridan's shoulder. "You're scheduled for Tylenol with a codeine chaser. . . . Say 'ah.' "

Sheridan showed the medical deputy his tongue and Hollander placed a pill there. Sheridan swallowed it down.

"Okay," Hollander said to the black deputy. "Get this one on the plane 'fore he starts flyin' without one."

And Sheridan was escorted to the steps up into the rear of the plane, as a Lincoln sedan pulled in with the starred USMS logo on its door.

The rider's-side door opened and Sam Gerard, in sport-coat, tie and jeans, lugging his travel bag, hauled his weary, disgruntled ass out of the sedan.

Deputy Hollander greeted him. "Welcome to the un-friendly skies, Sam."

Gerard grunted a laugh. "You're about the kind of stewardess I'd draw, Bill. So—we got some luminaries with us tonight?"

"Murderers, rapists, armed robbers. America's finest."

"I can vouch for the Conroys," Gerard said. "Their momma loves 'em, anyway."

And he trudged up a gangway at the front of the plane. A young blond deputy with a caterpillar mustache met him at the door and Gerard showed him his credentials and boarding papers.

"If I could have your weapons, sir," the deputy said, sounding like his voice had barely changed.

Gerard hated pushing fifty in a world of twenty-somethings. He handed over his nine-millimeter Glock, from under his shoulder; then his backup Colt .38, from his ankle holster; and finally, from his sportcoat jacket, his spare ammo, too. The deputy placed these possessions in a wire basket and slid the basket into a lockup area across from the forward john.

Gerard took a seat along the cold metal wall. The interior of the plane was military-aircraft spartan, stripped to the essentials. The forward cabin was separated from the main cabin, where the prisoners were confined, by a wire-mesh wall with a gate. Just behind the forward cabin's galley area, the crosshatch of steel provided a view of a dozen convicts-to-be, sitting trying to look like hardasses when most of them, Gerard knew, were, for all their misdeeds and muscle and attitudes, frightened kids inside—particularly those who hadn't done hard time before.

The prisoners faced forward, typical airplane seating, two seats on either side of an aisle that was constantly strolled by uniformed deputies. Handcuffed, belly-chained, feet shackled to the floor, the orange-suited passengers weren't going anywhere. Gerard buckled his seat belt, sitting facing another plainclothes deputy, chubby Jack Stern, whom Gerard knew, a little.

"Sam," Stern—already buckled in—said, with an acknowledging nod.

Gerard nodded back.

"Look at the bright side, Sam."

"And what would the bright side be, Jack?"

The chubby deputy shrugged. "This is one flight that's always on time."

And in the cockpit of the Federal Prisoner Transportation Service 727, the flight crew was indeed making its final checks, the pilot informing the control tower that F-PATS flight 343 was ready for takeoff.

"Point us towards Memphis," the pilot said, "then we're on to La Guardia and we call it a night."

Soon the 727 was moving down the runway, and then ascending over the vast army of fireflies that was Chicago at night, into a cool, clear, moonlit sky. And in the main cabin of the prison ship, Mark Sheridan was wondering if the lights would be dimmed for the passengers to sleep through the night flight; that near-darkness would aid him. . . .

Unlike the other prisoners, whose hands were cuffed together, Sheridan sat with his left hand cuffed to the seat and his right arm, with its elbow cast, free.

And as he looked around the cabin, he saw another prisoner looking his way, ever so briefly, and turning away, a thin Asian who couldn't be more than twenty.

The fugitive had noticed the skinny Asian on the bus, had noted his childlike face and ancient dead eyes, but he hadn't connected it. Now, seeing the Asian kid's eyes on him, those soulless gangbanger's eyes, Sheridan knew.

He knew he was in much more trouble than any of the other poor bastards on this plane.

Sheridan had the aisle seat; next to him was a massively

bulked-up redneck with a bald head and a Brillo beard and jailhouse tattoos all over him, included his wild-eyed face.

The redneck had noted Sheridan's appraisal of the Asian.

"Who you think you're lookin' at?" the redneck growled. His teeth might have been rotting lemon Chiclets.

"Nobody," Sheridan mumbled.

The wrestlerlike frame lurched forward, rattling his chains. "You makin' goo-goo eyes with that gook?"

Sheridan shook his head, no.

A low growl gradually turned into words: "Keep your bug eyes to yourself, boy. That's the future Mrs. Billy Ray Hazen."

The Asian stole another glance at Sheridan, but the fugitive kept his eyes forward, gave no indication he'd noticed the glance, to either the Asian or the Asian's would-be redneck "husband."

In the forward cabin, on the other side of the wire mesh separating the free from the incarcerated, Sam Gerard read the current issue of *Field and Stream,* which he'd picked up at a newsstand at O'Hare, the notion of a fishing trip (as planted by Catherine Walsh) sounding not half-bad. Or maybe it just made him recall the cabin on that lake he and Catherine had shared once, a lifetime or two ago.

Across from him, Stern was doing the *Sun-Times* crossword, occasionally seeking help from Gerard or any of the other three plainclothes deputies seated in the forward compartment.

"Eight letter word for 'fifty points'?" Stern wondered.

"Scrabble," Gerard said, not missing a beat.

"You think?"

"See if it fits."

"Yeah, it does! You like puzzles, Sam?"

"No."

And in the main cabin, the skinny Asian with the smooth child's face and eyes that held no more expression than black buttons was wagging his head to flag a deputy patrolling the aisle.

"Gotta shit," the Asian said.

The deputy, stocky, dark-haired, pale, said, "Keep a cork in it, sweetheart. We'll be on the ground in twenty minutes."

"I got flu. Gonna explode."

Hollander, the medical deputy, got in on this. "Ling, isn't it?" he said to the Asian. "You didn't say anything about flu back at Cook County."

"You want me to shit my pants? Real mess. Bad smell."

Hollander smirked humorlessly, shook his head, waved an okay, and within moments, the sad-eyed black deputy had joined the stocky white one to unbuckle Ling's belly chain, and his leg irons. Then, with one deputy in front, the other behind, the handcuffed Asian prisoner was escorted down the aisle toward the aft john, which was behind a wire-mesh grate. On this prison ship, a trip to the can did not mean a few moments of privacy.

Sheridan shifted in his seat, craning around to see that the Asian was now within the cage as the two deputies kept a close eye on him. The dead-eyed prisoner pulled down his orange pants with his cuffed hands and sat on the tiny toilet. He grunted and groaned and, eventually, the deputies looked away; the Asian smiled to himself, a barely perceptible smile, as he reached for the toilet-paper dispenser and, with deft fingers, removed an object that appeared to be a ballpoint pen from where it had been hidden inside the cardboard toilet-paper roll.

Sheridan could not see what the Asian was doing, exactly, not way down at the end of the aisle, through the heavy wire mesh, but he did see, or thought he saw, the trace of a smile on the Asian's face. That was enough to make Sheridan feel sure that the Chinese had sent the Asian.

"Do you want your black ass killed?"

Sheridan turned and the redneck's bloodshot eyes and awful yellow smile were an inch away.

"That's my bitch," the redneck said, "and I will not have you slobberin' on her with your eyeballs!"

His foul, tobacco-tainted breath was hot in Sheridan's face.

"I'm not interested in your girlfriend," Sheridan said softly.

The redneck's eyes flared; so did his nostrils, bull-like. "You callin' me a faggot?"

Sheridan said nothing. He was bringing his right arm over toward his left, to bring his casted elbow close to the fingers of his left hand, cuffed to the seat. His fingers worked at a tiny hole in the cast, which paralleled the pin in his elbow.

"I'm talkin' to you," the redneck blustered, leaning in. "What the hell you doin' there?"

Fuck this shit, Sheridan thought, and head-butted the son of a bitch, knocking him cold. With his right arm, Sheridan shoved the psycho redneck motherfucker back in his seat, where he slumped and might have been sleeping. A few prisoners noticed this but were only amused.

They did not notice that Sheridan was unobtrusively groping at his cast, trying to get the fingernails of his forefinger and thumb to catch the plastic coating of the Armani wire earpiece that he had snapped off Lieutenant Caldwell's glasses in the struggle on the floor back at the First Central District station, smuggling it out under his tongue, later embedding it in his cast.

In fact, just about the time that the Asian prisoner, Ling, was complaining of his stomach flu, Caldwell—about to read a book in bed, in his Naperville, Illinois, home—had put his glasses on, only to have them slide off and fall into his lap.

But even as the fugitive was easing the length of gold

wire from its tiny hole in the cast, the Asian prisoner was flushing the toilet to cover the click of the cocking of the .22 ballpoint pen. The next click would fire the single-shot weapon.

Ling, who was doing life without parole, knew he was on a probable suicide mission; but he also knew that his family, both here in the States and in Hong Kong, would be looked after. The Chinese mafia in America, after all, had close ties to the Hong Kong Triad, who were flourishing under the new Communist regime.

Sheridan was sliding one end of the gold-wire earpiece into the notch of his handcuff; he was sweating, but anxiety in this fugitive would never turn the corner into panic. He was cool, he was professional, and his hand did not shake as he worked the stiff wire in the handcuff's simple lock.

In the forward cabin, chubby Jack Stern was still at his crossword puzzle. " 'Split on ice,' " he said, seeking help from anyone who might offer it. "Seven letters."

"Banana," a plainclothes deputy offered.

"Bananas," Gerard said, not looking up from the article on trout fishing near Boulder, Colorado. "Plural."

"Yeah," Stern said, beaming. "Bananas. You sure you don't like puzzles?"

"Yeah," Gerard said, mildly irritated, and he unbuckled, leaving his magazine folded open to its place, and rose to go make himself some coffee in the galley down by the wire-mesh gate. Behind the fence-like barrier, Greg Conroy, shoulder bandaged, was seated over at the left; his brother Mike was up from Greg, on the right. Greg looked away from Gerard, while Mike glared at him. Gerard blew Mike a little kiss, and Mike sneered and looked out the window.

Chuckling softly, Gerard poured himself a cup of coffee, then looked to see if they had any half-and-half; he detested nondairy creamer.

As the manhunter searched for cream, the two deputies—the black somber one in front, the stocky pale one at the rear—were escorting the skinny Asian prisoner up the aisle. The fugitive caught this in his peripheral vision; he also noticed the Asian assassin, with a flick of the wrist, allowing something hidden in his orange sleeve to drop down into his palm.

Sheridan leaned into the aisle to face the oncoming deputies and their prisoner, who were coming up flush beside him now, and the Asian's arm jerked upward, like a robotic arm doing its job in an automated factory, and Sheridan knew at once that the object being aimed at his head, pointed at his head, was not a ballpoint pen, but a weapon.

A gun.

Though belly-chained, and even with his feet shackled to the floor, Sheridan—whose left hand was out of its cuff now—was able to lunge at the Asian, just as the Asian fired the .22 pen-gun, jarring his gun hand, sending the bullet flying narrowly past Sheridan's head, barely missing the slumped unconscious redneck who so admired the Asian, and punching through the window, which exploded into a sudden ragged impromptu doorway in the side of the plane, and as air shrieked through the gaping aperture, it was as if the plane itself were howling in pain from this wound inflicted by a skinny dead-eyed young man whose eyes came suddenly alive as he was sucked screaming out into a screaming sky.

Six

A full moon watched in mute witness as the heavens became home to hell. The Boeing 727 that was Federal Prisoner Transportation Service flight 343 heeled to the right, debris sucked out from within the plane—a blizzard of rubble, comprised of paperwork and life jackets and shoes and anything loose or anything that could be torn loose and ripped to shreds by the tornado of decompression within the cabin, flew backward, some of it into the night sky, some into the right and middle engines. The engine's turbines, like massive garbage disposals, did their best to grind up the debris, and failed, exploding, shaking the sky with man-made thunder, decorating it with bursts of orange and blue flame.

Within the cockpit, Captain Chris Kafer and First Officer Eric Hayes were doing their best to keep the plane in the air, Kafer calling "Mayday, mayday—F-PATS flight 343!" into his radio mike, working his voice above the bleating of an alarm klaxon.

In the cabin, those items that hadn't got sucked out flew

wildly about like birds caught in a wind tunnel. The stocky white deputy had followed the Asian into the sky, as if pursuing him; the black deputy was holding onto a seat for dear life, as were other deputies, wind whipping them mercilessly, and the prisoners, too, who were trying to catch the waving oxygen masks that had dropped automatically from above, batting awkwardly at them.

U.S. Deputy Marshal Sam Gerard was clinging like a spider to its web on the wire cage separating him from the main cabin and that sucking hole in the side of the ship, his stomach dropping to his shoes as the plane soared in its downward tilt. He had seen the Asian prisoner pointing and apparently firing something, a small gun, at another prisoner, a black guy; but the cause of this crisis was less important to him, at the moment, than simply surviving it.

Despite the efforts of the pilot and first officer to fight the plane's controls into submission, the 727—its engines coughing smoke, spouting fire, spitting sparks—pitched into a dive. Within the main cabin, the hard-bitten convicts swore and screamed and generally panicked, with the exception of Mark Sheridan, who with his uncuffed hands held tight to the arms of his seat, knowing that if he could live through this, he had a shot at freedom.

Gerard was facedown on his wire-mesh web, a trapeze artist who had fallen to his net, and as he clutched the steel mesh, feeling surprisingly serene, eyes filled with the gyrations of freaking-out prisoners, ears filled with their obscenities and the taunting howl of wind, he prayed for the welfare of his ex-wife and their son and asked forgiveness of his Lord.

Then the plane began to level out—still losing altitude, but equilibrium returning to the cabin—and Gerard let go of his wire-mesh cushion, which had become a wall again, the floor a floor again, properly under his feet, and he signed off with God to see if there was anything he could do to help keep himself alive awhile.

He staggered past Stern and Hollander, who were buckled into their seats, clutching the armrests, eyes like golf balls, and moved to the cockpit door, opening it.

The pilot was talking into his radio mike: ". . . lost two engines and need to make an immediate emergency landing."

They didn't need him bothering them, Gerard thought, and shut the door on them, returning to his seat and buckling in, even as the first officer's voice came over the intercom.

"We are about to make an emergency landing," the crackly voice said, and the shouts of fear and obscenity from the main cabin stopped as if shut off by a switch. "Sit forward and cover your head with your hands."

Even handcuffed, the prisoners could manage that, and they did, as the sound of landing gear doors opening, and wheels lowering, found its way above the wail of wind. An eerie sense of calm settled over the cabin.

Equally calm, though not eerily so, gliding down a rural highway below, his soul soothed by bluegrass from his radio, trucker Gary Meyers of Cedar Falls, Iowa, hauling eighteen wheels' worth of John Deere lawnmowers, was enjoying the ride—it was one of those rare clear nights where you could see everything, for mile upon mile.

Gradually the sound of an approaching vehicle worked itself above the bluegrass, interrupting his reverie, a peculiar sound, building to a roar that tweaked Meyers's attention, and made him wonder just what the hell kind of buggy was moving up behind his Peterbilt.

His side mirror gave him surprising news: the landing lights of a big motherfucking airplane (he did not recognize it as a 727—Meyers had never flown) were bearing down on him.

He hit the brakes, and they squealed like a hundred trailerloads of porkers, the thunderous airplane roar closing in on him, and he ducked down, as if aware that the 727's rear tires were at that moment barely missing the roof of his truck.

Then the huge plane was in front of him, billowing smoke, spewing flame, obviously a distressed aircraft trying to use the highway as a landing strip. Meyers jerked the wheel around as the Peterbilt skidded to a stop, jackknifing; up ahead, the airplane's tires hit the road, gray smoke rising like steam from the pavement.

In the cockpit, the pilot and copilot traded tentative smiles—so far so good—as the 727 barreled down the country highway, its brakes locking, the pilot steadying the wheel, staying on the road, a bully making oncoming traffic swerve out of the way, eyes wide behind windshields.

Relief rippled through the forward and main cabins, smiles forming, heads shaking, even some laughter erupting—the wheels were on the pavement, and they were rolling to a stop; they were going to make it!

But the pilot wasn't so sure. Up ahead, along the left side of the highway, like a tall fence, vertical lines in the moonlight, loomed a row of telephone poles; and within seconds, the left wing of the 727 began shearing through them, cutting them in half, tangles of wires descending, power lines sparking.

And in the main cabin of the prison ship, as that left wing battered its jarring way through the row of poles, relief was gone and alarm returned, obscenities rumbling like an engine starting up.

Impact upon impact, one sheared pole after another, took their toll, and the wing finally gave way, ripped from the plane like a wing from a roast chicken, taking much of the left undercarriage along with it, sending the plane atilt, on its left side, skidding down the pavement in a nails-on-blackboard screech of steel, with orange and blue flames streaming from its ruptured fuel tanks.

Horror gripped the passengers—prisoners and deputies alike—stilling the obscenities and screams and shouts, men frozen with fear and uncertainty as the crippled ship scraped its uncertain course down the rural highway, which was taking a right now, an inclined turn that the ship couldn't follow, and that the pilot couldn't do anything about. The right wing dragged along that incline, and was propelled upward, sending the plane slipping further to left, tilting even more, slamming its passengers to the left.

Missing its turn, the plane's fuselage smashed through a guardrail and plowed sideways down an embankment toward the waiting Ohio River, its shimmery surface holding the image of the placid moon. The plane made its careening way down the riverbank, ripping through trees that jolted the tail and left side engines until they finally separated from the ship in thunderous, flame-blossoming explosions.

With a few exceptions—Mark Sheridan and Sam Gerard, chiefly—the brutal men within the rotating ship were reduced to whimpering, weeping frightened children by the time the 727 finally flipped over into the river, making a tidal wave of a splash, destroying the placid moon.

It didn't take long for the river's surface to turn serene again, gently rippling around the floating, belly-up remains of the 727.

Within the dead ship, the cabin lights out and darkness descending, was a topsy-turvy nightmare world, prisoners dangling upside down, hanging like bats in a cave, held into their seats by their seat belts and shackles and chains, gripped also by a stunned silence, broken only by the sound of lapping water and crackling dying flames.

Then the plane seemed to shudder, unleashing a torrent of obscenity-laced shouts and panicky screams; the aft began settling, sinking, water gushing in through the hole in the side of the ship that the Asian's pen-gun had punched. Those prisoners hanging there, as the water below them rose up to greet them, struggled against their chains, freaking out in tears and terror. Two deputies were climbing up off the fuselage ceiling, which was now the floor, looking groggy but not obviously injured.

Gerard unbuckled himself with one hand and gripped an armrest with the other, then dropped nimbly to the ceiling. Before the lights had gone out, he had memorized the position of an emergency flashlight clipped to the wall; he yanked the Mag-Lite free, flicked it on and its ray caught the inverted face of Bill Hollander, dead in his upside-down seat, his neck broken.

"Shit," Gerard said softly.

Jack Stern and the young blond deputy were unbuckling themselves; Gerard helped them down from their seats, then crawled forward. Inside the cockpit, he helped the dazed pilot down; the copilot hung limp, neck broken.

Gerard moved to the forward exit door and, with the pilot's help, opened the hatch. This end of the plane was above water level, and in the clear moonlight the manhunter could see the riverbank and the rugged path the fuselage had carved through the trees. Safety was a hundred feet away, across the water.

Gerard motioned to Stern and the young deputy to join him; mussed, punchy, the two stumbled to his side.

"Is there an auto-release switch for these prisoners?" Gerard asked the young deputy.

"Yes."

"Well, hit it then. We want to jail 'em, not drown 'em."

The deputy moved forward, and speaking above the cacophony of screams and shouts and wailing from the rear, Gerard said to Stern, "I'm going back and try to get a rescue operation going. But these men are still prisoners. I want a couple of men on that riverbank, waiting with guns. Understood?''

Stern nodded, as the young deputy came up and asked, ''Are they loose?''

Gerard glanced back at the dangling, freaking-out prisoners. ''Does it look like it?''

The young deputy shook his head. ''The auto-release must be broken.''

''*All* the electrical's down,'' the pilot said.

Gerard put a hand on the young deputy's shoulder. ''Break out the guns, son. You and Jack and the captain here, head over to the shore and wait for me to deliver you some prisoners. Okay?''

The young deputy nodded, scurried off and came back with several wire baskets of sidearms, including Gerard's. Soon, Stern, the deputy and the captain jumped out of the plane into the water, and swam toward shore.

Using one of a ring of keys the young deputy had given him, Gerard—his nine-millimeter again in its shoulder holster—unlocked the cage door between the forward and main cabins, and, flashlight in hand, moved down into the sinking fuselage, under a ceiling of dangling deadbeats, where two deputies, one black, one white, met him.

''Gentlemen,'' Gerard said to them. ''We have work to do.''

They nodded.

Raising his palm like a traffic cop, Gerard shouted above the screams and wails: ''You will cooperate and stay quiet!''

The only sound now was the gushing of water through the gaping hole.

''I have men with guns on the shoreline,'' he said loudly. ''If you attempt to escape, you will be shot. Does anyone doubt my word?''

Cries of "No, no," "Fuck no," "Hell no," "Shit no" stopped when Gerard again raised his palm.

"Let 'em loose," he told the deputies, "one at a time, and let's get the hell outa here."

This elicited cheers, something Gerard had never before induced from felons.

The deputies began their task, unlocking belly chains and leg irons, helping the men down and dragging them toward the front exit, allowing the prisoners—one at a time—to drop into the water and begin splashing their way to the riverbank.

Gerard slipped out of his jacket and shoes. He moved down the slope of the ship toward the submerged rear of the fuselage, and suddenly a man dropped down in front of him, landing with catlike grace.

The manhunter, startled momentarily, did not know Mark Sheridan (or Mark Roberts) by name or otherwise, other than as one of the dozen faces of captured fugitives riding this prison ship. *Was this the guy that Asian had tried to shoot?*

Gerard said, "Going somewhere?"

"Just don't wanna drown."

The fugitive, whose right arm was in an elbow cast, held a piece of gold wire in his right hand; it reminded Gerard of nothing more than a wire-frame glasses earpiece.

"That the 'key' you used to undo your leg irons?" Gerard asked.

The fugitive nodded. "You looked busy."

"Now you're gonna be busy. You're helping me." He handed the fugitive the Mag-Lite. Gerard motioned to where the water was threatening to envelop the prisoners dangling at the rear. "Keep the light on their cuffs so I can unlock them. Fuck with me and die."

"Fair enough."

The plane shuddered again, the aft dropping sharply, manhunter and fugitive barely retaining their balance, the water now up and over five prisoners, who were sloshing and gurgling.

"Can you swim?" Gerard asked.

"Yes, sir."

"Good."

And the manhunter dove under the water, with the fugitive following. They worked efficiently together, the fugitive aiming the flashlight almost instinctively wherever Gerard needed it next. Two of the prisoners weren't moving, but three of them were, frantically, churning water with flailing arms. One of them was Mike Conroy—his brother Greg had already been taken to safety by a deputy—and Gerard unlocked him, and with the fugitive's help carted Conroy to the shoreline that was the slanting floor of the sinking fuselage; a deputy was waiting to drag Conroy to the fore exit. They had repeated the process with the second of the three surviving prisoners, when the ship shuddered again.

The black deputy took the prisoner from Gerard and looked at both manhunter and fugitive, saying, "We gotta get out of here, sir. Anybody left, better leave 'em."

"You go," Gerard said. He looked at the fugitive. "You want off, or you want to help me save that last poor bastard?"

The fugitive gestured with his head toward the water, and the two men exchanged a brief smile and dove back in. The last prisoner was still struggling, still alive, and the fugitive's flashlight beam helped Gerard free the guy, and the manhunter swam a longer distance this time, hauling the prisoner to the front of the nearly submerged plane, where the deputy no longer waited.

There was also no sign of the fugitive.

The ship shifted again, under the weight of the water it had taken on, and suddenly Gerard and his prisoner were underwater again; the manhunter grasped the man around the waist and propelled the two of them through the now-submerged exit door.

When they surfaced, the prisoner was barely conscious, and almost got caught by the current before Gerard grabbed him and lifeguarded him to the shore.

Jack Stern pulled the prisoner ashore as Gerard managed to haul his soggy ass out himself, collapsing onto his side on the bank, gulping air, washed in moonlight, glancing back at the plane, or anyway its nose, as it slipped under the surface with a gurgle from the river that seemed almost self-satisfied.

Soon the water's surface was placid again, gently rippling with the image of the moon.

And no sign of an escaped prisoner.

A fugitive.

Seven

By dawn the army of disaster's aftermath had moved into position on the Illinois side of the banks of the Ohio River, emergency vehicles and towering cranes, state and local police cars and mobile news units, the bustle and brouhaha drowning out the quiet sounds of a sunny morning, whose calm was reflected only by the half dozen mute body-bagged victims on the shore.

Observing this from a higher point, Sam Gerard, chilled to the bone on this pleasant A.M., face nicked and bruised, clothing still sopping even after several hours on shore, stood wrapped in a blanket like an Indian squaw, taking a paper cup of nondairy-creamer-polluted coffee provided him by a cheerful female deputy sheriff.

"There's plenty more where that came from," she said chirpily. "And don't worry about getting wired or anything. It's decaf."

He twitched a smile at her, as County Sheriff Patterson Poe—potbellied, potato-nosed, fiftyish, with wraparound sunglasses at odds with his good-ol'-boy demeanor—

headed over, barking a few commands at subordinates along the way.

"Found the two fellas that fell outa that plane," the sheriff told Gerard cheerfully. "That deputy, Clifford Willis? He turned up in a farmer's field—damn fall dug his own grave for hisself."

"Poor bastard," Gerard said.

"As for that Chinese, Ling? Sumbitch crashed through Harry Landers's farmhouse roof and landed right smack-dab in the damn bathtub. Looked like a big bowl of gumbo with a side of ribs."

"That's real colorful, Sheriff," Gerard said flatly.

Uniform still clinging damply, the black deputy who had helped ferry prisoners off the plane hustled up to Gerard, clipboard in hand; the soggy remains of the plane's manifest and various files were clipped there.

"Still got one prisoner unaccounted for, Marshal," the deputy said, and he held up the soggy file, displaying the photo of the black prisoner who had aided Gerard on the plane. "Mark J. Roberts. On his way to New York on a robbery/double homicide."

Sheriff Poe looked out at the river. "He'll probably turn up a floater, downstream, bloated and blue."

"He may turn up downstream," Gerard said, "but he won't be dead. The river didn't get this wily sucker. He's loose and he's running. . . . You got yourself a fugitive, Sheriff."

That seemed to give the sheriff pause, but only for a moment.

"Well, then," the sheriff said, hitching his gunbelt. "I guess we better find his ass."

At the base of the hillside, fairly near the riverbank, a triage tent with a platform floor had been erected, its canvas sides rolled up. Sheriff Poe stood within, a gaggle of local law enforcement gathered around him, as he played the big shot.

That was fine with Gerard, who was seated at a table off to one side, wrapped in his blanket, sipping his coffee. This was not his problem, and even if it had been, he probably would have bailed—somebody else from the USMS could take the necessary role in this. He was too beat-up and bushed to participate. For now he would just eavesdrop so he could bring up to speed whoever the office sent to replace him.

"Okay, everybody, listen up," Poe said. "We got ourselves a bone fide federal fugitive. Name is Roberts, Mark J. Fold out that map, there, darlin'. . . ."

A big map of the area—Illinois and adjacent Kentucky— was spread out by the female deputy like a tablecloth on one of the picnic-style tables.

"Okay," the sheriff said, whipping off his sunglasses, leaning over the map, gesturing with a wiggly finger, "let's talk roadblocks—general radius of ten, twelve miles—"

"Twelve minimum," Gerard said from the sidelines. "I'd advise twenty."

The sheriff and his people looked at the deputy marshal; Poe had the expression of a man who wasn't sure if he was being assisted or insulted.

"He's got a three-hour head start," Gerard said. "Average foot speed over uneven terrain, barring injury, is four miles an hour. But this is an extremely physically fit individual. And he probably swam, some. Twenty should cover it."

"Okay, then," the sheriff said, "twenty-mile radius, and that means in all directions, just like a big, uh . . ."

"Perimeter," Gerard said.

"Circle," Poe said. "Now, that'll start somewhere near . . . uh . . ."

The sheriff was studying the map; he scratched his head,

working his hand up under his Smokey the Bear hat, then he scratched his ass, then his head, again.

That did it. Gerard could not abide having a man in charge who could not decide whether to scratch his head or his ass.

Shifting into an overdrive he didn't realize he still had in him, Gerard rose, the blanket dropping in a flannel puddle, and moved to the table, where he gestured to the map with a thick pointing finger.

"Said perimeter to extend from Brookport downstream to Mound City," the manhunter said. "Block every bridge across the Ohio from Golconda to Metropolis to Cairo. Moving down from the Pulaski and Alexander county lines, check every hotel and motel and bed-and-breakfast, every hospital and veterinary, every backroad and backwater. Mr. Roberts is a resourceful and dangerous individual, wanted in a robbery/double homicide, and we can assume he will arm himself as soon as possible. Let's plaster him on the local TV until the citizens in your fair corner of the world are so familiar with our fugitive's face, they'll think they're related to him. . . . Anything to add, Sheriff?"

The sheriff was blinking. "No, uh, I think you've about covered it for now."

"Good. Then let's go, boys and girls."

The deputies and cops scurried to do that, then Gerard yelled out, "One more thing!", freezing them in place.

He lifted the paper coffee cup. "Could somebody get me something with with some goddamn caffeine in it? Coffee, Diet Coke, Mountain Dew, anything?"

The female deputy grinned and said, "You got it, Marshal."

"Thanks. And see if you can rustle me up a cell phone I can use."

The group dispersed, and Gerard hunkered over the map, wondering what kind of fugitive he was after. Had that plane crashed as a result of a failed attempt on the fugitive's life? If so, was the assassination attempt some simple jail-house beef, a lover's quarrel perhaps? Or was somebody trying to silence Roberts?

Because Gerard searched for escapees, he considered himself more manhunter than detective; he sought criminals, not the whys or wherefores of their crimes. Still, the puzzle of what had happened on that plane mattered to Gerard because it would help him understand the nature of the beast he was tracking.

The female deputy delivered a Diet Coke and a cell phone. He thanked her, she smiled, and he called the USMS Chicago office and instructed them to assign his warrants squad to the search.

Sheriff Poe shuffled up, his expression somewhat sheep-ish now. "Uh, Marshal, there's a slew of media up on the hill—TV, radio, papers—kinda chompin' at the bit."

Gerard glanced up the roadside and saw the reporters milling there; didn't take flies long to find shit. "I think you're up to handling that, Sheriff."

"All due respect, Marshal, but it's your investigation now. I'd appreciate it if you'd give 'em a word or two."

"All right," Gerard sighed, wearily, and trudged up to meet them, facing the out-thrust microphones, extended cassette tape recorders and cold glass eyes of shouldered Minicams with stoic indifference.

He was still approaching when the volley of overlapping questions began; he didn't recognize any faces—these were local news, probably from nearby Paducah.

An attractive blond woman asked, "What happened on that plane?"

"The Federal Aviation Administration will be here soon with that information," Gerard said.

"Was there a shot fired?" a pretty brunette asked. Most TV field reporters these days seemed to be young good-looking women, Gerard noted; not that he was complaining—that was how he'd met Stacia Vela, after all.

"That's another question better suited for the FAA," Gerard said.

A homely pockmarked male holding a cassette tape recorder posed a question; newspaper, not TV. Obviously. "We understand you have a fugitive. Was he the individual who fired the shot?"

Gerard said, "I didn't confirm that a shot was fired. Would you like to ask me how long I've been beating my wife?"

"Is it true your fugitive was with you on the plane?" the blonde asked. "Helping with the rescue efforts?"

Already, leaks to the press. Gerard would have to have a little talk with the law enforcement personnel here at the crash site.

"Marshal Gerard," the blonde pressed, "wasn't this fugitive seen helping you rescue other prisoners before he escaped?"

Gerard stared into the hungry faces and thrusting mikes and glass camera eyes and sighed. Then he flinched a smile and said, "That's right."

And every reporter there fired off another question at him, a blurred barrage out of which one question stood out: "Marshal Gerard, weren't you in charge of the Richard Kimble manhunt?"

It was going to be a long morning.

Roy Willy's World's Best Bar-B-Q was a fairly grandiose name for the shabby clapboard rib shack along the roadside, overlooking the crash site. People came from all around to Roy Willy's, however, and right now a dark-blue Suburban was pulling into the graveled lot.

Four United States deputy marshals hauling duffel bags clambered out of the rental utility vehicle: Robert Biggs, who'd been driving, his massive frame in a plaid shirt with solid-color tie, jeans and boots; Savannah Cooper, a leather vest over her denim shirt, ready to rock 'n' roll in blue cords and hiking boots; ponytailed Noah Newman, in a dark sweatshirt with the USMS badge logo on its breast, jeans, Nike hightops; and Cosmo Renfro—who also carted a shopping bag—spiffy in a peach Calvin Kline button-down shirt with diamond-pattern Perry Ellis tie, jeans and Hush Puppies.

They were immediately struck by the panoramic view of the river from the Roy Willy's lot, witnessing the arms of a pair of huge crawler cranes collaborating to lift the ragged, scorched, wingless fuselage of the 727 from the water onto the riverbank.

"Jesus!" Biggs said. "The Big Dog swam away from *that*?"

"That girl is definitely in need of a makeover," Renfro said of the fuselage.

Opening a door with a "CLOSED—PLEASE CALL AGAIN" card in its window, Gerard—his torn clothing still damp—stepped outside of the restaurant to greet his crew.

"We've commandeered this fine establishment, ladies and gentlemen," Gerard said. "Cosmo, do you have clothes for me?"

Renfro smiled weakly and nodded, hefting the shopping bag.

Cooper crossed to her boss, touching his elbow, saying, "Looks like you hung onto *your* wings, anyway."

"You doin' okay, Boss?" Newman asked.

"No," Gerard said. He took the shopping bag from Renfro, lifted out its contents: a lavender sweatsuit with silver racing stripes.

"Best I could do at the airport," Renfro explained.

Gerard's deadpan slow burn elicited smiles from his

team, but they knew enough to stop short of outright laughter.

Inside the restaurant, whose staff was entirely absent, the rustic place having been converted to a joint manhunt-task-force and crash-investigation headquarters, Gerard's people helped themselves to potato chips, candy bars and sodas.

"Pay as you go, children," Gerard said, demonstrating by borrowing five dollars from Newman to pay for the Roy Willy's World's Best Bar-B-Q T-shirt Gerard plucked from the wall behind the cash register. He placed the five spot on the counter, behind which he pulled on the T-shirt and climbed into the sweat pants; to pay for their goodies, as instructed, his people tossed coins and dollar bills on the counter, stealing glances and making remarks as Gerard changed.

"How much for a table dance?" Renfro asked.

"Now that you've been thoroughly entertained," Gerard said, coming around and going to the large map pinned to one rough-hewn wall, "let me bring you up to date."

As they sat at a nearby table, munching chips, sipping sodas, he filled them in on what he knew, including his suspicions that Mark Roberts had been the target of the assassin's bullet that had brought down the 727.

"Do you think this guy, Roberts, was really trying to help out on the plane?" Newman asked. "Or was he just looking for an opening to escape?"

"Yes," Gerard said. He let his people think about his response for a moment, then he turned to the map, and gestured to an area north of the Ohio River. "State Police picked up a shoe near Hillerman an hour ago, but we got nothing since." Then he turned back to them: "Now that I've given you that wealth of information, what have you got for me?"

"Jack squat," Biggs said. "This guy flat-out doesn't exist."

"I just imagined him," Gerard said.

"Called himself 'Mark Warren' in Chicago," Newman said, reading from a notepad. "But all his I.D.s were forged."

"Good forgeries, though," Renfro said. "Real professional."

"Why am I not surprised?" Gerard asked. "So much for Mark Warren—what about Mark Roberts?"

The churning thunder of a helicopter drawing closer caught their attention.

"So far," Cooper said over the drone, "he's nothin' but a picture and a set of prints on a federal warrant."

Out the window, a black copter was setting down in the graveled lot, right next to Roy Willy's neon sign.

"Jeez," Renfro said, "they really *do* come from all around for the ribs, don't they?"

The deputies went outside to meet the trio of men in suits and ties and dark sunglasses who were stepping from the copter, before its blades had even wound down. The arrivals moved through the minor cloud of parking lot dust the copter had stirred, like ghosts materializing.

Two of the men were from the same cookie cutter—in their forties, pale, patrician, dark-haired, slender as knife blades in their well-cut but anonymous dark suits—except that one of them—the one leading the way—had rather hawkish cheekbones to set him apart, and a flat black attaché case carried in his right hand. The third man was younger, no more than his late twenties, boyishly handsome with a swimmer's build made for his gray Brooks Brothers suit, which was set off nicely by a shades-of-blue patterned tie. He also had a mouth that seemed fixed in a faint, permanent smirk, which immediately rubbed Gerard the wrong way.

The hawkish leader of the trio looked over his welcoming committee and, seeing Gerard in the Roy Willy's T-shirt, said, "I'm looking for Deputy Marshal Sam Gerard."

"You've found him," Gerard said. "And you are?"

The leader withdrew a billfold, flipped it open to a set of credentials that were as flashy as a mail-order diploma. "Bertram Lamb, head of Diplomatic Security Service, New York office. This is Special Agent Frank Barrows . . . ," he indicated his near twin, then the younger man, ". . . and Special Agent John Royce."

Nobody offered to shake hands.

"Could we have a word alone, Deputy?" Lamb asked.

Gerard nodded as his deputies made la-de-da faces at each other, and stayed outside as their boss led the agents inside Roy Willy's. He steered them into the kitchen, the air thick with the smell of barbecue sauce. Lamb and Barrows took off their sunglasses, but Royce left his on.

Folding his arms, leaning back against a steel work counter, Gerard said, "What's cooking, gentlemen?"

Barrows said, "We'd like to discuss Mark Roberts."

"Okay by me."

Lamb asked, "What do you know about him?"

"Double homicide. Robbery. Flight."

Lamb set the thin black attaché case on the steel counter and snapped it open, withdrawing a manila envelope. He handed this to the deputy marshal, and with a curt nod indicated that Gerard should look inside.

He did. Half a dozen color photos of a grisly crime scene showed the bodies of two men asprawl on a cement carpet, apparently a parking garage. One of the corpses was blood-splotched, the other not, though both were obviously dead.

"These were not civilians," Lamb said.

"Yours?" Gerard asked.

"Mine."

"All information released regarding this matter," Barrows clarified, "was sanitized—national security."

"Okay," Gerard said. "So who is Roberts?"

"We don't know," Lamb said.

"You don't know?"

"He's an American with a service record—United States Marines—and that's how we identified his fingerprints at the scene. Otherwise, all we know is we've been chasing this man for over six months."

"We theorize he's a freelance assassin," Barrows added.

Gerard studied the gruesome photos. "Why did a freelance assassin hit two of your people?"

"I'm afraid that's on a need-to-know basis," Lamb said.

"And you don't figure I need to know."

"You know that your fugitive killed two government agents," Barrows said. "Isn't that enough?"

Gerard looked at the young agent, Royce. "Don't you ever say anything?"

"I only speak when I'm spoken to," he said. There was a glibness, a smart-alecky tone, that went well with the smirk.

"So," Gerard said. "Is my team working for you guys now? If so, I'd like to see that in writing . . ."

"That's not my intention," Lamb said. "This is still your investigation."

"Your reputation precedes you, Deputy," Barrows said. "We'd like you to continue administrating this pursuit. We want Roberts."

"We want him right away," Lamb said.

"We do 'right away,' " Gerard said. "That's our house specialty."

"Good," Lamb said. "Now, I'm sure you can understand the need for my office to be kept in the loop on this, every step of the way."

"I'll see to it you're kept up to speed," Gerard said.

"I've already taken care of that," Lamb said. "That's Agent Royce's job."

Gerard glanced at the young agent. "How exactly is it his 'job'?"

"He's joining your team, as of now," Lamb said.

Royce flicked a smile, saluted a little and Gerard shot him a brief, withering look, then said to Lamb, "No offense, gentlemen, but I don't have any openings for a diplomat on my team. If fast results are your priority, you'll find we can work faster without any outside . . . help."

"No offense taken," Lamb said, "but this isn't optional, Deputy Gerard. We have clearance directly from the U.S. Attorney General, as Marshal Walsh in Chicago will, I'm sure, be happy to confirm."

Barrows said, "Royce is one of our best men."

"I'm sure you'll find him useful," Lamb added, snapping shut his attaché case.

Within minutes, Lamb and Barrows were back on their black helicopter, rising into the blue sky in a cloud of tan dust. Gerard's squad gathered around him, their expressions of confusion tied to the continued presence—off to one side—of their third visitor.

"Special Agent John Royce of the Diplomatic Security Service," Gerard said, "has been assigned to help us."

Renfro shrugged. "Maybe he can teach the Big Dog to be more diplomatic."

That got some laughs, but not from Gerard, whose face was stony as Royce approached, black duffel bag in hand. The rest of the squad instinctively knew to give the two men some room, and moved to an outdoor picnic table, where they sat sipping sodas while Gerard and Royce spoke.

"If it's any consolation," Royce said, "I wouldn't like it, either, if I got somebody foisted—"

"It's not any consolation. Take off your sunglasses."

"What? Why?"

"I want to see your eyes."

Royce removed the glasses, tucked them in his breast suitcoat pocket; his brown eyes were long-lashed and almost feminine in their beauty. They had a disarming quality that took the edge off the faint smirk.

"Hi," Royce said.

Gerard asked, "How and why did you pull this duty?"

His mouth shrugged. "I volunteered for it. Those two agents murdered in that parking garage . . . well, I don't know about you, but the people I work with, they get to be like friends or family."

"This is personal, then."

"Yes."

"Then you're not going to fit in on my team. We don't allow personal feelings to enter in."

Royce's forehead tightened. "I think I can maintain a professional attitude."

"Ever collar a fugitive?"

"No. This will be my first."

"I hope you won't mind if we help you make it. You have a gun?"

The smirk blossomed. "Does a bear shit in the woods?"

"Don't get cute."

Royce withdrew a Colt .45 automatic from a shoulder holster, handed it butt-first to Gerard.

"Heavy hardware," the manhunter said. "You know, a nine-millimeter does much the same job without this bulk; they don't jam as easily, either."

"I'll take that under advisement."

"Let's see your backup piece."

"Don't carry one."

Gerard frowned. "Why not?"

"If that forty-five can't stop them, they're not human."

"Get a backup piece. A fugitive chase can get down and dirty. . . . You never know what contingency you're facing next, up against dangerous, wanted, *running* men." Gerard

65

handed Royce the .45 back, butt first. "And keep that tucked away unless it's time to use it. . . . All right, people!"

The warrants squad, seated at the picnic table, came to attention as their boss ambled over, commands tumbling out of his mouth, and as each of their names was called and their assignments given, the squad members rose and scurried off to carry them out.

"Biggs, get the director of the state police on the horn. . . . Cooper, this Chinese character, Ling, let's dig up some background on him, shall we? . . . Cosmo, see if Sheriff Poe has got anything new to report, and if he's standing on his dick, point it out gently to him. . . . Noah, you come with me."

Gerard was heading toward the slope down to the riverbank; and Newman, about to tag along, took the time to speak to their new team member.

"Never saw him take to somebody so quick," Newman told the diplomatic security agent.

And then Special Agent John Royce was standing, alone, in the Roy Willy's World's Best Bar-B-Q parking lot.

Eight

To a fugitive on the run in the woods, few sounds send the pulse racing faster than the baying of hounds, accompanied by their frantic slobbering as they paw and claw through the underbrush, and the snapping of branches underfoot as their masters follow obediently after them.

In the hours before dawn, scrambling through the woods, staying close to the river, knowing a bridge would have to eventually show itself, Mark Sheridan had lost a shoe—his poor left foot swaddled in strips torn from his shirt—and now, as dawn fingered its way through the trees, he knew from the sound of those approaching hounds that his shoe had been found.

Indeed, the Illinois State Police and deputies of Sheriff Patterson Poe were moving in a line along the edge of the Ohio River, their dogs incensed by the scent of a prison-issue rubber-soled canvas slip-on.

The barking and the baying echoed through the trees, propelling the fugitive onward, as he hobbled through the woods, high weeds whispering under his movement, twigs snapping under his feet, occasionally something sharp gouging his shirt-strip-wrapped foot, which was bloody and getting swollen. His elbow cast was soggy and bloody, as well. The mugginess of the morning was beading his black flesh, exposed by his shredded orange shirt, a glistening patina whose sleekness was occasionally disrupted by the nicks from branches and brush, and the bumps of mosquito bites.

Emerging from the woods, the fugitive slowed his run before he could fall tumbling down the rocky slope of a ravine that stood between him and escape. Behind him, the hounds yapped and howled and vegetation crackled and fluttered; below him yawned a steep, rugged ride down into a gully whose floor was a tangled parody of a forest, ugly weeds grown to grotesque trees. Telephone and power lines on utility poles spanned the nasty thicket-choked trench.

Sheridan's eyes narrowed, as he considered a risky but possible escape route; but even if he made it, those dogs and their masters might find their way around the ravine and back onto his trail. He needed to throw the mutts off. . . .

He unzipped his orange prisoner's pants.

It took a while to will himself to do it, as if he were at a urinal in a men's room with some guy sneaking a look; anybody could get stage fright under those conditions.

But finally the yellow stream of urine was sailing down into the thicket; using his penis as a paintbrush, Sheridan coated the rock-strewn drop-off, and the urine glistened like gold in the sunlight, catching green leaves like fresh morning dew.

Piss on you bastards, he thought, shaking off, putting himself away, and then, like the world's most nimble telephone repair man, he scrambled up a utility pole. At the top, he paused and considered the various lines snaking their way across the ravine, power and phone; the sturdiest of these, a power cable, would be his best bet. It would be insulated, meaning it technically shouldn't kill his ass . . . but Sheridan knew that, over time, that insulation could wear out.

What he needed to do was make sure he wasn't grounded; he had to become part of any potential circuit—so he leapt from the pole to the cable, grabbing on with his good hand. When he didn't start frying, he hooked his arm with the elbow cast up and over, and then his feet, the shod one and the cloth-wrapped one, and began to crab his way across.

If he didn't make it before the dogs and their masters cleared the woods, he would provide a fine target.

With the howling and rustling ever louder, he shimmied across, in agony, every muscle aching, every nick and cut burning, every bug bite itching, and after an eternity that was two minutes and fifty-seven seconds, he swung from the cable, letting go of it, leaping at the pole, clutching onto it and clinging there like a koala bear.

Then he climbed quickly down and headed back into the woods, and relative safety. But soon he realized he could no longer hear, no longer sense, the river; his entire sense of direction was askew. And in these dense woods, with their ceiling of branches and leaves, he could not get a fix on the sun.

Behind him, things were going better. The hounds had pulled the Illinois State Police and Sheriff Patterson's deputies out of the woods and to the edge of the ravine, where the scent of urine sent the dogs into an orgasmic frenzy. The dogs yanked their handlers down the sudden craggy slope and tumbling into the tangled mess below, trapping themselves.

Sheridan, looking for a bridge, came to a highway first, a four-lane—Interstate 24—and, getting his bearings as best he could, moved south, staying in the woodland parallel to the roadside, not wanting the Illinois Highway Patrol to spot his orange prisoner's pajamas. In a little more than half a mile, he came upon a rest stop, or an excuse for a rest stop—just a couple porta-potties and picnic tables and refuse barrels.

This wretched little pit stop at the moment had attracted only one customer—an eighteen-wheeler with an oversize tractor-trailer cab, whose driver was crossing the shallow graveled parking area to one of the plastic toilets, sending a sparking butt flying toward a refuse barrel, missing it. Pushing forty, he was a burly trucker with longish hair and a scruffy beard, a Budweiser baseball cap, jeans riding low over a beer belly, and a leather vest over a white T-shirt; he had the look of an ex-biker not quite ready to accept his age.

A fugitive does things he would not do in his normal life. Mark Sheridan was a violent man only in the sense that his life had taken him into a violent job, a job whose violence was justified by his government's needs. But even a good man, an unjustly accused man like Mark Sheridan, sent scrambling through a forest with dogs and men tracking him, can do things he would never, normally, do. Things to survive.

Things like slip into the cab of the tractor-trailer, knowing that he couldn't drive this big rig himself, that he would have to take a hostage, and then finding himself face-to-face with a hostage he hadn't planned on taking.

She was a frizzily-blond woman of perhaps thirty-five who had once been voluptuous but had crossed over into chunky, bulging her plaid shirt and faded jeans, fussing with some coffee at the kitchenette of the six-by-eight cabin, complete with TV and bunk bed.

"That was quick, Earl," the woman said, then glanced up to see a bedraggled, mosquito-bitten, blood-streaked, very black man moving toward her.

He covered her mouth with a palm, stifling the scream, her eyes—a pretty blue-green—wide above the blackness of his hand. And from the kitchenette counter, he grabbed a kitchen knife—small, sharp, potentially deadly—and he held its point to her throat, moving around behind her, putting the woman—who was breathing hard—into traditional hostage posture.

The cab door opened and her husky husband climbed in, saying, "Got that coffee, Martha?"

And the trucker looked back to see his wife with a knife to her throat, courtesy of a black bastard in tattered orange prisoner's apparel.

"Shut the door, Earl," the fugitive said. "I'm not lookin' for trouble—just a lift."

"Don't you hurt her," Earl said in a high-pitched voice that didn't suit him.

Earl's lower lip was trembling within the nest of his beard; Sheridan couldn't tell whether that came from worry or rage.

"I don't intend to hurt anybody. I'm just a guy in a bind—you've been in a bind before, haven't you, Earl?"

Earl said nothing.

"You got any weapons aboard, Earl?"

Earl shook his head, no.

"Okay, then. Just drive and everybody's gonna be fine."

They drove. The fugitive instructed Martha to curl up on the lower bunk and helped himself to a change of clothes, black T-shirt and jeans, Earl's size proving a little baggy on Sheridan, but preferable to Day-Glo orange. Then, kitchen knife nearby, he sat on the floor near Martha, using a small saw and pliers from a toolbox under the sink to work at getting the soggy, cracked cast off his elbow. He had helped himself to an extra pair of Earl's shoes—work boots—and they were a little big, but they beat the hell out of a single canvas slip-on and bloody strips of shirt. The strips and the pieces of the cast littered the cabin floor. Sheridan searched through cupboards, looking for a first aid kit, found one and applied an Ace bandage to his sore elbow.

He was aware that Earl had angled his rearview mirror so that the trucker could keep one eye on the road and the other on his unwanted passenger; but the fugitive couldn't blame the man. He felt bad about putting these apparently decent people through a hijack like this, and knew all the calming words in the world wouldn't take the edge off a knife-wielding escaped convict. That they were white and he was black added another dangerous element.

Earl was not aware, however, just how close an eye the fugitive was keeping on him. When the trucker moved ever so slightly forward, thinking his motion was barely perceptible, that it had gone unnoticed, feeling under the seat for the .38 Smith and Wesson snubby tucked there and shifting the rest of his concentration to the road before his hand emerged gripping the .38, the fugitive was on top of him in a blur, one hand grabbing Earl's arm, yanking it over, the truck swerving onto the shoulder, as the fugitive's other hand twisted the revolver from the trucker's grasp.

Instinctively, Earl began pumping the brakes, and Martha—on her way up to help him—was thrown forward onto her face, on the cabin floor. Her fingers found the knife even as the truck shrieked to a skidding stop, other cars and trucks honking angrily on their way around.

Sheridan was tossed against the rider's seat, but the gun wasn't dislodged, and he turned with it in hand and pointed it at Martha, whose eyes went wide as she dropped the knife. Sheridan reached his foot out and kicked it under the bunk.

Seated on the floor behind the rider's seat, Sheridan said, "You lied to me, Earl."

"Fuck you," Earl said.

"That's one thing you don't want to do, Earl, is fuck with me. The second to the last thing I want to do is hurt you. But the last thing I want to do is get caught. Follow?"

Earl, breathing hard, nodded.

"Get rolling again, Earl."

And the trucker rolled back onto the highway.

The fugitive was hefting the revolver. "If I wasn't so happy to have this, Earl, I might be pissed."

The next half hour or so was uneventful. The fugitive instructed Martha to take the rider's seat at the front of the cab and he, and his appropriated .38 snubnose, took the lower bunk. He rested without closing his eyes, though Martha occasionally glanced back to see if had fallen asleep; she even smiled at him, nervously, a few times, lamely covering herself.

Then Earl and Martha exchanged edgy glances, and Sheridan knew something else was up. He moved forward, leaned between them. A sign announced the Ohio River—the same body of water the fugitive had crashed into in that plane—and there it was, looming blue-green up ahead, and a bridge.

At the bridge's far end, a Kentucky State Police car barred the way. Another car was ahead of them as Earl slowed into the roadblock.

"Don't lose your cool, Earl," the fugitive said. "You've lied to cops before."

And the fugitive faded back into the cabin, ducking into the bunk, getting out of sight as a trooper sidled up to the cab, another officer waiting back at their vehicle.

"We have a fugitive at large, sir," the trooper said. "From that plane wreck."

"No shit," Earl said.

"Would you open your door, please?"

Earl did, and the trooper stepped up on the running board to peek in.

"He's an Afro-American, about thirty, six feet, hundred and seventy pounds," the trooper said.

"Ain't seen anybody like that, officer," Earl said.

"Me neither," Martha said, smiling too much, leaning forward. "We don't pick up no 'Afro-American' hitchhikers. Hope ya find him, 'fore he causes any more trouble."

She sure was chatty, Sheridan thought. Was she gesturing with her eyes or something . . . ?

And now the fugitive noticed, propelled there when the brakes had skidded earlier, his tattered strips of bloody shirt and the bloody husk of his shoulder cast, on the floor between the driver's and rider's seats.

She had signaled the trooper. Goddamn it!

Sheridan bolted forward, stuck the nose of the .38 behind Earl's ear and said, "Go!"

And the tractor-trailer lurched forward, the trooper tumbling from the running board, Earl slamming the door shut, .38 snout in his neck, the fugitive screaming, "Go go go!" as the rig plowed like a battering ram into the Kentucky police car, knocking it to one side, crumpling it like a beer can as the trooper standing guard there hurtled himself to safety, splashing into the river below.

By the time either trooper could do anything about it, the truck was gone; but within the vehicle, the passenger with the gun was fumbling with a road map. At the town ahead—West Paducah—this highway connected with another interstate. But the troopers would be out in force.

He needed to disappear.

Symbols on the map, signifying swampland, suggested an alternative, however unpleasant.

"Turn up there," he told Earl, gesturing to a gravel side road.

As much fun as Earl and Martha had been, it was time to get back out on his own.

Nine

The fuselage of the dead 727 lay like a dinosaur's carcass on the Ohio River bank; within the fallen beast moved smaller organisms—creatures not of decay but of analysis, poking through the muck and debris that littered the floor, braving the oppressive reeking atmosphere in a darkness broken only by occasional slants of light through ruptures in the hull.

Using a mini-Mag-Lite, Gerard—wearing a sport jacket and tie and jeans, a care package of his clothes having arrived thanks to Catherine Walsh—searched the floor around the area where Mark Roberts had sat; the beam picked up a familiar object, caught in the goo of mud that had seeped into the ship.

"What's that?" Royce wondered. He had filed down the aisle right after Gerard. Renfro, Newman and Biggs were lined behind them, like passengers aboard a ghost ship, anything but eager to take a seat.

"Looks like a ballpoint pen," Gerard said.

He plucked it from the muck and held it up to the Mag-Lite's beam.

"But it isn't," Royce said.

Gerard twisted the "pen" open, disassembling it into the components of the single-shot weapon it was. The spent shell casing was nestled within.

Newman leaned in for a look. "I don't suppose that weapon belonged to one of the deputies."

Now Renfro crowded in. "Naw, I don't think zip guns are standard issue on Federal Corrections prisoner transports."

"We're damn lucky this didn't get sucked out in the sky with that fella, Ling," Gerard said.

"I never even *saw* a pen-gun before," Renfro said.

"I have," Biggs offered, peering over the heads of his smaller colleagues.

"Yeah?" Renfro asked, mildly impressed.

"I think it was *The Spy Who Loved Me*. Or maybe *Goldfinger*."

Renfro rolled his eyes, then his attention returned to the deadly little weapon, the pieces of which were in his boss's palm. "But what's this doin' here? Spy shit like that."

Gerard handed the pieces to Renfro. "Send it into the lab. Maybe they can tell us."

"Tell us what?" Renfro wondered.

"Whether it's a custom item, handmade, or actually manufactured somewhere, country of origin. . . . Let's de-plane, shall we, children?"

On the riverbank, the deputies—liberated from the musty, fetid odor of the plane's carcass—sucked in fresh air. Cooper, cell phone in hand, was coming down the hill from the rib shack, a certain urgency in her step.

"Boss," she said, approaching, "I got something on your shooter in the plane."

"Good."

"Vincent Ling—on his way back to the pen after losing his appeal. Life sentence for murder, no possibility of parole. He's a hit man, Sam—enforcer for the Chinese mafia."

"Could I borrow your handcuffs?"

Despite the vital information Cooper was imparting, Gerard's attention was drawn elsewhere.

"What?" Cooper asked, already taking her cuffs from her purse. "Sure. . . ."

Off to one side, facing the river, Royce stood, using his cell phone.

Gerard took the cuffs, smiled his thanks to a confused Cooper, held up his hand to silence her before she said anything else, and stepped up stealthily behind the diplomatic security agent.

"Pen-gun," Royce was saying, "Korean—'Stinger' XL-17, standard twenty-two-caliber. Amazing it was still on there, but Gerard's got an eye, picked it right out with a little flashlight—"

"I have ears, too," Gerard said.

Royce swiveled, his mouth dropped like a trapdoor, his eyes wide open and innocent.

"The better to hear you with," Gerard said, and grabbed the phone from the young agent's hand and tossed it into the water, where it plunked like a stone.

"What the hell do you think you're doing?" Royce demanded, holding his now-empty hands in front of him. "That's my phone, my *personal* phone!"

Fast as an eyeblink, Gerard slapped Cooper's cuffs on Royce, whose expression was a symphony of outrage and shock.

"You're under arrest for obstructing a federal investigation," Gerard said.

The deputies had seen this confrontation building and were slowly gathering, amusement tickling their faces.

"You have the right to remain silent," Gerard continued.

"Oh, come on, who are you kidding? This isn't convictable."

"It's arrestible," Gerard said brightly. "Should you wish an attorney—"

"Are you crazy?" He turned to Renfro. "Is he crazy? Is he stark staring nuts?"

"Maybe not 'stark staring,' " Renfro said. "But he's definitely a carrier."

"My superiors aren't going to like this one little bit," Royce said, huffily.

"I'm your superior," Gerard reminded him. "And I like it fine. . . . Sit down and shut up."

Royce just looked at him.

Gerard sighed, shook his head and shoved the younger man to the ground, where he landed in a sitting position, more or less.

Biggs moved in, hands on his hips, and was shaking his head, as if he were witnessing something unfortunate, or sad. "See, when you know something he doesn't," Biggs said, "and you don't share it with the class? Teacher gets pissed off."

"Get me out of these goddamn handcuffs, Deputy," Royce demanded of Gerard, holding up his locked-together fists. "Right now."

"Get out of them yourself," Gerard said casually.

The deputies had circled around and were smiling openly now; Renfro was chuckling. Royce began to understand the fraternity house nature of his situation and grinned at them.

"Okay," he said, just as casually.

He got to his feet. Glancing around at the deputies, he centered on the smirking Renfro and moved toward him. Renfro's smirk froze as the cuffed hands rose to his shirt pocket and Royce lifted out the deputy's Ray-Bans. He stepped back, quickly removing the wire temple piece from the sunglasses—Renfro said, "Hey!"—and in less than ten seconds, the diplomatic security agent had worked the wire piece in the cuff notches and the handcuffs were shaken off his wrists, falling to the soft earth of the riverbank.

"What's next, kids?" Royce asked. "Cow tipping? Maybe t.p. Sheriff Poe's place?"

Cooper bent to pick up her cuffs. "That's pretty slick, Slick."

"Thank you," Royce said.

"Very damn slick," Newman agreed.

"Way cool," Biggs nodded.

"Fuck you, guys!" Renfro said, snatching back the wire-frame temple. "The prick busted my Ray-Bans!"

"Arrest me," Royce suggested.

"All right, all right, back to school," Gerard instructed his charges, and they began to scatter up the hillside.

Then to Royce, Gerard said, softly: "I don't mind you reporting in—that's your job. But the next time you withhold something from the group, your ass is gone."

"Fair enough," Royce said with a nod, and he fell in step with Biggs and Newman, heading up the hillside.

Cooper had hung back. She was looking at her handcuffs. "Man, I never saw *that* before."

"I have," Gerard said.

Minutes later, inside, Gerard stood at the map, and pointed to a red pin—Hillerman.

"Based upon where that shoe was found," the manhunter said, "I suggest we get on the radio and move the perimeter south—our fugitive may've already made it into Kentucky."

Renfro was bent over his cell phone, listening intently, talking occasionally.

"Statistically," Royce said, leaning back in a chair, tenting his fingers, "there's a greater chance he'll go toward the nearest metropolitan city—St. Louis, most likely."

"We're chasing a man," Gerard said, "not a statistic, Mr. Royce."

Renfro snapped his cell phone shut, got to his feet and moved to the map. "Our fugitive was spotted near Metropolis."

"Royce said he was headed to a metropolitan area," Newman offered with a grin.

Gerard frowned at the map. "Where is Metropolis, anyway?"

"Due north of Gotham City," Biggs said.

"Quiet, Biggs," Cooper said.

"An eighteen-wheeler rammed a roadblock fifteen minutes ago," Renfro said, tapping the map. "And they just found it outside West Paducah. Heading south."

"Like I said," Royce said good-naturedly, "he was bound to move south."

"Roberts held this trucker and his wife hostage," Renfro continued. "They dropped him off before they got to West Paducah. They say he headed right toward the swamp."

"The swamp," Gerard said. His eyebrows raised; so did his voice: "We're gonna need boats."

"I hate boats," Renfro said.

"Get me boats, Cosmo."

"Boats you shall have."

"Get the van ready," Gerard announced, but the deputies were booking already, swinging into action, packing up their field office, gathering their gear, as Renfro punched numbers into his cell phone.

"Yeah, say, Lester, yeah, it's Deputy Renfro from Chicago, that's right. . . . We're gonna need boats, you know, like they use in swamps. What do you call 'em? . . . Swamp boats. Yeah—make it swamp boats."

Within minutes the warrants squad had loaded up the Suburban and rolled.

Ten

A fugitive often faces unpleasant options, and the boggy area where the Ohio River gave birth to the Tennessee River was not a travel route Mark Sheridan would have chosen under normal circumstances. Within minutes of leaving Earl and Martha Chambers by their eighteen-wheeler along the country side road, Sheridan had found a fishing boat—a rowboat—tied to a small ramshackle pier. Sheridan was a city boy, but due to his military background, his specialized training, the wetlands landscape that stretched before him did not intimidate him.

As an avenue of escape, as a means of confusing his pursuers, the marsh was a godsend; the hungry wet ground would swallow footprints, the moist plant life would give way easily, bending to his touch, not snapping into a tracker's sign. He could move quickly through, or hide himself away; either way, when he emerged from the marsh, those hunting him would have no means of determining his direction.

Using the sun as his compass, Sheridan—in the dark T-shirt and jeans appropriated from the trucker, whose .38 special was in the fugitive's waistband, a box of shells in a pants pocket—rowed deep into the swamp, as shore and wading birds alternately watched and skittered away, the occasional snake slithering greenly by like moving vegetation in the murky algae-kissed water. Perhaps an hour had gone by when a distant thunder that was the rumble of a helicopter signaled that the search in the swamp had begun. He stroked down a creek sheltered by cyprus.

At the edge of the swampland, the afternoon moving into dusk, a caravan of law enforcement had pulled in around the eighteen-wheeler, the trucker and his wife answering questions posed by Deputy Marshals Noah Newman and Robert Biggs, telling them the tale of the savage wild-eyed black man who had so terrorized them.

Deputy Marshal Sam Gerard stood atop the truck's cab, slowly scanning the marshy landscape through Zeiss field glasses; the sinking sun was abandoning the swamp, and Gerard knew that the world they were about to enter would only grow darker.

Deputy Savannah Cooper was at the rear of the Suburban, double-checking their communications gear. Royce, his Brooks Brothers suit absurd in this backwoods setting, was removing a small pair of black binoculars from his duffel bag.

Cooper glanced curiously at the binoculars, and Royce smiled his boyishly ingratiating smile and explained, "Thermal imaging—picks up on heat."

The minions of Sheriff Patterson Poe had been replaced by deputies and volunteers from the local police auxiliary sent by Paducah's sheriff, Elroy James. These assorted trackers were backing up boat trailers hooked behind their patrol cars so that sleek flat-bottomed airboats, with their aircraft-style propellers encased in mesh cages, could be unloaded down into the swampy waters.

Sheriff James, mustached, shovel-jawed, mightily paunched, sidled up to Deputy Marshal Cosmo Renfro, who was in the process of disgruntledly spraying Off insect repellent onto every exposed portion of his body, and onto his clothing, as well.

"Won't get far in that boat he swiped, boys," Sheriff James stated, removing sunglasses the dying sun had made irrelevant. He had tiny black-bean eyes. "No motor, fella that owns it says."

"I hate boats," Renfro said to the sheriff.

"I wouldn't suggest goin' wadin' in that snake pettin' zoo, Deputy."

The sheriff wandered off and Renfro, with the hand that didn't hold the Off canister, slapped his arm; he looked up at Gerard, who was still panning the swamp with his field glasses.

"I just swatted a bug with the head of Vincent Price," Renfro said, "and the ass of a B-52."

"Hope it wasn't on the endangered species list," Gerard said, lowering the glasses.

"I hate fucking boats," Renfro repeated, "I hate fucking bugs, I hate fucking snakes. . . . Did I mention I hate fucking boats?"

Gerard hopped down off the truck cab, the moist ground underfoot a hint of the humid landscape to come. "You brought that up, yes."

Notepad in hand, Biggs ambled over, a humorless smirk digging into his cheek. "I got bad news and I got bad news."

"Give me the bad news first," Gerard said.

"Our fugitive got a .38 off that trucker."

"Sweet. Now let's have the bad news."

"There were six rounds in the gun and a dozen more in a box of cartridges he also took."

"Well. We wouldn't want this to be too easy, would we?"

Sheriff James, eavesdropping, sauntered over to say, "Don't make no difference. Your man's gonna be dead from snakebite by mornin', anyhow. I'm gonna repeat my objection to undertaking a search in this area after nightfall."

"Duly noted, Sheriff," Gerard said, his face as blank as his voice. "Thank you for your cooperation."

With this news of an armed fugitive, Biggs headed to the Suburban to break out the Kevlar-lined quilted field vests, which soon the entire warrants squad was wearing; even Royce traded his Brooks Brothers jacket for one of the bullet-proof vests.

"If I could have your attention please," Gerard yelled, calling for the troops to gather around him, not just his squad but the sheriff and his deputies and the auxiliary helpers. "We're going to divide up—one of my federal deputies with each one of you. We will spread out and search this swamp. Who is the best tracker here?"

Four of the men, including Sheriff James, raised their hands—everyone except a potbellied, unshaven civilian in a Skol cap and ancient coveralls, who was chewing a chaw no bigger than a baseball.

Gerard smiled to himself. "All right, then—which one of you is the ugliest, most inbred redneck sonuvabitch out here?"

By way of reply, the scruffy tracker cackled a laugh and spat a yellow-brown streak of tobacco juice into the mud.

"You come with me," Gerard instructed him.

Deputy Cooper began to hand out walkie-talkies to the rest of the warrants squad, and to the sheriff and his deputies and volunteers; these were different units than the locals were used to, and some quick instructions were needed.

"How long you plan to be out there?" Sheriff James asked Gerard.

Gerard didn't respond.

Cooper was saying, "Okay, gang—everybody com-check with me on channel three."

"You eyeball our man," Gerard told the assembled group, "send up a flare, call for backup and stay in your damn boat. He is armed and dangerous. He has military training, and heroics can get your ass killed. Understood?"

"How long you all gonna keep us out there?" the sheriff asked, again, getting irritated. "We got bowling team to-night."

"We will be out until we find our man," Gerard said. "Those of you on the bowling team will have to put your balls on hold."

That made the scruffy civilian tracker cackle again, and the warrants squad members were suppressing smiles.

Soon they had stepped into the long narrow airboats, easy-to-operate vehicles, sans clutch and brake, that the local deputies, seated in back, piloted by pedal. Royce was in the boat next to Gerard's, and the deputy marshal called out to his newest team member.

"That advice went for you, too," Gerard told the boyish agent right before they took off. "I don't like my people getting killed, even a goddamn diplomat. You be careful."

"Always," Royce said.

Then the boats were skimming over the shallow scummy surface of the swamp, the sunset glowing over the waters, tinting the grays and browns and greens an eerie orange until shadows lengthened into darkness. The airboats parted company, separating down arteries, the squall of birds and the hum of insects summoning them deeper into the primordial world.

Capable of speed, the airboats slowly prowled the channel, as a light fog settled in, riding the water like wispy white hair on a balding codger's scalp. The night was chilly, the air dank. High-power searchlights were mounted on the front of the shallow boats, and these were left for the passengers—Gerard and his team—to man, beams stroking the water and the land, as if you could tell the difference. The orchestral din of insect noise mounted, as the swamp swallowed the searchers, and their searchlights—which they guided with one hand, guns poised in the other—barely penetrated the fog. When the moon came out, huge and yellow, it provided no help, merely staining the darkness with its mocking jaundiced eye.

A fugitive often faces unpleasant options, and Mark Sheridan, hearing the buzz of approaching airboats, confronted with the weaving beams of searchlights like swords piercing the magician's box that was the bog, guided his boat to the shore of a small cypress-choked island. Sliding the boat onto the bank, he quickly covered it with leaves and brush, as quietly as possible, until it was camouflaged enough to risk leaving. Then he padded deeper into the island and, with the same nimble grace he'd used to scale that utility pole, sought a hiding place in the mossy obscurity of a cypress's upper branches.

Sheridan clung there and waited, and minutes turned into hours. Bugs courted him, but otherwise he was not uncomfortable, and cool air whispered through the cypress leaves; this was as close to a rest as he'd had since those few minutes in the bunk on the truck.

Finally the monotony was broken: he could see one of the boats moving down his channel, cutting through the low-lying layer of fog, the eye of a searchlight coming his way. The fugitive did not feel threatened; the searchlight would not penetrate his mossy hiding place, nor would it uncover his camouflaged rowboat.

But then the searchlight winked out.

Now, in a near pitch-darkness tinged yellow by moonlight, Sheridan's keen night vision made out the two figures in the boat—someone at the rear, guiding the airboat, another figure standing toward the bow. Adjusting something he was holding up to his eyes. . . .

And Mark Sheridan, himself a field agent well acquainted with the toys of espionage, felt a chill that had nothing to do with the weather. If those binoculars were a thermal model—explaining the need to turn off the searchlight for a better look at the landscape—then the man standing at the bow of that boat would be clearly viewing the world in a monochrome green, with white blurs indicating the heat of animals, their movements leaving signatures.

If heat signatures were lingering on the rowboat—on the ends of the oars, for example—and if those traces of heat were picked up by thermal binoculars, ghostly white handprints glowing through the camouflage of brush, then the fugitive was moments from discovery. The figure at the bow was slowly scanning past the hidden rowboat now, moving toward Sheridan's cypress. The fugitive clutched his branch, knowing that if those were indeed thermal binoculars, more blurs of white on the trunk of the cypress would send the man's binoculars searching higher.

Damn, it was so hard to tell in the fog and the dark and the blur of moonlight—was the man at the bow looking at him? Had Sheridan been spotted?

Diplomatic Security Agent John Royce whispered into his walkie-talkie: "Got a visual," so softly it could not be heard above the symphony of insects. "Sending flare."

And Royce signaled the sheriff's deputy at the rear of the boat, but the deputy piloting the boat—unnerved by this breakthrough—fumbled with the flare, firing it directly into the water, turning the water bloody red in a fizzling foaming fuckup.

This was all the fugitive needed to know his cover had

been blown, and he dropped from the tree and dashed toward the island's interior.

Royce required no thermal binoculars to see, and hear, the fugitive fleeing.

"Get this over to the bank," he snapped at the deputy, "then load up another flare and fire it off." Then into his walkie-talkie, Royce said, "Going after him!"

On the adjacent artery of the labyrinthian marsh, Gerard responded into his walkie-talkie: "No! Goddamnit, Royce, stay in that boat!"

Then Gerard's eyes were pulled to a flare streaking the sky in a crimson arc.

The manhunter yelled to his scruffy guide, "Go! Go! Go!"

Elsewhere in the swamp, the other searchers in their airboats, having seen that same flare, were heading in that direction; but Gerard was closest, and he soon heard the loud rustling and, on a nearby island, spotted the slashing rays of what had to be Agent Royce's Mag-Lite beam, as the young agent pursued the fugitive through the thick underbrush.

"Pull into that bank!" Gerard said, and in moments the boat had lurched to a stop, and Gerard leapt onto the sodden shore. He looked back at his tobacco-chewing guide and asked, "Can you steer this around to the other side of the island?"

"Do frogs fuck in the water?"

"Do it, then," Gerard said. "Remember, he's got a gun."

The tracker grinned brownly, lifting the double-barreled shotgun he'd been cradling in his lap. "This ain't licorice."

With a curt nod, Gerard charged into the island, plowing through reeds, high grass and brush, feet sinking into the muck at times, slowing him, but never coming close to stopping him. Ahead, through the twisted tangle, the beam of Royce's tiny flashlight danced like a laser light show.

The fugitive, however, was not on the island—though he was close to it. Sheridan had caught sight of his pursuer, a figure in a quilted jacket, the thermal binoculars necklaced around him, a big handgun—a .45?—clenched in one hand as a small Mag-Lite probed ahead of him. The fugitive considered shooting him, maybe winging him, but the gunshot might alert the other pursuers, and Sheridan didn't want to risk killing the bastard.

They were nearing the edge of the island when a sudden fluttering movement—a crane disturbed by the ruckus of their running—distracted the pursuer, causing him to turn toward the flapping wings of the bird.

Sheridan took that opportunity to slip into the water. He swam swiftly, quietly, behind tall grass; only his eyes and his gun-hand rose above the pond-scummy surface. His pursuer—slim, dark-haired, young, but yes, armed with a .45 automatic—stood at the island's edge, the beam of the Mag-Lite searching the green-skinned water.

And the fugitive rose from the water behind him, placing the nose of the .38 against his pursuer's temple.

"Not a sound," Sheridan said. "Don't move, either. . . ."

"I'm Royce with Diplomatic Security," he said. "You're making a mistake."

"You fuckers made the mistake. Give me your piece—slowly."

Royce's hand loosened around the .45 as the fugitive lifted it out of reluctantly lax fingers.

"Atta boy," Sheridan whispered.

"So what happens now?" Royce asked, his casual words not masking his fear.

But Sheridan didn't reply; a third voice did: "Drop those guns, please!"

A beam of bright Mag-Lite hit Sheridan's face, but it

didn't blind him; the voice and the flashlight belonged to that deputy marshal from the plane.

The fugitive shifted, putting Royce between him and Gerard, the beam of the Mag-Lite off of him and onto his hostage now.

"Gerard, U.S. Marshals Service," said the figure behind the eye of the flashlight, emerging from the shadows of the island. "You are under arrest."

The deputy marshal held a nine-millimeter in his fist, his expression as blank as the yellow moon's above.

Keeping the nose of the .38 at Royce's temple, Sheridan aimed the .45 toward the approaching manhunter, who, seeing this, stopped in his tracks.

"Mr. Roberts," Gerard said, his tone conversational, and just a little weary. "It's been a very long day for us all. Let's try to end it on a positive note, shall we?"

"I agree," Sheridan said. "Dropping your gun would be a start."

A blinding beam of light stabbed Sheridan, coming from his right, and the fugitive shifted again, blinking frantically, managing to keep Royce between him and Gerard, never offering a target, not to the marshal or the new arrival, the party guiding the airboat whose searchlight had hit him.

"If everybody walks away breathing," Gerard said, working his voice up over the sound of the airboat's fanlike propeller, "everybody wins."

Sheridan's vision returned, more or less, and he could see that the pilot of the airboat was a cracker with a nasty-ass double-barreled shotgun, the boat gliding in ever closer. The cracker was grinning through his beard, as if enjoying the notion of blasting Sheridan's black ass to smithereens.

"What do you think my odds are, Deputy?" Sheridan asked over Royce's shoulder. "How long will I last after you take me in? I was in custody on that plane when they tried to ice me—or have you forgotten?"

"Nobody in my custody dies," Gerard said. "You did the right thing on that plane, Roberts—do the right thing now."

Helicopter thunder was overhead, a spotlight knifing down through the mossy trees; engines of other airboats approached, their spotlights catching the fugitive, too—both Sheridan and Royce were washed ghost-white.

"End of the road," Gerard said, not unkindly. "You're caught. It's over. Time to go home."

"Time for you to go," Roberts snarled, and he took quick but careful aim with Royce's powerful handgun and fired off two rounds at the deputy, point-blank.

The bullets slammed into Gerard's chest, knocking him off his feet, sending him tumbling back into the muck; but even before Gerard had landed, the fugitive had fired another round into the searchlight on the nearby airboat, shattering the glass and sending the rustic tracker and his deadly shotgun diving into the water, scurrying the hell away.

When Sheridan turned to shoot out that searchlight, however, it gave Royce the opportunity to squirm loose; rather than flee, Royce grabbed for the .45, the weapon the fugitive had commandeered from him. In the night, the sound of other deputies reacting to the gunshot, urging their guides to move faster toward the island, merged with the helicopter roar to provide a backdrop to their struggle; but that struggle was brief: Sheridan cuffed Royce with the trucker's .38, knocking the young agent to the sodden ground, only in the process, the .45 slipped from Sheridan's grasp, onto the mud bank.

But Sheridan still had the .38; no need to waste valuable time retrieving the second weapon.

So the fugitive did what a fugitive does: he ran, as if he were heading into the interior of the island, the whir of airboat engines building, signaling the imminent arrival of more deputies with guns; but as soon as he was lost in the darkness, the fugitive sidestepped and slipped into the water again, gliding as smoothly as a snake, long seconds later bobbing surreptitiously to the surface to watch the boats converging on the site of the shooting, voices shouting, ''Gerard's been hit!'', ''He shot the boss!''

Then Sheridan's eyes, equally snake-like as they hovered barely an inch from the water's surface, closed as if he were about to drop off to sleep; instead, he ducked into the water, so gently he left barely a ripple on its skin, swam silently under water, and away.

Eleven

Shortly after dawn, in a sawhorsed-off area of the parking lot of a health clinic on the outskirts of Paducah, Kentucky, a helicopter touched down, perking up the cordon of media who were being held back by Sheriff James and his men and local police officers. From the copter stepped United States Marshal Catherine Walsh, her brunette hair tossed by the churning of the slowing copter blades, as she held down the hem of the skirt of her black pinstriped power suit as it lifted over shapely legs. Deputy Marshal Cosmo Renfro ran to meet her.

"How is Sam?" Walsh asked Renfro.

"Two broken ribs and a bad temper," Renfro said. "The ribs will improve."

"God bless Kevlar," she said. "But two forty-five slugs fired at point-blank range, even into bulletproofing, can mess you up. I want to talk to his doctor before I talk to him."

"No problem."

Walsh and Renfro ignored the shouted inquiries of the

media, and entered the clinic, where in the waiting room the screen of a television tuned to CNN was filled with images of the aftermath of the 727 crash—body bags on the shore, the fractured fuselage getting craned out of the river and some generic shots of the swamp area where they had chased the fugitive.

Unwittingly interrupting an argument in progress, Marshal Walsh acknowledged her people with a nod and they stood and smiled and nodded nervously back; the warrants squad had not freshened up—they had come here straight from the swamp, and were soiled and smelly and surly.

Renfro delivered Walsh down the hall to Dr. Conrad Visage, the fortyish physician who had attended Gerard, while the deputy marshals resumed their bickering.

"You weren't supposed to leave the goddamn boat," Newman said to Royce. "What the hell were you doing, leaving the goddamn boat?"

The usually laid-back, ponytailed deputy was hovering over the diplomatic security agent—once again in the jacket of his Brooks Brothers suit—who sat diffidently cleaning the mud from his .45, which he had retrieved from the muck on the island.

"I had a visual on the fugitive," Royce said calmly. "He was on the run. If I didn't pursue him, there was a good chance he might get away."

"He *did* get away!"

Savannah Cooper, eyes hollow with no sleep, stirring nondairy creamer into her paper cup of coffee, paced over to put in her two cents.

"All you had to do was ask me for a backup piece," she said, "and I'd have fixed you up. We got plenty of armament. Sam *told* you to get a backup piece . . ."

"You didn't listen!" Newman said.

Royce slipped the .45 back under his jacket, into his

shoulder holster. He shrugged with his mouth. "I never needed one before."

"You needed one this time!" Biggs said. He was collapsed into two chairs, one extended as a footrest; but he was gesturing angrily in the air, like a pissed-off musical conductor. "Sam coulda got killed 'cause of you!"

"Well, he didn't."

Newman grabbed the seated Royce by the jacket front, two fists wadding the material, hauling him bodily out of the chair. "I'm gonna make you eat that smart-ass look—"

"Newman," a voice said.

Newman, Cooper, Biggs and Royce—who seemed unconcerned that the front of his jacket was being grabbed—turned toward the voice, which belonged to Deputy Marshal Sam Gerard, standing at the mouth of the nearby hallway in a hospital gown, the wrappings and bandages binding his chest and rib cage glimpsed here and there. Walsh was coming up behind him, chatting with Dr. Visage, and Renfro was at Gerard's side, carting the bullet-dented Kevlar vest.

"Noah, let's be more diplomatic with our diplomat," Gerard said. "Put the State Department down. We're professionals; we don't take these things personally, remember?"

Newman twitched a non-smile and released Royce, who coolly smoothed out the front of his jacket.

Gerard leaned against the wall and asked, "Anything new on our fugitive?"

Biggs rose, shrugging. "We got a three-state manhunt going—Kentucky's blanketed, interstate highway roadblocks, the enchilada. Every law enforcement agency in the United States, except for Alaska and Hawaii, is on the alert."

"And?"

"Nada. Zippo. Suddenly he's D.B. Cooper."

Behind him, Gerard heard the doctor saying to Walsh, "Marshal Gerard should be able to rejoin his team in a couple of days. We're going to keep him here on painkillers and under observation—internal injuries don't always show up right away—and as badly bruised and shaken as he is, he needs to take it easy, at the very least until tomorrow."

Gerard glanced back—his side killing him—and said, "Couple days R and R, got it. Thanks, Doc. . . . Give me a few moments with my people, would you? I need to give 'em some guidelines."

"Certainly," the doctor said, and exchanged smiles and nods with Walsh, and disappeared down the hall.

"Pull that Suburban around," Gerard said, "now."

He headed back into the examining room where he'd spent the last several painful hours, and was pulling the hospital gown gingerly up and over his bandaged body when Catherine Walsh entered.

He turned, naked but for his bandages and jockey shorts, and said to his superior, "Hand me my pants, would you?"

She did.

He grunted and groaned getting into them; she had to help him some. "Threading a needle would be easier," he said.

"So," she said, "how's it feel nearly getting killed?"

"If he was trying to kill me," Gerard said, zipping up, "I'd be dead."

"You think he shot you in the vest, on purpose."

"No question."

"Never occurred to you he might've missed?"

"I don't think we're dealing with a man who misses."

Her eyes tightened. "Who *are* we dealing with?"

"I'm not sure," he said, reaching for his shirt. "Has anyone told *you,* yet?"

She lifted an eyebrow. "No. I just know he's a security risk of some sort."

Gerard nodded toward the door. "That's why our pistol-packing diplomat is among us."

She helped him into the shirt. "Aren't you wondering why I'm here?"

"It's an important investigation." He winced and grunted as his arms went into the sleeves. "And you still love me."

That made her smile, just a little; she held her palm out and in it were two disfigured .45 slugs. "Thought you might like these," she said.

"Thanks," he said, taking them, pocketing them. "They make nice reminders."

Now her mouth tightened. "That's why I'm here, Sam."

He put on his tie, using a wall mirror—she was behind him and he looked at her as he tied it. "Don't play games with me, Catherine. You know I hate games."

"I'm here to take you off this assignment."

He wheeled to her. "What? Why in hell?"

"This has become personal. And that breaks your own primary rule, doesn't it?"

"It isn't personal, Catherine." He lifted her chin gently to make her look directly at him. "Do you see any anger in me?"

". . . No. But you were on that plane when it went down. You are by definition personally involved, and keeping you on skirts violation of USMS policy, at best. This should be handed to someone more dispassionate. . . . We're going to let someone else catch him, Sam. Anyway, you're injured."

"Do you seriously believe I'm incapable of performing my duties, Marshal?"

"Of course not. But—"

"No 'buts.' Let me do my job."

She turned her back to him. "It's not just *your* tail on

the line. If I make the wrong decision here, keeping you on the case when I shouldn't, and then you screw up, Sam—''

He put a hand on her shoulder. "I know. There are people who know our history. If it looked like you were giving me special treatment . . .''

She glanced over her shoulder at him. "I do love you, Sam.''

"I know.''

"But if it comes down to my job and yours . . . ,'' she smiled gently, ". . . don't think I won't shitcan you.''

Moving with that fluid, feminine grace even a severe suit couldn't hide, she left him there.

"I know,'' he said.

Gerard was cautiously climbing into his sport jacket when a knock came at the examining room door.

"Shit,'' he said to himself, afraid the doctor had caught him; he'd been hoping to avoid that dance.

But it was Royce who stepped inside.

The smug young agent had a sheepish expression. "Can I have a minute?''

"You can have ten seconds.''

The smirk twitched, somehow conveying both regret and embarrassment. "Look, I made a mistake, okay? I'm used to working alone.''

"You and I were lucky I was the one that got shot.''

Royce frowned in confusion. "Lucky how?''

"If Roberts had shot one of my deputies, you'd be the one in the hospital and I'd be on suspension or in jail.''

His eyes widened with amused surprise. "And here I thought we didn't take our work personally.''

"We don't,'' Gerard said. "I do.''

Royce swallowed, shrugged, said, "Anyway, I just wanted to say that.''

"Get a backup piece.''

"Okay."

Royce gave Gerard the ingratiating little boy smile and ducked back out. The deputy marshal gathered the rest of his things, took a piss and went out to the waiting room where his people were gathered.

Soon Gerard and his deputies were exiting the clinic, ignoring the shouted questions of the media behind the local police barricade. Over in the sectioned-off portion of the parking lot, Catherine Walsh was getting into her helicopter.

"Coop, Biggs," he said, "you stay in the field and run the operation; we'll stay in close touch from home base. With our man doing a Jimmy Hoffa, Chicago is as good a place as any to run things from. Cosmo, where's David Copperfield?"

"Mr. Magic Handcuffs?" Renfro turned to his fellow deputies. "I dunno—anybody seen the boy genius?"

"Slashing his wrists?" Newman posed hopefully.

"Somebody go find him, 'cause we're leaving for the airport right now." Gerard glanced over as Catherine Walsh's helicopter lifted noisily. "And I want him with us. . . . We're going to find out how that gun got on that plane, and who 'Mark Roberts' really is . . . and it just could be our State Department exchange student may hold the answers."

Twelve

An innocent man who is a fugitive is a criminal; while innocent, he is fleeing the law, by definition a wrongful act. But the wrongfulness of the false accusations against him take precedence, and a fugitive, labeled by law and circumstance a criminal, must commit crimes to survive. And to a fugitive, survival is everything.

Mark Sheridan ran until he ran out of night. When he emerged from the trees into daylight, he looked like a man who had survived torture, his stolen clothing tattered and leaf-flecked, his body mud-caked, flesh bedecked with bug bites, gashes and nicks, blood glistening along the whiplike welts of leaves and branches from swampland and woods.

Had he seen himself, Sheridan would have been shocked by the animal wildness of his eyes. But a fugitive is a man reduced to an animal, whose animalistic nature comes to the fore as a means of survival.

And to a fugitive, survival is everything.

He was on the edge of a small town—Eddyville, Kentucky—the commercialized outskirts where fast-food restaurants, car dealerships, strip malls and the like flourished.

Food, he thought. *Wheels. . . .*

He hadn't eaten in a very long time, and the thought of McDonald's or Wendy's was like contemplating a feast. But even in a backwater burg like this, a bloody, muddy raggedy man like Sheridan would attract unwanted attention. Plus, he had no money. He was just a scavenging animal that had crawled from the woods. . . .

Harold Beckey, of Huntington, Indiana, came to Eddyville, Kentucky, from time to time, for two reasons: his in-laws lived here, and the fishing at the nearby lakes was killer. His wife, Jeannie, was understanding about him taking several days out of their annual visit to the folks to go off fishing by himself. An insurance salesman whose business was people, Harold much preferred the company of catfish, bass and perch. It was a relief to trade all the glad-handing and ass-kissing of clients and prospective clients for the simple pleasures of solitary fishing.

Harold was dressed in full fishing regalia—from his downturned sailor's cap adorned with fishing lures through his plaid shirt and bib overalls to his tall boots—and was hosing down his camper in the cinder-block stall of the Eddyville Self-Service Super Wash. He had no good reason for washing his camper, and later he would kick himself for doing so; but even on a solitary day of fishing, it just wasn't in Harold's character to start out in a camper splattered with mud, which his camper was, filthy from the storm they'd got caught in on the drive down here.

About the same size as Mark Sheridan, Harold was a pleasant-looking man with a fish-belly-white complexion—as much as he loved the sport, he hadn't fished once all summer, the demands of his business too great—and he was physically fit for his age, forty-three. Like Mark Sheridan, Harold Beckey had been an athlete in high school—albeit swimming and golf, as opposed to football and basketball—but unlike Mark Sheridan, Harold Beckey had not trained as a field agent for the government.

As Harold wielded the metal wand attached to its hose, blasting the muck and crud off his camper with the high-pressure spray, he imitated the motion of casting his rod. He did this several times, each with more exaggeration, and suddenly the water stopped. Harold wondered if, in his silliness, he had broken the device, and turned toward the wall where the hose connected.

A man was standing there, holding the hose, crimping it, stopping the flow—a black man, in shredded clothing, spattered with mud, shaggy with leaves, a mess of a man replete with red cuts and lacerations and the bumps of bug bites.

"How about giving me a wash while you're at it?" the man asked.

"Stay away from me," Harold said.

A fugitive does things he would not normally do. A fugitive does things to survive.

Mark Sheridan withdrew the .38 from the deep pocket of trucker Earl Chambers's pants and pointed it at the fisherman.

"Clean me off," he said. "And don't try anything cute . . . like trying to knock the gun out of my hand with the spray."

The fisherman nodded, and complied. Muddy water, stained red with blood, ran down off the fugitive onto the floor, pooling down the drain; the water was hot, steamy but not scalding, and it felt good. He did not close his eyes; he studied the fisherman through the mist, making sure the man in the ridiculous attire didn't try anything.

The water ran out—the fisherman's seventy-five cents' worth was up—and Sheridan said, "Thank you. What's your name?"

"Harold."

"Harold, I'm in some trouble and I need some help. I don't want to hurt you, and I won't, as long as you help me."

"What do you want?"

"I want you to get into your camper. You're going to drive me."

". . . Where?"

"East."

"I'll be missed. People are expecting me . . ."

"I don't think so. I think you're setting out on a day's fishing trip, all by your lonesome. Now, we've talked enough. Someone comes along, we're both in trouble."

At first, Harold drove, taking Highway 65 east to Louisville; but at a rest stop on 71 North, Sheridan—dressed in jeans and a blue plaid shirt he found in the back of the camper, and which fit him just fine—took over. Harold had been no trouble, but after his experience with the trucker and his wife, the fugitive decided to take no chances. He found duct tape in a cupboard and tied Harold up with it—hands and feet and mouth—and stowed him on the lower bunk.

It was an uneventful day of driving; the normal feel of it was comforting to Sheridan, and only when a highway patrol car would glide by him did he experience a twinge. Though his picture was on TV and in the papers, his regular features made him fairly anonymous, and the swollen bug bites and nicks only served to make him look different from his picture; at a truck stop, he bought various toiletries and used a shower provided for truckers.

Clean, clean-shaven, wearing Harold's sunglasses and in Harold's clothing, he was able to sit at the counter in truck stops, and spending Harold's money, eat several big meals along the way—an enormous bacon-and-eggs breakfast, a meat-loaf lunch and by suppertime, in Ohio, he was ready for a steak.

He was not bothered by being a thief; he was surviving. He had apologized to Harold, and told him he'd pay him back one day, but Harold's bugged eyes over the duct-tape slash of a gag told Sheridan that his hostage wasn't taking these promises very seriously.

At a rest stop outside Columbus, Ohio, Sheridan stepped from the camper to use an outdoor pay phone for a long-distance call, feeding the hungry phone coins courtesy of Harold's change-filled ashtray (meters and tolls).

"Joe's Java," a woman's voice said.

"Marie Bineaux, please."

"She's working right now."

He had to cup the receiver to avoid the nearby interstate noise, particularly the roar of passing trucks. "Well," he said, "she's the one that sold me the grinder, she should have to explain how the damn thing works."

"Okay, okay. . . ."

Over restaurant sounds, he could hear the woman calling out, "Marie—it's for you!" Then after a few moments, the woman's voice again: "Some guy with a question about a grinder you sold him."

"Hello," Marie's voice said without enthusiasm. "This is Marie."

"God, baby . . . hearing your voice makes me feel alive again."

"Mark?"

"Let's not use that name again, okay?"

"Just a second . . . it's a portable, I can take it in the back room. . . ."

The restaurant sounds increased, then abruptly disappeared.

Then Marie's voice was saying, "Is it really you?"

"It's really me."

"Are you hurt? How could you survive that terrible crash? I saw what was left of that plane, on TV—"

"I'm fine. Not hurt, but I am in trouble."

"I know. Oh, Mark, I know. Your face is all over everywhere . . ."

"Listen to me, Marie . . ."

". . . they keep saying you're a criminal, the TV, the papers, they say that you murdered two people? That can't be true!"

"It isn't. Anyway, not the way they say."

"What do you mean? That sounds like you *did* kill them. . . ."

"Not the way they say. It was self-defense."

The whoop of a siren announced the nearby presence of a highway patrol car. Sheridan whirled, but the car was pulling over an eighteen-wheeler along the nearby highway.

"What was that?" Marie asked, frightened.

"Nothing. Just real life. . . ."

"Where are you?"

"I can't tell you. You're better off not knowing."

"Seems like there's a lot of things about you I don't know. They're saying your name is Mark Roberts."

"That's not my name, baby."

"Is 'Warren' your name? What's going on? I just don't know what to believe, anymore."

He gripped the phone tight. "Believe that I love you. Believe that I am the man you knew in Chicago. Believe everything I've told you about my feelings for you."

"Oh, Mark. . . ."

"There are things I can't tell you about myself, but believe me when I say that I did not do what they claim I did. Baby, I've never lied to you."

"But you've kept things from me."

"To protect you. Do you believe me?"

"I want to. It's just . . . I'm so confused, and scared."

"I understand that, but you don't have to be scared, baby. Nothing for you to be scared about."

"I'm scared for you."

"Look, I'll call again soon, but baby, the police are going to find you. Soon. They're going to tell you more lies about me, and they'll even threaten you."

"Threaten me?"

"They'll say you're an accomplice, but you're not. First of all, I haven't committed the crimes they say I have. And you didn't help me escape, and you don't know where I am, do you?"

"No."

"They're going to try to get you to help them catch me. Don't tell them anything, and remember, they can't hurt you, you've done nothing wrong."

"What is going on? What are you going to do?"

"Clear up a mess. It was a mess I was trying to hide from, but now I know I can't."

"Will I . . . Will I ever see you again?"

"Of course you're going to see me . . . but I could use your help. I don't like involving you in this, but there's no one else I can trust. I can trust you, can't I, Marie?"

"Of course you can, Mark. I love you, you know that."

"It may be dangerous. And you need to understand, if you do this, and I'm not able to clear myself . . . those threats from the police, they won't be as empty."

". . . I would be an accomplice."

"I'm afraid so. Will you help me, anyway?"

The silence on her end lasted forever: three seconds.

Then her voice returned: "What do you need me to do?"

Hope flowed through him; it was a relief to feel something besides fear and stress.

"There's a key I hid in your apartment," he said. "I'll tell you where it is. . . ."

Thirteen

The next morning, in the midst of the Chicago Loop, just blocks from the financial district, a small army of national and local media—news vans wearing satellite dishes, remote crews armed with Minicams and microphones, milling reporters with their cassette recorders in hand—was encamped outside the glass-and-steel highrise of the Everett M. Dirksen Federal Building on South Dearborn, within which were the offices of the United States Marshals Service.

But the deputy marshals the media was waiting to ambush did not use that entrance; they came in under the street and went safely up to their offices high above, and would exit the same way.

In the corridor, outside the main USMS office, a stony-faced Deputy Marshal Sam Gerard—brown elbow-patched jacket fitting a little tight over his bandaged rib cage, brown tie flapping on his yellow shirt, blue jeans brushing black boots—was catching up with Deputy Marshal Frank Henry. Thirty-seven years of age, black, handsome, trimly mustached, Henry was probably Cosmo Renfro's chief competition for best-groomed deputy in the Fifth District.

"NYPD sending over their original homicide casebooks on 'Mark Roberts'?" Gerard asked him.

"On the way, FedEx." Henry—looking crisply professional in his pale blue shirt and tastefully patterned darker blue tie with creased navy trousers—was taking a small notebook from his shirt pocket as they walked along. "Then there's this Marie Something."

"Who?"

He referred to a notebook page. "Marie Bineaux—she's the woman at the hospital who was there when 'Roberts' was arrested. . . . She paid his bill."

"Sounds like true love," Gerard said, pushing open the glass office door. "Find her."

"Good as done, Sam."

Before they split off on their separate ways, Henry followed Gerard into the main office of the United States Marshals Service, Fifth District, a sprawling bullpen, its many metal desks not partitioned off other than by the occasional file cabinet. Because of this—and despite its rather low, tile-and-fluorescent-lights ceiling—the expanse had a feeling of openness, amplified by a wall of windows looking out on the city. Only the ubiquitous gold, blue and white USMS star logos on the off-white walls, and the sporadic memo-spotted bulletin boards, indicated the law enforcement nature of these surroundings. Right now the room was alive with activity, as the office mobilized for a major manhunt.

Gerard did not have a private office, but he and his desk took up a considerable area by a corner window. He was on his way there when he stopped at the desk he'd assigned to Diplomatic Security Agent John Royce, who—in another Brooks Brothers suit, a tan one—was giving both Renfro and Henry a run for their money in the Best Dressed Man competition.

Gerard tapped on the edge of the desk, which Royce was still in the process of organizing. "Wouldn't you think," Gerard said, as if posing a hypothetical question, "there would be security cameras in that United Nations garage?"

The young agent shrugged with his mouth. "I know there are."

"Then security-cam tapes must exist."

"Undoubtedly."

"So find the date and time of those murders 'Roberts' committed, and get me the security-cam tapes that go with them."

The know-it-all smirk was back, as Royce shook his head. "We'll never get clearance for that."

"I'm sure you're mistaken. You see, we have a liaison with the State Department working with our lowly warrants squad. And I'm sure he will be able to get that clearance and get me those tapes. He's kinda on my shit list and is looking for a way to get off."

Royce's smile was faint and the smirk was nowhere to be detected in it. "You'll get the tapes."

"I love it when a plan comes together."

Spotting Gerard, Deputy Noah Newman, in a USMS T-shirt and jeans, rose from his desk and came quickly over; a brief awkward moment passed between him and the diplomatic agent he'd braced in that rural clinic the day before.

"CPD says Mark Roberts's apartment was nothing more than a crash pad," Newman told his boss. "Few sticks of furniture, pallet on the floor. Hardly a thing in the fridge. Portable TV with rabbit ears. No phone hookup. Neighbors barely remember him."

"Personal effects?"

"A few clothes. No books, no magazines, no tape or CD

player. Clock radio, is all. But here's the really weird part—no fingerprints in the place.''

Gerard blinked. ''He lived there, and didn't leave a print?''

''Not a one.''

''What did he do, wear gloves around the house?''

Royce said, ''He must have wiped the place for prints, every time he left.''

''Who the hell does that?'' Gerard asked.

''Somebody who's a risk to national security,'' Royce said.

Gerard turned to his ponytailed deputy. ''Look, Noah—go back and canvass the neighbors yourself. You may come up with something Chicago's finest missed. And I want you to check out where he worked.''

''That's my next stop—Powkowski Towing.''

Gerard raised his eyebrows. ''Something keeping you here?''

''Not a thing.''

''Take Agent Royce with you.''

Newman and Royce exchanged blank looks.

''You girls are going to have to learn to get along,'' Gerard said. ''Royce, take some of your James Bond, Batman utility-belt shit along, whatever the hell it is you pack in that black bag of yours. If Roberts left anything behind at his place of employment, I want it gone over with a high-tech-tooth comb.''

''Roger that,'' Royce said, rising.

''Get anything good, call me on the Bat Phone.''

Royce grinned and nodded, and he and Newman quickly exited, side by side. Did Gerard's heart good.

He moved to his desk, where his phone was ringing. It was Renfro, calling from O'Hare Airport; Gerard had sent him out there to check on the Federal Prisoner Transportation Service hangar, where the 727 had been serviced be-

110

fore its ill-fated flight—where somebody either in the employ of, or sanctioned by, the Bureau of Prisons had managed to sneak a pen-gun into that roll of toilet paper.

"We covered all the maintenance employees out here who had access to the plane," Renfro said, "except for one guy—Kevin Peters."

"What's his story?"

"That's in the pending file—he's out sick today."

"That's an interesting coincidence."

"Isn't it?"

"I hate coincidences. In fact, Cosmo, I do not believe in coincidences. Find his ass."

"My thinking precisely."

"Who's out there with you?"

"Niebuhr and Hertel. They're taking the B.O.P. workers through a second round of questioning."

"Then it's on to Final Jeopardy—we move to full background checks: associates, family, any sudden change of personal habits, bank records, medical records, you know the routine."

"I'm on it."

"We're gonna stand on these people till one of them squeaks."

Gerard had barely hung up the phone when it rang again. This time it was long-distance—Deputy Marshal Robert Biggs.

"What have you got?" Gerard demanded.

"We're at a rest stop off the Pennsylvania Turnpike, just outside of Harrisburg," Biggs said, working his voice up over traffic noise. "Roberts took another hostage—fisherman with a camper. The guy made Roberts's photo, no question. Name is Harold Beckey, insurance salesman from Indiana. Guy's pretty shook up . . . Coop's interviewing him in depth right now, 'fore the ambulance carts him off to the hospital."

"Did Roberts injure this civilian?"

"Not really. He's just freaking out from what happened to him. Roberts jumped the guy outside of Eddyville, in a car wash, stuffed him, bound and gagged, in back of his own camper. At some point Roberts dumped the camper at this rest stop, and got some other ride. No idea yet what that might be, but we'll do a canvass."

"How long has Mr. Beckey been there?"

"Guy doesn't really know. Six hours, maybe."

"Have Cooper type up the full interview and fax it here."

"Okay . . . what else do you want us to do? We haven't slept in two days."

"Stay on our fugitive's trail. Like the song says, you can sleep when you're dead."

"What song?"

"Biggs, you have no culture, but the Big Dog loves you anyway."

Gerard hung up, and stood, moving across the main office and into the adjacent "war room," a brown-paneled chamber whose central conference table was surrounded by electronics, monitors and the occasional wall map. The manhunter moved to a map dedicated to the Roberts investigation, dotted with pins that represented sightings, the most recent of which was the marshland in Kentucky. He placed a pin next to Harrisburg.

When Gerard got back to his desk he found the FedEx packet waiting, containing the NYPD homicide casebooks; he began going through them, but they weren't very illuminating. Less than an hour had gone by when the phone rang.

Newman said, "Roberts has a locker here at the towing garage."

"Do we need a warrant?"

"Nope. Mr. Powkowski says help ourselves."

"What's the address?"

Within fifteen minutes, Gerard was breathing in the smell of grease and oil as he entered Powkowski Towing on Goose Island near Cabrini Green. Wreckers and wrecks filled stalls on either side, a police band radio chattering in the background; but few human beings were in evidence. Outside a glassed-in office area at the far end, Newman was interviewing a grizzled, heavyset citizen in a smudgy jumpsuit, presumably Powkowski, the proprietor.

A wrecked tow truck took up a corner of a garage—was it really salvageable?—and Royce was at work in gloves and ultraviolet specs, using a handheld laser gadget on surfaces he had brushed with red-orange powder. The process involved Royce scanning the prints into his laptop, and made Gerard feel about as sophisticated as a Swiss Army knife.

The kneeling Royce, noticing Gerard, and looking like a spaceman in his goggles, said, "I've found a number of fingerprints so far, and I've faxed them back to the office."

"Any matchups?"

"Not with Roberts's prints. This guy is so good it's unreal. So far his fingerprints aren't in the cab, on the equipment in the trunk, aren't anywhere."

"Starting to sound like he wore gloves to take a piss. . . . Biggs and Coop just found a guy near Harrisburg, Pennsylvania, tied up in his own camper. He I.D.'d our man."

"Harrisburg," Royce said thoughtfully. "I told you he'd head north."

"He's heading east."

"Northeast. Maybe you should start listening to me."

"I always listen to you, Royce. I just don't pay attention. But maybe you can tell me something."

"Yeah?"

"Why is our ruthless assassin, this 'security risk,' going out of his way not to harm his hostages?"

Royce had no answer for that.

Gerard wandered down where Newman was talking to the man who indeed turned out to be the towing garage owner, Chester Powkowski.

"He was a helluva worker," Powkowski said. He had a florid mottled face bloated with indulgence, with hairs growing out of the damnedest places. "Never caused no trouble, quiet and knew his stuff, never no lip, wish I had a hun-erd like him."

"My associate here," Gerard said, gesturing toward Newman, "indicates you've said we can have a look in Mr. Roberts's locker."

Powkowski made a farting sound with his lips. "No skin off my ass."

So much for loyalty to a helluva worker.

Soon, in the employees' locker room, as Gerard, Newman and Powkowski looked on, Royce was working technological wonders again, this time on the formidable padlock on Roberts's locker. The young agent unrolled a small kit and used a "quick mold" tool, inserting its pliable tip into the lock and copying the key signature; then, using a spray can of CO_2, he froze the tip. He inserted the hardened tip—now a key—into the locker, clicking it open with ease.

"Whoa," Newman said, impressed. "David Copperfield strikes again."

Royce grinned at the praise, removed the padlock and opened the gym-style locker; it was empty but for a Cubs gym bag on its shelf. The young agent hauled it down, set it on a nearby dressing bench and drew back the zipper.

A nauseating stench, an exaggerated version of the familiar aroma of stale socks, shorts and sneakers, knocked all of them back.

Recoiling even as he zipped the bag quickly shut, Royce said, "That's been there awhile!"

"Some nasty shit," Powkowski confirmed.

Royce left the zipped bag to examine the inside of the gym locker. "Wonder if this is worth hitting with the laser . . ."

But Gerard had picked up the gym bag, and unzipped it again.

"Jesus, Boss!" Newman said. "Take it outside, would you? That sucker's ripe."

Gerard slid down the bench; the foul odor was making his eyes water, but just the same, he managed to empty its reeking contents on the cement floor, and peered within the bag, blinking away his tears.

"Too many gadgets can numb the senses, Mr. Royce," Gerard said.

Royce was covering his nose and mouth. "My senses seem to be working just fine."

"Not really." Gerard lifted out the false bottom of the bag and held it up, waving the heavy cardboard around a little. "That stink was a fence meant to keep you kiddies out."

They gathered around, ignoring the smell now.

Within the bag were a .38 revolver, a well-stuffed money belt and fake passports in several names, each bearing a photo of the same handsome black face of their "Mark Roberts."

"It's a 'bug out' kit," Royce said, examining the items. "Standard E and E training."

"What's that?" Gerard asked.

"Escape and evade. Basic intelligence training. Rule number two: always have a backup plan."

Newman said, "I must've missed rule number one."

Royce's familiar smirk came into play. "Don't leave anything behind they can use against you—like fingerprints?"

"You remember *those* rules," Newman said with a nasty

edge in his voice. "Why can't you remember ours?"

"Children," Gerard warned. He thought about what Royce had said, and said to the young agent, "But he did leave his prints behind—in that U.N. parking garage."

Royce's eyes narrowed and he began to nod. "What makes a careful man like this, a guy who wipes his apartment clean every time he leaves, get sloppy at such a crucial moment?"

"I hate puzzles," Gerard growled. His cell phone rang and he answered it, with a surly "What?"

"My," Deputy Henry's smooth voice said, "are we retaining water today? Thought you'd be pleased that I found the girl."

"Marie Bineaux?"

"Herself. You want the address?"

Gerard listened to the address once, said, "Got it" and told Royce and Newman, "Found his lady."

Then Gerard turned to Powkowski and gestured to the gym bag and its secret contents, as well as the spilled smelly gym clothes on the floor. "I'm gonna send somebody right over to pick up this garbage."

"Hey, I ain't about to touch it," Powkowski said.

"Thank you. Gentleman, let's get of here. No offense to you, Mr. Powkowski, but this place stinks."

Fourteen

The anonymity of a big city is the perfect hiding place for a fugitive, but Mark Sheridan—in Harold Beckey's plaid shirt and jeans, wearing a spirit-gummed-on mustache, the result of a stop at a theatrical supply shop—had returned to New York City in hopes he might stop hiding. Lost in the sidewalk stream of Manhattan pedestrians, Sheridan had returned to the scene of the crime—a crime he had not committed, not really—to put an end to the running.

At the end of East 42nd Street, Tudor City rose behind a leafy park, respectable, quaintly Elizabethan; among the leaded glass, half-timbering and turreted stonework were well-maintained neighborhood shops. Sheridan, a duffel bag in hand, stood across from one of these shops—Tudor Tobacconist—and watched; when he was reasonably convinced the place wasn't under surveillance, he jaywalked through light traffic, crossing through late-morning sunshine, and slipped inside.

Pleasantly assaulted by the heavy aromas of the shop's pungent wares, Sheridan passed between the glass-and-wood counters of cigars and pipes on either side of the narrow space, winding through displays of smoking paraphernalia and bric-a-brac, skirting a Yuppie-ish couple browsing at a shelf of collector plates. He made his way toward a sliding-glass-doored humidor room at the rear, beside which—behind the counter, smoking a cheroot, reading the new issue of *Cigar Aficionado*—sat the proprietor, J. Starkweather Henke, "Stark" to those who knew him well, "Sarge" to a more elite group that included Mark Sheridan.

Stark was in his early forties, blade-thin, hawkish-faced with a well-trimmed mustache and goatee, his steel-gray hair in a military buzz cut, his tan shirt buttoned to the top, his darker brown pants pressed and creased, looking as razor-sharp as their wearer. Though his eyes touched base briefly with Sheridan's, as the fugitive pretended to browse, nothing on Stark's face betrayed their familiarity.

As the fugitive perused the shop's merchandise, Stark put his magazine down and swiveled on his seat to a small safe behind the counter, dialed it open to remove a bulky manila envelope. Then Stark rose and headed for the humidor room. Sheridan, giving a display case of cigars a cursory once-over, followed moments after.

Within the small, air-sealed, humidity-controlled chamber, the far and right walls were stacked with cigar boxes on cedar shelves, the cedar smell threatening to drown out that of tobacco; the wall at left, however, consisted of oak-paneled lock boxes, safety deposit boxes of a sort, often bearing the brass nameplate of the cigar club that had rented the box. A well-dressed gentleman, who had withdrawn a few precious cigars from his club's box, was in the process of locking it back up as Sheridan entered.

When the customer had exited, Stark turned and his well-grooved face carved itself out a grin. "What are *you* doin' still alive?"

They had ducked into a side area, at left, where the glass doors would not reveal them.

"I had a good teacher," Sheridan said.

Stark handed him the thick manila envelope. "You sure as shit must have, to get all the way from the fuckin' swamp to the Rotten Apple in one piece. I must be damn good."

"Yeah, Sarge," Sheridan chuckled, opening the envelope, "it's all you, man."

The fugitive examined the contents of the envelope: blank passport, credit cards, cell phone. Everything he had asked Sarge to come up with.

"Phone's clean," Stark said.

"I expected nothin' less. Hear anything interesting?"

"Just that you're one very popular son of a bitch."

"How popular?"

Stark's eyebrows lifted over eyes sunken with experience. "Large dollars. The kind Swiss bank accounts are made for."

"Dead or alive?"

"That second word wasn't part of the equation. This is an open contract, available to every buddy fucker in the business."

Sheridan flinched a non-smile. "They almost succeeded on that prison plane."

"Close only counts in horseshoes."

"Tempted, Sarge?"

He shrugged. "Depends on whether you're the rat bastard traitor they say you are."

"What do you think?"

"I think people change."

"Don't buy into their bullshit, Sarge—I was set up from jump street."

"Who by?"

Sheridan sighed, shook his head in frustration. "If I

knew that, I'd know who to squeeze. Somebody on the inside. I got coded instructions, through the usual channels, just a routine drop . . . then the shit hit the fan.''

"And now you got good guys and bad guys jockeying for position with each other to take your sorry ass out.''

"That about sums it up.''

Stark's eyes narrowed. ''What the hell are you doin', showin' back up after six months?''

"Thought I could disappear—hell, I was ready to cash it in, even before this. How much of this cloak-and-dagger bullshit can one man take?''

"But they found you.''

Sheridan laughed once, humorlessly. ''More like bad karma caught up to me.''

"The man that said bad luck is better than no luck at all didn't know jack shit. . . . So, bro—what's your next move?''

"Find the son of a bitch that set me up.''

"And get righteous again?''

"Hallelujah.''

A smile creased the hawkish face. ''Anybody can do it, Sherry, it's you.''

"Got a key for me?''

Stark raised a fist from his side and tossed a small key to Sheridan, who snatched it from the air and moved to the wall of private oak-paneled lock boxes. He unlocked the door of one, opening it to reveal stacked cigar boxes within.

"Take it all with you now,'' Stark said, '' 'cause I don't want to see you back here again.''

Sheridan frowned over his shoulder at one of the few people he trusted on the planet. ''Don't you believe me, Sarge? Don't you believe it happened like I said?''

Stark's expression might have been disappointment, or maybe frustration; Sheridan couldn't tell. But the voice was weary as J. Starkweather Henke said, ''Maybe I didn't teach you so good, after all. Don't you know in the spook biz, ain't no such thing as right or wrong or truth or lies. Comes down to who's left standin'.''

Stark moved to the sliding glass door, pausing to say, "Good luck. I'll catch the rest on CNN."

"Sarge . . . thanks."

Stark nodded, slid the glass door open, slipped out into his shop and slid the door tightly shut, as the fugitive began transferring the cigar boxes from the locker to his duffel bag.

Sheridan checked several of the boxes, just to make sure they hadn't been tampered with—they were as he had left them: stuffed with thousands of dollars in money bricks.

The fugitive paused, toward the end of the process, to remove a thick stack of hundred-dollar bills from one of the money bricks, shoving the fat wad of cash into his pocket. Then he finished filling the duffel bag with cigar boxes and moved back out through the shop, not even acknowledging his old colleague.

Money, particularly a lot of money, is a fugitive's best friend; it buys silence, it buys cooperation, it buys things a normal citizen could never buy. Finding an apartment in Tudor City was next to impossible; but the slightly bizarre, twenties-era neighborhood, with its brick gothic towers topped off by manor house–like crowns, was exactly the location he craved for what he needed to accomplish. Five building superintendents informed him that there were no vacancies whatsoever, but the sixth let slip that an elderly tenant had "just kicked the day before yesterday."

The super, a round-faced, balloon-bellied guy in his fifties, wore a food-stained T-shirt and jeans; he was leaning against the doorjamb with a can of beer in one hand and an ash-drooping cigarette in the other. "But there's a wait-in' list longer than your dick—nothin' racial implied, y'understand."

"I only need it for a few days."

"Hey, does it look like we rent by the hour around here?"

Sheridan showed him a business-size envelope that he had filled with hundred-dollar bills; his thumb flicked along the edge of the money, riffling it seductively.

The super's eyes bugged. "How much is that?"

"Five thousand. I'll be gone in a week."

"Let me show you around."

The old woman's furnishings were still in place; the musty smell of old age and even death hung in the air.

"I can move this junk out, if you like," the super said. "She didn't have no relatives so I was plannin' to offer it furnished."

"It's perfect," the fugitive said.

"Phone's dead. You want it hooked up, I'll have to—"

"No. Fine."

"All righty, then. That'll be cash in advance."

Sheridan handed the super the envelope; the man looked inside the envelope, to make sure a switch hadn't been pulled.

Thumbing the bills, he was grinning at his good fortune when something like a thought passed across his perverted cherub's face. "You ain't gonna boil Vietnam kids and keep their heads in the fridge or anything, are you?"

"Why, is that more?"

"Hey, just keep the noise down, and the place is all yours, pal."

The super stepped outside and the fugitive locked the door behind the man. Then he tossed the duffel bag on a coffee table and sat on the sofa facing it. From the bag he took new clothes he'd bought. Then he lifted out the cigar boxes, all of which contained bricks of money, with one exception. That box, marked with a red felt-tip slash, contained a .45 handgun with several spare ammo clips and a passport.

What was called, in the trade, a "bug out" kit.

With the help of the yellow pages by the dead phone, he used his cell phone to call several electronics stores; it took him several tries to find an outlet that could fill, with in-stock items, his want list of electronic and computer gear, and was willing to deliver. He used one of the credit cards Stark had supplied to secure the order, but let them know he'd be paying cash. He wanted delivery as soon as possible, and they were able to comply—he'd have everything by end of the business day.

Pleased, Sheridan went to the window, to air the place out, and to enjoy the view of the United Nations complex—the slender slab of the Secretariat Building, the General Assembly Building with its dish-shaped dome, the green glass skyscraper of the UN Plaza Hotel.

"Perfect," he repeated.

Fifteen

The address was on Fullerton Avenue, on the edge of Bucktown, a gentrified Chicago neighborhood alive with restaurants, galleries and storefront theaters—one floor up from the street, an apartment over a coffeehouse.

Newman knocked, with Royce just behind him on the small landing; Gerard was laying back, standing on the couple steps below the landing, leaning on the railing. He had already given instructions to the younger men, each of whom carried a manila envelope, on how he wanted this interrogation handled.

"Nothing," Newman said.

"Try again," Gerard said.

Newman knocked again, and kept knocking.

Finally the door cracked open and long-lashed brown eyes, lovely feminine frowning eyes, peered over a chain. "Yes?"

"Marie Bineaux?" Newman held up his badge in its black leather holder. "U.S. marshals."

"What's this about?"

Her voice had a kiss of French accent.

Newman was coolly polite. "We'd like to ask your co-operation in a murder investigation, ma'am."

"What? You can't be serious. . . ."

"May we come in?"

The slice of her pretty face visible in the cracked door flinched in irritation; but then the door closed and the chain was undone and she opened it for them.

The three men trooped into the tiny two-room studio apartment, which was eclectically furnished in a funky yet tasteful array of secondhand furniture, deco touches mingling with nouveau and fifties modern. The smell of oil paints greeted them; an easel with an unfinished painting stood over by the window, a palette and other oil painting paraphernalia scattered nearby, a number of unframed paintings, oil on canvas, leaned against the walls. A few of the paintings—pastel impressionist-influenced Chicago street scenes, mostly—hung unframed on the walls. The kitchenette looked rather slovenly, perhaps betraying this young woman's state of mind; she was certainly nervous, smoking, a slenderly attractive brunette in a hastily belted blue terry-cloth robe.

"Do you have names?" she asked, with mild indignation.

Gerard and Newman identified themselves, and the younger agent said, "John Royce with Diplomatic Security."

Her brow tensed. "Not a marshal?"

"It's a joint investigation," Royce said, with a bland smile. He removed a photo from his manila envelope. "Do you recognize this man?"

Marie Bineaux looked at the photo of "Mark Roberts" and said, "I've never seen him before."

"Really?" Royce said, amused. He flashed his smug smirk at Gerard and Newman. "Never met him?"

"No. I'm sorry. Is there anything else?"

Gerard stayed in the background, wandering casually about the apartment, glancing here and there.

"Well," Royce said, "you could explain why you'd pay the hospital costs of a perfect stranger."

Newman took out a photocopied receipt from his manila envelope and held it up for her to see. When her eyes avoided it, Newman helped: "A receipt from Chicago Memorial. It's Mark Warren's bill, paid in full. . . . Isn't that your signature at the bottom?"

She said nothing; she looked at the floor and sucked on her cigarette and blew smoke out and tapped her foot.

"We can verify your signature, Miss Bineaux," Royce said. "You paid Mark Warren's bill, didn't you?"

Ignoring the query, she wandered to a couch and plopped down, stabbing out her cigarette in a black ceramic ashtray on a blue-glass deco coffee table. She folded her arms, crossed her pretty legs and sat mutely, as if waiting for them to get tired of asking questions and go.

Gerard was in the kitchenette, where on the refrigerator a series of photos was magneted—several conspicuous empty spaces indicated a few photos had been removed. In one photo Marie Bineaux looked glowingly beautiful, beaming radiantly at the camera; the setting was outdoors, a garden, and in the background a tow trunk could be glimpsed.

Newman came over to her and asked, "Are you in this country legally, ma'am?"

Her eyes flashed. "I'm on a student visa."

The soft features of Royce's face hardened. "Green cards get pulled for infractions much smaller than aiding and abetting a fugitive. Are you familiar with federal harboring laws?"

"Of course, you'll get to extend your stay in this country five to ten years," Newman said. "You won't be kicked out of this country until you get out of prison.''

Her eyes were narrow, her lips trembling, as she asked, ''Why are you threatening me this way? If I know this man, is it a crime? I've done nothing wrong.''

''Mark 'Warren' has,'' Royce said.

He emptied the manila envelope on the coffee table before her, ghastly images spilling out, dead men in graphic full-color close-up.

The woman gasped, covered her mouth, turned away.

Royce, with casual sadism, lifted a photo and said, ''Diplomatic Security Service Special Agent Neil Kasinski. He has three kids; *had* three kids. Notice how the blood is starting to darken? Eventually it turns almost black. But the photographers got there quickly enough to capture the red.''

''Please . . .''

He nudged another photo with a finger. ''DSS Special Agent Sam Harmon. Notice there's no blood, but you see the peculiar posture of his neck? Necks aren't designed to do that, you know. Your boyfriend killed this man with his hands. Tidier, but just as effective.''

''Stop doing this. Please stop doing this . . .''

Gerard was back in the living room area, admiring the paintings.

''I understand that Mark Warren is somebody you trust,'' Royce said quietly. ''A friend. These men, these dead men, they were my friends.''

''I don't know anything about this! I haven't heard from him, and I won't be. We argued after I paid that bill.''

''Argued?''

''When he got in trouble with the police. He wouldn't tell me why, so we argued.''

''When did you have an opportunity to have this argument? I'm under the impression he was arrested in your presence, and taken off to jail, and you never really talked to him again.''

127

"I don't want anything to do with him, if he's this kind of person. I'm not going to see him again."

"So you do know him," Newman said, stepping forward, an edge in the usually easygoing voice. "You lied to us."

"That's a federal offense right there," Royce said, shaking his head with mock regret. "Shame to see you lose your visa. . . ."

Gerard, standing looking at a painting, suddenly barked, "That's enough!"

Royce and Newman turned and looked at Gerard with apparent surprise.

"Put that garbage away," he said, nodding toward the grisly photos fanned out before her.

Royce quickly scooped them into the manila envelope.

Gerard sighed wearily and strode over to where the woman sat. "You'll have to forgive my young associates. Maybe you can understand their zeal, when you consider the seriousness of this crime."

She said nothing, but her eyes were large and her expression had thawed.

"I apologize for these shock tactics," he said. "I shouldn't have allowed them, but I got distracted."

She frowned, not in irritation this time, but confusion.

Gerard gave her his best smile, gestured toward the canvases. "These paintings. They're really quite striking. They're yours?"

"Yes."

"You have talent." He reached inside his coat. "If you think of something that you think we should know, you can call me there."

He held out one of his cards to her and she took it, with a noncommittal nod.

Heading out, with Newman and Royce bringing up the rear, Gerard paused and glanced back at her as she followed them to the door. "Say, I noticed some photos on your refrigerator. Taken in a garden . . . outside?"

"What about them?"

"Whoever took those photos has a kind of artistic touch, too."

"Friend of mine took them."

Gerard lifted his eyebrows. "He's good."

"I don't remember saying it was a 'he.' "

"Just sort of figured. You had that look, in the photo, you know? The young love look?"

She frowned, Gerard's soft soap apparently starting to irritate her as much as the shock approach. "Listen, I was getting dressed for work. I'm going to be late because of you. If there's nothing else . . ."

"No. Nothing. Fine."

Gerard's gesture of good-bye was half wave, half salute, as she opened the door and he moved out onto the landing.

"You're wrong about him," she called out.

She was talking to Gerard, but Royce—the closest of them to her—asked, "Why do you say that?"

She nodded toward the manila envelope in Royce's grasp. "He couldn't have done those things."

"Sometimes you think you know a person and you really don't," Royce said. "Your boyfriend committed cold-blooded murder, and he probably will again. He will lie and he will cheat and he will use anybody to achieve his ends. . . . I'm relieved to hear you've decided not see him again."

Before she closed herself back within the apartment, Gerard noted the troubled expression on the pretty face. They had left her with something to think about.

On the street, walking toward their government sedan, Gerard said, "Ah, those oldies but goodies . . . but notice it only took my one good cop to balance out your two bad cops."

"Did we get through to her?" Newman asked.

"She's an icy bitch," Royce said.

"On the contrary," Gerard said, "that is a passionate young woman. She loves that man."

Newman's eyes narrowed. "Is that good for us, or bad?"

"It is wonderful. Noah, set up surveillance on Ms. Bineaux round the clock, and get Judge Rubin to give us a phone tap for here and at her job. Mark Roberts knows that woman loves him, knows she will do anything for him, and he will contact her. Bet my Bears tickets on it."

A car honk caught their attention, and Renfro, in a blue Ford government sedan, had drawn up alongside them.

"Got somethin' for ya, Boss," Renfro called out.

Gerard went over and leaned at the rider's window like a waitress taking an order at a drive-in. "Tell me you've found our sick maintenance man."

"I have found Kevin Peters," Renfro said from behind the wheel, holding up a faxed photo of a vacant-eyed guy with glasses, thinning hair, mid-twenties. "I have also found an interesting piece of information: two days before that plane you were in crashed, a twenty-K deposit was made by an offshore bank to the account of Peters's sister."

"Must be a close family. Where is our sick generous boy now?"

"His wife says he went to the gym to take a sauna and get the poison sucked outa him."

"That may take more than a sauna. What gym?"

"Windy City—over on West Ogden."

Gerard got into Renfro's sedan, calling out the window to Newman and Royce. "Noah, get on the Bineaux woman and I mean that in the nicest way. Agent Royce, get me those U.N. security-cam tapes!"

From Bucktown to West Ogden was less than fifteen minutes by car, but it was as if they'd taken a spaceship to another planet: the neighborhood, near where the Martin

Luther King riots had taken place, was a misbegotten collection of vacant lots, burned-out buildings and boarded-up storefronts. The ramshackle brick building with the off-kilter "WINDY CITY GYM" sign was a noble survivor in this barren landscape.

Dusk was settling as they left the sedan on the street and headed inside—a "CLOSED" sign hung in the double doors, which were open—moving past an unattended reception counter, where a television blared a boxing match, and up wide rickety wooden stairs past a weight room with stationary bikes and running machines to a big open gym with a boxing ring at its center, heavy bags and speed bags on the perimeter. The place had seen better days but apparently generated enough up-and-coming pugs, and area businessmen wanting a workout or a steam, to stay barely alive.

Right now, however, tumbleweed was blowing through the joint.

Renfro frowned as he took in the deserted room. "What is this, *Rocky* meets *Night of the Living Dead*?"

"Somebody's here," Gerard said, nodding toward the muffled sound from the showers. A paint-blistered sign, no older than Prohibition, said "LOCKERS" over a doorless double doorway, and the two deputy marshals were headed that way when they practically bumped into a short, slender, thirtyish Asian in gray sweats, carrying a gym bag.

"Excuse me," the Asian said, smiling reflexively, stepping around.

Renfro stopped him with a question, holding up the faxed photo of Kevin Peters with one hand and his badge in its leather holder with the other. "Seen this guy around? He a member?"

"Sure," the Asian said. He had a rather cultured voice. "Don't know his name, but he works out here. He was here, earlier."

Gerard and Renfro exchanged glances.

The Asian gestured with a thumb. "Check the showers. I think there's a few stragglers back there. He might be one of them."

Gerard nodded his thanks and the Asian moved on.

"Cosmo," Gerard said, "see if anybody's around. Somebody's gotta be in charge of this rathole."

Renfro nodded and headed back downstairs, as Gerard moved cautiously through a bulletin board–lined hallway into the locker room, which smelled only a little better than the contents of Mark Roberts's gym bag. Water pooled on the cement floor and used towels were haphazardly tossed about—neither the clientele nor the attendants here seemed to take much pride in the place. The hiss of steam and the drilling of jetting water drew Gerard around behind the lockers, where the wall was lined with a row of individual stalls with ancient, cracked plastic curtains. Only one stall was in use.

"Hello!" Gerard called. His hand was on the butt of the nine-millimeter holstered under his arm. "Kevin Peters!"

No answer, other than the hot pounding rain within the shower stall.

"Peters!" Gerard yelled, almost screaming. No way the guy couldn't have heard that; that would have damn near woken the dead. . . .

With that in mind, the manhunter yanked back the shower curtain, *Psycho*-style, and found Bureau of Prisons maintenance worker Kevin Peters pretzeled within, slumped on the floor and against the wall of the cement booth, water pounding down and diluting the blood streaming from his slashed throat in red ribbons over his naked physically fit form, the pinkish water finding its way to the drain, gurgling down, gurgling down.

Nine-millimeter in hand, Gerard hurtled down the steps three at a time, footsteps echoing like gunshots, the whole building seeming to shake and rattle under his weight, his ribs and the muscles around them burning and aching like hell, and at the bottom he practically collided with a pale, wild-eyed Renfro on his way to the front door from the reception counter.

"Attendant got his throat slashed," Renfro said, nodding back toward the counter where the boxing match blared.

"So did Peters," Gerard said, as they bolted onto West Ogden. Light traffic was gliding by as dusk darkened into night.

No sign of the Asian.

"Fuck!" Renfro said.

"You know who we just let waltz outa here?" Gerard asked, then he answered himself: "The guy who paid to get that pen-gun on the plane!"

"Shit!" Renfro said, shoving his gun back into his shoulder holster. "Why the hell are the Chinese out to snuff Mark Roberts?"

Gerard turned slowly to Renfro. "Why don't we ask our liaison with the State Department?"

"Why don't we?" Renfro said.

Then they headed back inside the Windy City Gym to call the Chicago PD.

Sixteen

The streets of a teeming city are populated by individuals who, out of protection, submerge themselves into the masses; for all the famed personality of New Yorkers, on the street they become, for the most part, invisible men and women, ignoring each other, not wanting to invite trouble or hassle, preferring to disappear within the safety of the throng.

Such invisibility is perfect for a fugitive, as Mark Sheridan discovered when, wearing an anonymous working man's jumpsuit and with a clipboard in hand (his duffel bag in the other), he was able to blend in among the various deliverymen and maintenance personnel at the rear of New York University Medical Center on Second Avenue at 30th Street.

Further cloaked by dusk, Sheridan lingered by the loading dock, watching from a distance with a stopwatch in hand as a uniformed driver, pushing an empty handtruck down the ramp, returned to his panel truck to unlock its rear door and pile another load on; on the side of the truck were painted the words "KNICKERBOCKER PHARMA-CEUTICAL SUPPLIES, INC." The driver had done this four times so far, and the average time he'd taken, to go inside and return, was three minutes—never more than four, never less than two minutes and change.

When the driver had wheeled another load up and inside, Sheridan moved quickly to the rear of the truck and, using two small picks, unlocked it faster than most people could have with a key.

Slipping inside, leaving the doors ajar, the fugitive moved between stacked cartons, looking for boxes with the label "CAUTION—RADIOACTIVE MATERIALS" surrounding the distinctive fanlike radiation symbol. Before long he found them, stacked together, designated "Medical Isotopes." Using a box-cutter, he quickly opened one of the cartons and fished through smaller boxes of vials, until he found one labeled "Chromium 51." He placed this in his bag, put the opened box on the bottom of a stack of similar boxes and checked his watch.

One minute and forty seconds gone.

Looking among other boxes, shopping with a particular item in mind, he stopped when he came to a stack of smaller boxes, each marked "MEDI-JECTORS"; he took two of these, dropping them into his bag.

When he slipped back onto the cement, locking the door behind him, he was at just over two minutes. He was half a block away, on foot, heading back to Tudor City, by the time the driver wheeled his handtruck back down the ramp.

A fugitive grabs sleep when he can. Mark Sheridan returned to his apartment and willed himself to take a nap, setting the small clock radio he'd bought to wake him at one A.M.

By one-forty A.M., a refreshed Sheridan had begun a dangerous exercise that, for almost the next two hours, found him hanging precariously in various locations along a high ledge up under the eaves of an old brick office building on

Seventh Avenue. Frequently shooing away pigeons, constantly fighting his own innate fear of heights, the fugitive affixed small video cameras into position for various views on a gothic brownstone across the street; he would check the camera placement by referring to a handheld TV, a Sony Watchman, on which images of the various entrances and exits of the building in question could be seen.

Back in his apartment in Tudor City, Sheridan got to work. Throughout the remainder of the night, actually the early morning hours, he assembled an elaborate video surveillance system that involved jury-rigging and customizing of, among other things, a direction-finding head and the innards of a spectrum analyzer, plus the linking up of several Watchmen, VCRs, a high-end laptop and a thirty-five-inch television that dwarfed his living space. The smell of smoldering solder filled the room with the incense of electronics.

At dawn he took time out to go down and have a quick breakfast in a neighborhood coffee shop, and then it was back to work, hunkered at a kitchen table strewn with tools and electronics equipment, fine-tuning the setup, encrypting his laptop commands. At seven-thirty A.M. he used the remote control to zap the big TV to life, its screen divided into quadrants, each fed by another surveillance camera. The four-way split-screen view showed every entrance and exit of the gothic brownstone, including where two New York City uniformed police officers stood guard at the front entry. . . .

Of the Chinese Consulate.

Sheridan moved into the bathroom and threw cold water on his face; exhaustion was a luxury he could not afford. Perhaps later today he could allow himself an hour nap. Right now he had more work to do, starting with using an eye-dropper to load one of his two Medi-Jectors with Chromium 51.

Throwing on a sport coat, into a pocket of which he dropped his cell phone, Sheridan—Medi-Jector in one hand, a customized Watchman in the other—headed out of his apartment, ready to make a field test. When Sheridan stepped from the elevator into the small lobby, a world-weary postman happened to be trudging by, heavy bag slung over his shoulder, having filled the apartment-house boxes.

Sheridan fell in step alongside him, and as they jockeyed for position at the revolving doors, the fugitive considerately allowed the postal worker to go first, taking that opportunity to shove the Medi-Jector against the mailbag and shoot its contents into the bottom of the bag. The only sound was a soft *thwick*.

The building's doorman stepped aside for Sheridan as he exited, stopping at a trash bin to drop in the used Medi-Jector. The fugitive sucked in the fresh morning air, listening to the Manhattan symphony of honking horns and snarling traffic, and followed the mailman down the street, winding among the upscale pedestrians of Tudor City, switching on his specially modified Watchman, slipping on its headphones. Onto its small screen popped a compass-style direction indicator above which tiny, pulsing LED numbers indicated signal strength.

The mailman disappeared around the corner, and the fugitive let him, laying back, standing back away from sidewalk traffic, by the window of a corner restaurant. He cradled the Watchman headphones around his neck, then took the cell phone from his sport-coat pocket and pushed a digit that recalled a stored number there.

It was answered on the first ring: "Yes?"

That woman's voice again, Marie's boss, rising above restaurant clatter; he asked to speak to Marie, no bullshit story about a grinder this time.

He could hear the woman yelling, "Marie, you post my

number on the net, or what? Every time this thing rings, it costs me money!''

And he heard Marie saying, ''I'm sorry,'' and then the restaurant noises cut off and the voice of Marie, ducked into the back room, said tentatively: ''Yes?''

''Hi, baby.''

''Mark! Oh, God, Mark, it was a nightmare!''

''The cops found you.''

''It was *horrible* . . .''

''I told you they would. Did you handle them like I said?''

''I tried, but they didn't believe me.''

''I'm sure they didn't. They'll be watching you every second now. But you mustn't give any sign you know they're there.''

''Okay . . . okay. Mark . . . they said horrible things. They showed me these awful pictures. Did you kill those men?''

''Yes. In self-defense. It's not the way they're telling you. If you don't believe me, I understand.''

''Oh, Mark, of course I believe you.''

And there was no guile in her voice; this was not a woman who had been turned by the police—Sheridan knew her too well. He still had an ally. She still loved him. As he did her.

''Did you find the key?'' he asked.

''Yes.''

''Then just do everything the way I told you, and everything will work out. The two of us will be together, soon. Keep your energy up. Eat an apple.''

''I will. A big one.''

He smiled at their silly code; even playing the espionage game, they sounded like foolish lovebirds. ''You know I love you, baby.''

138

"I know. And I love you, too, Mark. That is your name isn't it?"

"Yes, baby. I'm Mark, all right. Your Mark."

And he hung up, hoping he wasn't just heedlessly manipulating this wonderful woman. That she hadn't become *his* mark.

Time to resume his experiment. He slipped the Watchman phones back on, listening to a signal tone, watching the screen. Processing this mix of audio and visual information, the fugitive turned the corner, walked a block, then turned another corner. He glanced up from his screen.

The postman was exiting one building, trudging toward another, a doorman tipping his hat.

Neither rain nor hail nor sleet, Sheridan thought to himself, *can stop me on my mission.*

Satisfied that his field test was a success, the fugitive stopped in at a twenty-four-hour photo shop, had a passport picture taken and headed back to his apartment. Before long he was sitting at the kitchen table, looking up from laminating the picture onto his forged passport, smoothing it in place with a white-gloved thumb, keeping an eye on the four-way surveillance screen's views of the gothic building that was the Chinese Consulate.

"Where are you," he asked the TV, "you miserable son of a bitch?"

139

Seventeen

The manhunter pursuing a fugitive frequently leads a life filled with dead ends; such a chase, more often than not, is not a linear affair, but a journey of detours, loops and corkscrews. After spending nearly two hours with Chicago PD at the scene of the Windy City Gym murders, Deputies Sam Gerard and Cosmo Renfro returned to the offices of the USMS at the Everett M. Dirksen Building. Night had settled over Chicago, but neither man had even considered going home.

Renfro moved toward his desk to check on the status of the Marie Bineaux surveillance and phone taps, while Gerard headed through the openness of the main office into the smaller world of the dark-paneled, underlighted electronics chamber where Diplomatic Security Agent Royce and Deputy Marshal Carla Holt were settled in at an audio/video station.

Holt, a bespectacled curly-headed blonde in a tan cardigan, was alternately at her computer keyboard and manually working dials and switches, attempting to synchronize three images—dark, murky, high angles of a parking garage—on a trio of side-by-side monitors, right down to the seconds that ticked off on their time/date indicators.

Gerard took in the stacks of VHS videotapes on the central conference table nearby; interspersed with wire-and-paper containers of Chinese take-out, the smell of which enveloped the room, the tapes were prominently marked "U.N./CLASSIFIED."

"Tell me what I want to hear," Gerard said.

"These are indeed the security-cam tapes of the U.N. garage hit," Royce said, swiveling from the monitors toward the warrants squad leader. "They just arrived by messenger."

Gerard allowed himself a smile. "And how did Houdini manage to pull this out of wherever he pulled it?"

For once the smug smirk didn't seem so annoying. "Called in a couple markers," Royce shrugged. "Lamb and Barrows don't exactly know we have 'em."

"Remind me not to hate you anymore," Gerard said, drawing a chair up to where he could peer between, and over the shoulders of, Holt and Royce.

Renfro stuck his head in and said, "Sam, we got full surveillance on Marie Bineaux, with taps on her phone and where she works and even her boss's cell phone."

"Excellent," Gerard said. "Join us."

Renfro came over and pulled up a chair by Gerard. "We got Evans working the night shift, and Henry'll take over tomorrow."

"Carla," Gerard said, "when you get done here, grab yourself a good night's sleep. I want you in that surveillance van with Deputy Henry. You're the best damn techie we got."

"Maybe so," she said wearily. "But you may not think so when you see what I've got for you. . . . Here we go."

Gerard squinted from one grainy, poorly contrasted image to another. "Are these copies? Agent Royce, I expected the damn originals."

"These are the damn originals," Royce said, some glumness working into his voice.

"Terrific," Gerard said. "What is this, underwater photography? I thought Jacques Cousteau was dead."

"It's technology at its low-end finest," Holt said, tossing her own smirk back at her chief. "VHS tape on the slowest speed known to man, cheap security cameras, in a poorly lighted parking lot. What you see is what you get."

On the middle monitor, a blue Lincoln Continental with diplomatic license plates was swinging into a stall. The driver's-side door opened, and a figure stepped out, a slender man in a dark suit and tie, a rather large black briefcase in his hand. But the parked car was in shadow, and the individual was clinging to the darkness, moving to a nearby pillar and assuming a posture of waiting, the briefcase figleafed before him.

"Can you zoom in on his face?" Gerard asked.

"Yes, but it'll still be dark," Holt said, her fingers flying at her computer keyboard, digitally enlarging the frame. Suddenly the lights of a passing car threw a momentary spotlight onto the figure.

"Freeze that!" Gerard said.

Holt did, pausing all three decks simultaneously.

The driver of the Lincoln was well illuminated now, his face clearly visible. He was an Asian, and his was a familiar face.

"Son of a bitch!" Renfro said. "It's our pal Benihana from Windy City Gym!"

"That's a Chinese face," Royce said, "not Japanese."

"Yeah, yeah, yeah," Renfro said, "but any way you slice it, that's Mr. Ginsu Blade."

"Are you on-line to print images?" Gerard asked.

"Absolutely," Holt said.

"Well, give me that middle screen."

"You got it," Holt said, and the laser printer across the room hummed as the face of Kevin Peters's assassin printed out.

"Okay, Carla," Gerard told her. "On with the show."

On the middle screen, the Asian, briefcase in hand, was turning to the left (his right) in apparent reaction to a sound that wasn't picked up by the meager microphones of the security cams. But on the first monitor, the one at left, a taller man, probably six feet, had walked into security-cam view; like something out of an old detective movie, he wore a hat whose brim was tugged down and an overcoat, and, like the Asian, he carried a similar big black briefcase; from the overhead angle, his face was a mystery. He seemed to walk from the first screen into the second as he and the Asian exchanged nods.

And briefcases.

"Some kind of a drop," Renfro thought aloud. "Money for information, information for money. . . ."

They were still zoomed in on that middle monitor, but even so, the mystery man's face remained obscured by his hat brim and the general shadows.

"Show me Overcoat's face," Gerard demanded.

Holt's fingers worked both the keyboard and manual controls. "Sorry. Too damn dark. . . . Garbage in, garbage out."

"Overcoat could be Mark Roberts," Renfro offered.

"Sure could," Gerard agreed.

The mystery man was exiting the middle monitor, and soon had reappeared on monitor one, going back the way he came.

"What's this?" Gerard asked.

As the Asian was moving back toward his parked vehicle, a tall figure in a brown suit, a Caucasian, apparently in his thirties, had entered the third monitor, the one at right, and was moving toward the left, quickly. Soon the tall man appeared in the middle monitor and approached the Asian, who looked at him in what might have been recognition as well as confusion and perhaps fear.

The fear was justified, because the tall man seized the briefcase, jerking it from the Asian's grasp, shoving the Asian onto the cement.

"Freeze that!" This time the command came from Royce. Holt did so, all three monitors freeze-framing, and he leaned in, the electronic glow on his face emphasizing his astonishment. "That's . . . For Christsake, that's Kasinski!"

Renfro frowned. "As in, Special Agent Kasinski?"

"That's him," Royce confirmed. "What the hell's going on here?"

"Let's print that, too, shall we?" Gerard said.

Holt did, and as the laser printer hummed, Gerard said, "Continue."

The monitor screens came to life with their murky but compelling images. On the monitor at left, the mystery man in the overcoat had spun around, hearing the scuffling. He seemed about to head back toward the Asian when a figure from the shadows jumped him from behind.

"Freeze that fucker!" Gerard shouted, and Holt did.

The attacker's face had caught some light, just when Gerard had requested the freeze frame, revealing the attacker to be another male Caucasian, his regular features contorted in aggression as he put an automatic, possibly a nine-millimeter, to the mystery man's head.

"Christ," Royce whispered. "That's Agent Harmon. . . ."

Gerard said, "Print it, Carla." Then to Royce he directed, "Didn't your boss Lamb indicate Mark Roberts ambushed your agents?"

"Kinda looks the other way around," Renfro offered.

Royce said nothing; his smirk was nowhere in evidence, and his face was a morose putty mask.

"Let's see more," Gerard told Holt, nodding toward the screens.

The monitor at left showed the man in the overcoat reaching in back of him, to get both his hands on his attacker's neck. With a quick, deadly twist, like an obscene chiropractic move, the mystery man broke Agent Harmon's neck.

"Oh God," Royce breathed.

Holt had gasped, and both Gerard and Renfro had sucked air in, as well; this was not easy to watch.

Then Agent Harmon was dropping to the pavement, to assume the familiar death sprawl from the crime-scene photos, and the man in the overcoat—who seemed to be Mark Roberts, but whose face could not be determined in these dark, murky goddamn images—plucked the gun from Harmon's limp fingers.

The awful tableau continued as Agent Kasinski ran from the middle monitor, where the Asian lay limp on the pavement, into the monitor screen at left, by which time his gun was drawn. Kasinski fired at the mystery man, who ducked behind a parked car, returning fire, twice, with Harmon's gun, in a muzzle-blast blur, shots sounding like firecrackers on the lousy audio, though the tape effectively caught the howl of agony as Agent Kasinski took first one, then another gunshot to the chest.

"Jesus," Royce whispered, eyes tearing up. "Shit."

Kasinski went down and assumed his familiar, bloody crime-scene posture. Then the mystery man was emerging from behind the parked car to cautiously examine the two bodies; he seemed to be checking their identification, and their credentials, and his body language betrayed surprise, or at least Gerard thought he read that there.

"Don't miss *this* show," Renfro said, nodding toward

the middle monitor, where the Asian was waking up, pushing to his feet.

And drawing a nine-millimeter automatic from under his suit coat.

Just as the mystery man was standing—both black briefcases in hand now—the Asian began firing at him. The mystery man dove for cover, dancing as bullets zinged nearby, ducking behind another parked car.

"What the fuck is going on here?" Gerard demanded.

The Asian was still shooting, and return gunfire came from the mystery man's hiding place, and then the Asian, dodging bullets, leapt back into his car. Soon the Lincoln started and backed up and squealed out of the middle monitor even as on the first monitor, the mystery man was moving out into the open, presumably to take a better shot at his latest assailant.

Then the Lincoln appeared in the left monitor, bearing down on the mystery man as he spiderwebbed its windshield with his gunfire, and the mystery man—awash for a moment in the lights of the Lincoln—dove for safety.

"Freeze it! Show me his goddamn face!"

Holt's fingers flew at the keys but she was shaking her head, her face squeezed with frustration. Whatever enhancements she tried—pulling up image size, increasing brightness—failed to pull the features into any kind of focus.

"That could be Mark Roberts," Gerard said.

"It's a black guy," Renfro said.

"That really narrows it down. . . . Carla, continue."

And now the mystery man in the overcoat—a briefcase in either hand—seemed to run from one monitor to another; when he hit the third monitor, at right, Gerard said, "Hold it there, please!"

Holt froze the tape, and Gerard said, casually, "Cosmo,

how was it again that the State Department boys linked Roberts up to this crime?''

"Straight fingerprint match, Sam.''

"From the crime scene, right? This crime scene.''

"Right.''

"They matched the prints of the man who never leaves prints; good trick. Agent Royce, remember that point you brought up? That this world-class assassin, who wiped his apartment clean of prints, who wore gloves to work, wouldn't likely get sloppy at the scene of a double hit?''

"That always bothered me,'' Royce admitted.

"Carla,'' Gerard said gently, "take us in a little closer, would you?''

Everyone studied the frozen image of the man in the overcoat as Deputy Holt zoomed in.

"Get right in on the hand gripping that briefcase. Good, good . . . now, children—where's Waldo?''

"Goddamn!'' Renfro said.

"Shit,'' Royce said softly. "He's wearing gloves.''

"That's right,'' Gerard said, tapping the screen, where the white hand of the black man clutched a briefcase. "He's wearing gloves, so he *didn't* leave his prints at the scene— and he didn't initiate the attack, either. Boys and girls . . . we have been had.''

Within minutes, Gerard stood before the desk of his boss, Marshal Catherine Walsh, in a dark-paneled private office that looked out upon the Loop, and whose walls were adorned with framed award certificates and citations of merit, as well as photographs with mayors and other local politicians and celebrities, and state and United States congressmen.

But the picture Catherine Walsh was examining at the moment was fresh off a laser printer: a freeze frame of video whose subject—an Afro-American male in an overcoat—was blurred, but whose white-gloved hand was not.

Gerard pointed to the print, poked it. "They lied to us, Catherine. They fucking lied to us. We were operating from a faked warrant."

Her brown eyes narrowed; otherwise her face, framed pleasantly by brunette arcs, betrayed no opinion of the case he was making, nor did her tone as she interjected, "Faked? You really think so?"

"There's no way in hell they could have linked him to that crime scene. The only fingerprints he could have left were inside those gloves, which I don't exactly think he would dump near the bodies. He was the victim of an ambush, Catherine—not the perpetrator."

Something like amusement twinkled in the brown eyes. "You're not usually one to question the wisdom of those issuing warrants, Sam. You're not a detective, you're a manhunter, remember?"

He flinched a frown. "Well, I'm sick of chasing a man who in all likelihood is in New York City from my Chicago office. And who is this Chinese asshole who keeps coming up like bad chow mein? I can tell you somebody who knows—Bertram Fucking Lamb, head of Diplomatic Security, also in New York City. And his flunky what's-his-name, Frank Barrows."

"What do you want to do about it, Sam?"

He batted the air, as if swatting an imaginary fly. "The whole damn deal stinks to high heaven. I never believed in conspiracies, Catherine, I always laughed at the chuckle-heads who thought the CIA killed Kennedy, who thought the FBI set up Martin Luther King. But this smells like a government conspiracy, and I don't like being part of it."

"Nor do I."

He was pacing. "It's all in Manhattan, Catherine—the U.N., Lamb, the Chinese guy is from there, and probably our fugitive's there now." He leaned on her desk. "I want four tickets to New York—me, Cosmo, Noah and the diplomat. Biggs and Coop are on the road, in Pennsylvania, still trying to track our man . . . we can pull them in easily enough.''

''And move the entire investigation to the field, in Manhattan? Not pass the ball to the New York office—''

''No way! It's our case.''

''But is our case finding a fugitive, or nailing Lamb and company?''

''Yes.''

She thought about that, then said, ''Sam, I'm not authorizing four tickets—''

''For God's sake, Catherine, we're getting close here. I need those tickets. Bill the goddamn State Department for 'em.''

She smiled and laughed a lovely liquid laugh he hadn't heard in much too long. ''I was saying . . . we'll need *five* tickets. I'm going with you.''

Eighteen

To a fugitive, time is precious, and so far today had been one long waste of it for Mark Sheridan.

After running his successful field test with the help of the U.S. Postal Service, the fugitive had studied his split-level surveillance images throughout the remainder of the morning and into the afternoon. On the few occasions that he went out—for a quick meal, to invest in transportation (purchasing from a Honda dealership a small motorbike that he could keep with him in the apartment)—he had recorded the surveillance images, and reviewed them a screen at a time on one of his Watchmans, even as he continued monitoring the ongoing surveillance on the TV.

Now this afternoon was frittering itself away with no sign of his man, and Sheridan was fighting the despair that can dog any fugitive. Had he wasted that irreplaceable time, expending energy and now days in assembling and manning this hodgepodge James Bond-ish surveillance system? Perhaps his man was no longer in New York; the bastard could be back in Beijing, for all Sheridan knew.

Then, shortly after two, a chauffeured Lincoln Continental drew up in front of the Chinese Consulate and dropped off a small man in a black suit, who quickly disappeared inside the gothic brownstone. Sheridan sat forward; he felt suddenly alert, and yet dazed, as if he were imagining this.

He was taping everything he monitored, so he quickly played back what had just happened on a Watchman screen: the face of the man in black was not visible, but it seemed to be an Asian, it could be his man. It could be Chen.

In fact it was, though Sheridan did not yet know that for a certainty, just as he had no way of knowing that his prey had spent the entirety of yesterday halfway across the country, in Chicago, Illinois, personally tying up a loose end called Kevin Peters.

So Sheridan watched and waited; this time he didn't have to watch and wait long: within ten minutes, the Asian was slipping out a rear exit of the consulate, skirting delivery trucks, and his face was clearly visible.

"Son of a bitch!" Sheridan exclaimed with glee, an emotion that had been foreign to him for days. "Got you!"

Chen was moving down the alley, and was quickly out of frame, but not before Sheridan had seen what the Asian was carrying in one hand: a big black briefcase.

Sheridan sprang to action, plucking the small motorbike from where it leaned against the wall and rolling it, and himself, out of the apartment.

The elevator ride seemed to take forever, but actually within one minute the fugitive was wheeling the motorbike through the lobby and out into sunlight and traffic noise and dirty looks. This was not the first time he had shadowed Chen—he knew the man's ways, he knew the man's haunts. So despite the several blocks that separated Sheridan from the Chinese Consulate, he had a good shot at grabbing the Asian's tail right now.

Pointing the motorbike down East 42nd, Sheridan raced toward Sixth Avenue, where he figured Chen would be doing his usual subway 'dodge. God smiled on the fugitive and Sheridan hit the lights, and then there the subway station was, beckoning from the end of Bryant Park.

And there Chen was, coming up out of the subway, having gone down one subway stairwell to double back up here, and foil anyone trying to tail him.

Such a small bag of tricks, Chen, Sheridan thought, smiling tightly, pausing on the motorbike, watching as Chen hailed a cab. *Next stop, Chinatown. . . .*

And the fugitive's prophecy was soon fulfilled, the motorbike tailing the taxi as it moved east on 42nd, turning right on Fifth Avenue, going south, on its way to Chinatown.

The crowded crinkum-crankum streets of Chinatown provided a noisy, gaudy cover for what the shadowing Sheridan needed to do. He chained his motorbike to a tree grating and slipped into the sidewalk stream of humanity, Asian faces mingling with *guey low faan,* the "foreign devil" tourists who kept the neighborhood's hundreds of restaurants thriving, with their windows of hanging cooked ducks and doorways leaking exotic aromas. Chen would be headed toward one of his two favorites, Joe's Shanghai on Pell Street, or the Sweet 'n' Tart Cafe on Mott.

Joe's it was, and as much as Sheridan craved a portion of the restaurant's specialty—a crab-and-pork "bun" dumpling—he lingered across the way, near a food store proudly displaying fresh squids, where he had a view through the front window of Chen at his table. Ordering. Eating. Meeting no one.

Chinatown had the highest bank-per-capita ratio in New York City, and, after his late lunch, dark-suited Chen and his briefcase moved along Canal Street past the traditional herbalist shops, tea parlors, dim sum joints and fruit-and-vegetable-laden stalls, as well as the newer, brightly lighted jewelry and electronics shops, and slipped into one of them.

The fugitive waited outside the bank, but glancing through the front window he could see Chen approaching a bank officer, receiving a glowing greeting, and being ushered respectfully toward a back room. Sheridan had no doubt that the black briefcase was being loaded up with bricks of money, like those he had transferred from the briefcase he'd taken from the U.N. parking garage to cigar boxes in that humidor locker room.

When Chen exited, less than ten minutes later, two Asian men in dark suits accompanied him, but they were not slight, slender creatures like Chen, rather taller, bigger men, bodyguards the bank had provided.

Sheridan didn't mind. He wouldn't have feared taking the bodyguards on, but it didn't really matter: he wasn't after Chen's money—he had money. But this told him something important: the exchange was not going down today. These bodyguards would, as Sheridan had witnessed in the past, accompany Chen back to the Chinese Consulate.

The money exchange would go down tomorrow.

Sheridan quickly walked the Chinatown streets back to his motorbike, unchained it and was able to follow, discreetly, another cab bearing Chen (and his bodyguard contingent) back up to midtown in gathering traffic as rush hour approached. Eventually, the Asian—accompanied by his two bodyguards—returned to the consulate, entering a side door.

It was almost as if Chen were making it easy for him. It was almost as if Chen understood that the fugitive was not after the Asian's money, or the Asian himself; as if Chen knew that the fugitive, turned manhunter, was after larger game.

Nineteen

Earlier on the same day the fugitive's surveillance of the Chinese Consulate proved productive, three manhunters—one of them a woman—stepped from a cab in front of the glass tower housing the U.S. Department of State Mission to the United Nations on the corner of First Avenue and East 45th. The morning was sunny and a mild breeze teased the hem of the dress of the slenderly attractive woman's gray suit.

Deputy Marshal Sam Gerard, Marshal Catherine Walsh and Diplomatic Security Agent John Royce had come directly from La Guardia, where their red-eye flight had delivered them; none of them looked any too fresh. Deputy Marshals Cosmo Renfro and Noah Newman had remained at the airport—Renfro's luggage had been lost—and would meet them at their hotel, with their baggage (Cosmo's excluded of course); playing a hunch, Gerard had specifically requested that the USMS travel service have them booked at the International House on Seventh Avenue near West 40th.

Going up the stairs and into the building, Catherine—who had taken time at La Guardia to touch up her makeup and did look quite presentable—flashed Gerard a look of warning.

"Let me do the talking, Sam," she said. She carried a slim brown-leather attaché. "This requires something called 'finesse.' "

"I know what finesse is."

She smirked at him. "Your idea of finesse is grouping slugs together."

He shrugged. "That does take finesse."

Their I.D.s were inspected at a sophisticated security checkpoint, complete with airport-style metal detectors, and soon Walsh had checked in with the young, black female receptionist in the lobby, who sent them to the seventh floor, where Walsh checked in with an older, white male receptionist who ruled a large, open, modern waiting area. Royce sat. Walsh sat. Gerard paced.

"You told him to tell Lamb we were here?" Gerard asked.

"Of course," Walsh said.

"Gave all three of our names?"

"Didn't you hear me?"

"No. I was keeping a respectful distance. Plus, that waterfall sculpture makes it hard to eavesdrop."

"Lamb knows we're here. He knows it's important. Patience."

"That's listed in the dictionary somewhere after finesse, right?"

She nodded, her hands folded delicately in her lap, legs sleekly crossed, as she waited.

And waited.

Gerard's pacing was threatening to wear a groove in the marble floor when Walsh asked, "How long have we been here?"

That was all the encouragement Gerard needed. "Long enough," he said, and moved past the receptionist, who yelled, "You can't go in there!"

Gerard did not reply, nor did Walsh, who was following on his heels; Royce, tagging after, smiled at the wide-eyed receptionist, saying, "Apparently you've been misinformed."

In the hallway, busy offices on either side of them, Gerard said, "Guide me, Agent Royce."

Royce caught up with Gerard and gestured ahead. "It's down here—end of the hall."

The bronze door plate said, "Bertram Lamb, Department Head," but Bertram Lamb said nothing as the marshals charged into his office, Royce bringing up the rear, seeming somewhat embarrassed by his own presence.

It was a spacious chamber, dark paneling intermingling with flat pastel plaster walls wearing such ornaments of diplomacy as framed certificates and photos of Lamb posed with assorted heads of state and diplomats; the wall facing the doorway consisted of windows that looked out on the United Nations complex. To the left was Lamb's massive desk, but the head of the Diplomatic Security Service was not seated there. He was down at the end of the central conference table, with his clone Frank Barrows and three other anonymous dark suits, filling low-backed, leather-upholstered chairs that had cost the taxpayers plenty.

"Don't get up, Mr. Lamb," Catherine Walsh said, stepping forward, taking command. "You make a better target sitting down."

So much for finesse.

Lamb's pale, hawkish features took on faint amusement. "I take it you're not here to deliver our fugitive."

"We've suspended that operation," Gerard said.

Lamb arched an eyebrow. "Really? On whose authority?"

"Mine," Catherine said. "I've frozen the manhunt until we can sort through the horseshit disinformation you've been feeding us."

Now Lamb played faintly offended. "Excuse me?"

Gerard said, "Your people planted Mark Roberts's fingerprints at that crime scene."

"That's a serious and outrageous accusation," Lamb said calmly. "You had best watch what you say, in front of these witnesses, Deputy Marshal Gerard."

"Maybe we should stop talking," Catherine said, resting her attaché on the conference table and reaching within to withdraw a small stack of video laser prints. "You know what they say about pictures being worth a thousand words. . . ."

She thrust before Lamb the video print of the mystery black man's white-gloved hand, clutching a briefcase; the gloved hand was circled heavily in red marker. Lamb swallowed, as if finishing a distasteful meal, and passed the print to Barrows.

Barrows studied it and the blandly handsome diplomatic agent's eyes flashed with anger. "Where the hell did you get these, Gerard?"

Catherine answered for him: "From the U.N. surveillance tapes."

Both Lamb and Barrows shot accusing glances at Royce, who said, rather stiffly, "You assigned me to Gerard's team. I used my contacts to acquire evidence. I don't remember you giving me any guidelines that would preclude my doing that."

Lamb didn't reply, neither did Barrows; perhaps Royce had squelched them with the truth, or maybe they just didn't want to reprimand him in front of outsiders.

Nodding at the laser print, Lamb said to Barrows, "Do you know anything about this?"

"His prints *were* found at the scene."

"Who by?" Lamb snapped. "I want the provenance of that evidence traced."

"I'll look into it immediately," Barrows said, but he remained in his comfortable chair.

"*I* can help with you the 'provenance' of those prints," Gerard said, stepping forward. "You people had them on file. Roberts or Warren or whoever the hell he is . . . he's one of yours."

Somehow Lamb's pale features turned a whiter shade.

"Same as Kasinski and Harmon," Gerard said. "He was one of your own agents."

As Lamb whitened, Barrows reddened; all they needed was a third diplomatic agent to turn blue and they'd have the goddamn flag.

"I'm waiting to hear I'm wrong," Gerard said simply.

Lamb and Barrows exchanged glances.

Marshal Catherine Walsh said, "I want an answer to Deputy Gerard's question, gentlemen, and I want it now . . . or the next person I discuss this matter with will be seated behind a desk at the Justice Department in Washington, D.C. You are familiar with the attorney general?"

Lamb's color, what little there was of it, returned and he twitched a little smile, saying to Barrows, "Fetch the Sheridan file, would you, Frank?", then to the rest of the seated suits he said, "And if you gentlemen will excuse us . . . I'll be taking the marshals into classified territory."

The other diplomatic agents rose and scurried away, their faces blank with uncertainty as to what their proper reaction should be; Royce, however, made no move to leave—he had arrived with the marshals, and he would stay with him.

Within five minutes, they were seated around the conference table, as Gerard accepted from Lamb a thick file adorned with various security and classification warnings. From the file Gerard lifted a photograph of the man he had been chasing: Mark Roberts.

"Mark Sheridan," Lamb said. "As I told you, he was a Marine."

"Special Forces," Gerard said numbly, reading from the file.

Lamb nodded. "Also ex-C.I.A., black ops branch. We recruited him in '93 and, up until last year, he was one of our resident 'kites' here in New York."

"I'm not familiar with that term," Catherine said.

Royce said, "A kite is an agent who works alone, and with no official connection—if something goes wrong, the string is cut, and the kite is on his own."

"That gives us deniability," Lamb said.

"And why would you need deniability?" Gerard asked. Then he answered his own question: "Sheridan was one of those agents doing the government's dirty work."

Lamb nodded, slowly.

Gerard sighed. "That can breed a dangerous lack of morality into a man."

"Yes it can," Lamb admitted. "And somewhere along the line, Sheridan went wrong. He became what you, in your line of work, would call a 'bent cop.' "

From within her attaché, Catherine withdrew a laser print she had held back: the face of the Asian.

Lamb whitened again. "Where did you get that?"

"From the same security-cam tapes," Catherine said. "Who is he?"

Lamb turned to Barrows, who merely shrugged in defeat. Then Lamb said, with quiet reluctance, "Xian Chen. Cultural attaché to the United Nations—representing the People's Republic of China."

"Isn't that interesting," Gerard said. "You received information from us, last night, about the Kevin Peters murder? An attendant at that gym was killed, too, you know."

"Yes, yes," Lamb said, somewhat impatiently.

Gerard flicked the laser print in Lamb's hands. "That's

the guy who did it. He brought the 'culture' of slashing throats to Chicago yesterday.''

Barrows said quickly, ''He's back in New York now, according to our intel.''

Gerard blinked. ''Really?''

Barrows nodded. ''Arrived in the wee hours this morning, via private Lear jet, belonging to the People's Republic. You see, 'Cultural Attaché' Chen is in reality an agent of Chinese intelligence.''

Gerard glanced at Catherine; neither of them betrayed a feeling they shared: they had wandered in way over their heads, into the arcane, cloudy and seedy world of espionage.

''For the past two years,'' Lamb was saying, ''we've known we had a mole in the State Department, peddling secrets to the Chinese. We suspected Chen was the bag man for the Chinese, the man physically exchanging money for secrets.''

''A tail on Chen led us to Sheridan,'' Barrows explained. ''We knew of an exchange set to go down in that parking garage, between Chen and Sheridan; agents Kasinski and Harmon were assigned to intercept that exchange, and take Sheridan in.''

''In,'' Gerard asked, ''or down?''

Lamb twitched a frown. ''It was to be an arrest. We don't liquidate.''

Not unless you assign one of your black-ops kites to do it, Gerard thought; but he said nothing.

''The timing was off,'' Barrows continued, voice colored with regret and embarrassment. ''Sheridan showed up early, our guys were apparently a little late; the whole thing went abysmally south.''

''I've seen the tapes,'' Gerard said solemnly.

''Bottom line,'' Barrows shrugged, ''Sheridan was better than we were.''

"Apparently he's better than us all," Lamb said pointedly to the manhunters who had not yet brought Sheridan in.

With quiet frustration, but no anger, Catherine asked them, "Why did you keep this from us?"

"Matters this delicate are strictly on a 'need to know' basis," Lamb said wearily. "It was a judgment call, perhaps a poor one, that you would not need this information to do your job. We believed your people would quickly apprehend him. . . . After all, the investigation was headed by the man who brought in Richard Kimble."

Gerard shifted uncomfortably in his comfortable chair.

"We believed the whole issue would be cleaned up internally, and swiftly," Lamb concluded, then added, "Perhaps our confidence in Deputy Gerard was . . . misplaced."

Gerard stared at Lamb stonily, then gestured to himself and Catherine and said, "We're the good guys. We chase bad guys. Question is . . . which the hell are you?"

"Deputy Gerard," Lamb said, "I apologize for my rude remark . . ."

"And by the way, which the hell is Mark Sheridan?"

"I'll admit it was a mistake to withhold information from you . . ."

"You left out the fabricating evidence part."

Lamb patted the air with his palms. "I have no knowledge of those fingerprints being faked, and as you've seen, Agent Barrows is assigned to that matter. The fact remains Mark Sheridan killed those two agents—you saw it on the tape yourself."

Gerard lifted an eyebrow. "It looked like self-defense to me."

"I understand Sheridan shot you in the chest, twice," Barrows said to Gerard. "You, a law enforcement officer, were holding a gun on him. Sheridan, a fugitive, shot you— was *that* self-defense?"

Gerard had no answer for that. But the mention had started his ribs aching again.

"Context is everything, Deputy Gerard, Marshal Walsh. And I apologize for withholding the true nature of that context, for national security reasons."

"Where do we go from here?" Catherine asked.

"Not to the attorney general, I trust," Lamb said, with an unexpected smile. Then his patrician features turned somber. "Mark Sheridan is still at large, armed and dangerous, and until we have him in custody, we will not know the extent of the leak, or how much damage has been done to the United States government, not to mention American interests here and abroad."

Gerard was thumbing through Sheridan's file.

"You have as much information now as we do," Lamb said. "What do you intend to do with it?"

Gerard shrugged, but there was an edge of fire in his matter-of-fact voice.

"Do what I do," the manhunter said. "Find him."

The International was an older hotel, the accommodations just fair, showing the roots of their most recent remodeling in the 1970s; Gerard had booked a suite for himself to share with Renfro and Royce, with Newman across the hall in a room he'd share with Biggs. Deputy Savannah Cooper would be sharing a suite with Marshal Walsh, although the marshal would be working at the New York office of the USMS, coordinating efforts with the State Department, NYPD and the local marshals.

"What are we doin' in this dump?" Renfro asked sourly, feet up on a coffee table. He was combing his hair—which is to say, his toupee in his lap—revealing, among friends, that he was cueball bald. Newman and Royce, sipping room service sodas, were seated nearby, as if they were all watching the room's television, which wasn't switched on.

Night had fallen; the afternoon had been spent going over the Diplomatic Security Service file on Mark Sheridan. Biggs and Cooper, en route by rented Suburban from Pennsylvania, were overdue.

The big event since arriving in New York was a call from Agent Henry saying a cell phone call from "Roberts" to Marie Bineaux at work had been intercepted; they were backtracking the outgoing cell site, but it would take time and some dealing with red tape to get the information shaken loose.

"It's not so bad," Newman said, glancing around the slightly threadbare suite. "We're close to Times Square."

"They've turned it into Disneyland," Royce winced.

"Seriously," Renfro said, "who booked us into this rat trap? Marshal Walsh? What is this, a theater package? She takin' us all to *Cats*?"

"*I* booked it," Gerard said. He was standing at the window; his ribs were aching and in his right hand he was absently rolling the two spent slugs that had broken them. Souvenirs from Mark Sheridan.

"You booked it?" Renfro said. "What, sentimental reasons? Is this where you arrested Angela Davis in nineteen-sixty-somethin', or somethin'?"

"We need a twenty-four-hour surveillance on the Chinese Consulate," Gerard said, still at the window.

Renfro snorted. "So where's the Chinese Consulate?"

Gerard gestured with his head and the three younger men gathered round the window.

"There," he said, nodding toward the view of the gothic brownstone just down, and across, the street.

Newman said, "How did you manage this? You didn't find out about Chen bein' the Chinese cultural attaché till this morning!"

"Call it instinct, call it intuition," Gerard said. "The way the Chinese kept turning up, the national security, State

Department dance we been doin' . . . hit goes down in the United Nations parking garage. I figured being across from the Chinese Consulate just might come in handy.''

"The Big Dog rules," Renfro said, with no sarcasm.

"Hell of a sniffer on ya, Boss," Newman said, not a little awe in his voice.

Newman moved back to his chair, and Renfro went to a mirror to adjust and further comb his hairpiece. Royce lingered near Gerard.

"Think you might ever consider leaving the marshal's service?" Royce asked him quietly.

"Why?"

"I just think you could do well on a, uh, more sophisticated playing field."

Gerard smiled a little, oddly touched by this gesture. "If you're offering a recommendation, thanks but no thanks. I guess I'm more at home in the wilds of Chicago."

"And the swamps of Kentucky?"

Royce's smirky smile seemed less irritating to Gerard, now that he knew the man.

A rather frantic-sounding knock at the door ended their conversation. Newman went to answer it and Royce followed.

Savannah Cooper was first inside, then Biggs, both lugging their bags; in USMS sweatshirts and jeans and boots, they had the look of drenched dogs that had dried in the sun.

"I need a life," Biggs moaned.

"Maybe there's one after death," Newman offered.

"Then kill me now."

"You're three hours late," Gerard said, ambling over, tossing his slugs in his palm like Captain Queeg playing with steel ball bearings.

Biggs flopped into a chair, which wheezed under his weight. "That's what I kept telling those maniacs on the

Jersey Turnpike when it stopped dead, but they wouldn't listen.''

''You're bunking with Marshal Walsh,'' Gerard told Cooper. ''But hang here for a while—our liaisons from NYPD are supposed to drop by, any minute.''

''Marshal Walsh, huh?'' Coop said. ''Excellent opportunity for brown-nosing. . . . Why the long face, Cosmo? Miss me?''

''No,'' Renfro said. He had not acknowledged his colleagues' appearance as yet, still engrossed in combing his ''hair.'' ''I miss my two-hundred-dollar white bucks. I miss my Armani jacket. I miss my Nicole Miller tie. I miss my new toup, which happens to be the most expensive the Hair Club for Men has to offer. But I did not miss you, Cooper, nor will I this hotel or this town when we leave, which can't come too soon to suit me.''

''Nice to see you, too, Cosmo,'' Biggs said.

''In case you didn't gather,'' Newman said, ''his panties are in a bunch cause the airline lost his luggage.''

''I have this idea,'' Renfro said, ''this excellent idea. When an airline loses your luggage, they should be required to give you free tickets to wherever your luggage went. I mean, why should my shit go to Hawaii and not me?''

''You can borrow some of my shirts, Cos,'' Biggs offered.

Renfro turned from the mirror. ''Do I look like I could fit in one of those pup tents?''

''Well, you're on your own for underwear,'' Biggs said. ''*Those* I could fill.''

The phone rang and Gerard answered it.

''Sam,'' Deputy Henry's voice said, crackling with long-distance and cell-phone static. ''Holt and me are at O'Hare.''

''Why in hell?''

''Marie Bineaux led us here. She just used a key to unlock one of those long-term lockers and retrieved a brief-case. Then she bought a ticket to—''

''New York City.''

''That's right! You want us to grab her, or—''

''Hell no! Follow her!''

''To New York?''

''To New York,'' Gerard affirmed. ''Join the party; more the merrier. You take her flight and I'll arrange to have New York deputies meet you. Which airport is she coming in at?''

''JFK.''

''No problem. Any news on that cell-phone trace?''

''That's the other reason I called; we just got it. They've narrowed the call to a cell site in Manhattan. Third Avenue and Forty-second Street area.''

Gerard jotted that down on a hotel notepad.

''Good work, Deputy,'' Gerard said. ''Check right in when you get here, no matter the hour.''

''You got it, Boss.''

Gerard hung up. Royce was looking at the note pad, at the words ''Third Ave & 42nd.''

''That's not that many blocks from here,'' the young agent said.

''Sheridan's damn near a neighbor,'' Gerard said.

A knock drew Gerard to the door, saying, ''Bet that's the NYPD,'' and it was: two plainclothes detectives, both male—a Korean who introduced himself as Detective Kim, and a chunky white dick named Stans.

''We're supposed to report to Deputy Marshal Sam Gerard,'' Kim said, still in the hallway.

''You're doing that right now,'' Gerard said. ''But I'm going to need more of you . . . Come in.''

And Gerard called his chatty deputies to order, saying, ''Hope you're all rested and eager to get out on the streets and explore this fine city. . . .''

"Tonight?" Renfro asked, eyes wide, toupee askew.

"Tonight," Gerard said. "Sorry, no *Cats*. We'll go till midnight, then start again at dawn."

Soon only Gerard was left in the room, standing at the window, contemplating the view of the Chinese Consulate, tossing the spent slugs in his palm. Out on the streets, the door-to-door search was under way, the deputies and Royce and the two NYPD detectives, plus uniformed cops they'd brought in, checking every hotel and apartment house in a four-block radius around the cell site of Third Avenue and 42nd Street.

Somewhere out there, his fugitive was burrowed in, maybe feeling safe. He would find him, Gerard would find him; but the manhunter couldn't help wondering if Xian Chen, the throat-slashing cultural attaché, was across the street right now, snug in that Chinese Consulate, secure in his cloak of diplomatic immunity.

Now, there was a bird the Big Dog wouldn't mind bagging.

Twenty

The loved ones of a fugitive react in varying ways—denial
. . . even faced with clear evidence, a mother may reject her
child's guilt; disavowal . . . a harsher-minded parent might
turn away an offspring on the run; even betrayal . . . handing son or daughter over to the law. If child or spouse is
clearly guilty of a crime, should unconditional love extend
into aiding and abetting? When her man may be guilty, but
swears not, when her intellect tells her he may be lying but
her heart says he is not, what does a woman in love do?

Marie Bineaux flew from Chicago to New York bearing
the thick manila envelope withdrawn from a locker at
O'Hare Airport, using the key her lover Mark had hidden
in her apartment. Hand-carrying the important envelope in
a leather briefcase, traveling in sweatshirt and pants, she
was not aware that Deputies Frank Henry and Carla Holt
were on the same plane, or that they had followed her from
JFK Airport to the Tudor Hotel on East 42nd Street, not
far from the U.N. or that Henry and Holt had watched from
a government sedan (in the company of the two New York

deputy marshals who had picked them up) as a porter took her backpack and suitcase from the cab and into the hotel.

Her room had already been booked for her—by Mark—so early check-in was not a problem; and when the bellboy carried her bags into her small but nicely appointed room, with its dark hardwood furnishings, gold-and-blue wallpaper and English-style ambience, she found the message light on the bedside telephone winking at her.

When she was alone in the room, she sat on the edge of the double bed with its rich royal-blue brocade spread and retrieved her voice mail.

"This is Alfonsito from Saks," Mark's disguised voice said. "Your dress is ready."

She grinned at his silly accent; what country was that supposed to be? Opening her briefcase, she removed the manila envelope and transferred it to her backpack. She craved freshening up—she had managed to sleep a little on the plane, and needed to wash the oily film from her face, to brush her teeth and make herself feel human again. Glancing at her watch, she realized she had just enough time for a shower.

While Marie Bineaux was showering, little more than a block away, Deputy Noah Newman—bleary-eyed, frazzled from last night's fruitless canvass, already tired from an effort that had begun on these streets at dawn—was showing a doorman in Tudor City a photograph of Mark Sheridan.

The white, thirtyish, heavyset doorman didn't look at the photograph any more carefully than he had Newman's credentials; so the deputy wasn't convinced he had the most observant citizen Manhattan might have to offer.

"Nope," the doorman said after a glance, "haven't seen him. Sorry."

Newman sighed. He went ahead with the routine; it was his job. "Look at a couple more."

"Different guy?"

"Same guy. He may have changed his appearance."

And Newman showed him the first of several computer-doctored photographs of Sheridan, this one with glasses and a mustache.

"Wait a minute, gimme that," the doorman said, suddenly interested. "This guy I've seen. He rented an apartment couple days ago. . . . Y'ask me, he musta slipped our sleazeball super a few bucks on the side, 'cause there was a long waitin' list for that old gal's place."

Newman's cell phone was out faster than a gunfighter's six-shooter, and within fifteen minutes—about the same time Marie Bineaux, looking and feeling fresh in a black knit top and jeans, wearing the backpack, stepped into a cab, asking to be taken to Saks Fifth Avenue—a mix of uniformed and plainclothes NYPD had surrounded the Tudor City apartment building.

Gerard and Royce were in the hallway outside the fugitive's apartment, poised on either side of the door, weapons in hand, the young man's .45 held in a double-handed grip, the deputy marshal's nine-millimeter in one hand and his walkie-talkie in the other. Within the apartment a radio was playing—an oldies station, Aretha Franklin spelling out her need for "Respect."

Then the radio clicked off.

Gerard's eyes met Royce's in mutual understanding: their fugitive was in there.

Gerard lifted his foot, said into the walkie-talkie, "Move in!" and kicked the motherfucker in, splintering it to shit, then shouldering through into the small apartment, Royce bursting in behind him, even as Biggs shattered the glass on the fire-escape window, reached around to unlock and shove it open, and crawled in with Renfro close on his tail. Everybody with guns in hand. They had the little living room surrounded.

170

But the little living room was empty.

Empty of their fugitive, that is. It was filled with electronics gear that had Royce wide-eyed with admiration.

"Damn!" Gerard barked. His gun was still out. He checked the kitchenette and the bedroom, carefully but quickly. Nothing. Little sign anyone was even inhabiting this space.

Except for all the high-tech equipment.

"He's got a timer controlling the lights and the radio," Royce said, kneeling by the sofa. "For that lived-in look."

"Our boy does like his toys," Renfro said, patting the top of the thirty-five-inch television. "If the local evidence locker's short on space, they can ship this baby back to Chicago with me."

"Renfro," Gerard warned, as he prowled the apartment, feeling surly.

Renfro plucked a remote control from the nearby kitchen table and pointed it at the TV, clicking it on. *Baywatch* bikini babes pranced and jiggled across the screen.

"Nice picture quality," Renfro said. "Check out the skin tone."

"Turn that off," Gerard snarled.

"No, wait a second," Royce was saying. He had zeroed in on the laptop on that same table. He pulled up a chair and sat; began typing.

Suddenly the beach bunny images were replaced by a four-way split screen—surveillance angles on a familiar gothic brownstone.

Biggs said, "S.O.B.'s got a better surveillance setup on the Chinese than we do!"

At this moment, Marie Bineaux was stepping from a cab and across the sidewalk to, and through, the brass revolving doors of Saks Fifth Avenue. She moved briskly through the plush marble-floored world of glittering display cases, breathing in expensive air touched with the memory of a thousand perfume spritzers, ignoring the tinkling anonymous piano artistry of somebody working his or her way through the works of Andrew Lloyd Webber.

As she rose with the escalator to the women's fashion department, Marie was unaware that Deputies Frank Henry of Chicago and Jackson of New York were in low-key pursuit. Had she known, however, she would not have been surprised: Mark had warned her.

Stopping at a counter, she asked a chicly attired, terminally bored saleswoman if a dress had been put aside for Marie Bineaux.

"Oh yes, Ms. Bineaux," the saleswoman said, pretending to brighten. "Your husband picked it out himself, yesterday. He'd like you to check the size."

Soon Marie had been ushered to an empty stall in the changing area, still unaware that Henry and Jackson—two bulls in a dress shop—were nearby, doing their best to look inconspicuous, getting fish eyes from rich women trying on Paris fashions. Had they known Saks was the Bineaux woman's destination, they would have sent Deputy Marshal Carla Holt in their stead.

"Can I take your backpack?" the saleswoman asked, as Marie was about to shut herself in the stall.

Marie blinked. "Is that required? I only have one item, here, to try on. I hope you're not suggesting—"

"Certainly not! Keep it with you, if you like."

"Thank you," Marie smiled. "I'm carrying valuables with me, and you never know who you can trust."

The saleswoman said nothing, and seemed vaguely offended, before wandering off.

Within the cubicle, Marie was pulling off her blouse as she kicked off her running shoes; then she shimmied out of her jeans and slipped into the slinky little black dress. She was wearing nothing under it but panties—she wore no bra—but something was rubbing her. Quickly she discovered a small note pinned to the underside of the waist of the dress.

In Mark's cursive handwriting it said: "Mirrors. Employees only."

She frowned, stepped from the cubicle, carting her backpack with her (as Mark had instructed), and moved into a viewing area where mirrors faced each other, broken only by the entrance to the alcove and a door marked "EMPLOYEES ONLY." For a moment she had got caught up admiring her slender, shapely form in the smart little dress, when in the nearest mirror she saw the "EMPLOYEES ONLY" door crack open and Mark gesture to her.

She went to him, and he pulled her into what seemed to be an electrical closet.

Then she was in his arms and they were kissing, hungrily, happiness and sadness blurring together until there was no difference.

Reluctantly, Mark drew away from her enough to say, "We don't have much time. There are deputies right outside. Do you have it?"

She nodded and withdrew the envelope from the backpack. Mark opened the clasps, quickly checked the contents and smiled tightly. Then he tucked the envelope under his arm and drew her to him, again.

He looked at her, in the skimpy little dress, with open admiration, grinning as he said, "Black *is* your color."

"Always," she said, and she fell into his arms, and they kissed again, tenderly, sweetly.

Then whispering in her ear, he spoke words not of love, but of escape.

Outside, Deputies Henry and Jackson (one of the New York deputies) had settled in at the nearby lingerie section, Henry reasoning that a lot of men bought their wives or girlfriends that kind of "Victoria's Secret stuff." It seemed the least conspicuous place they could find near where the

Bineaux woman was changing clothes; plus, a little TV monitor was showing a promotional video of sexy fashion models in flimsy undies. When his cell phone rang, Henry jumped like it was his wife who'd caught him.

"Henry," he answered.

"Henry," Gerard's voice echoed nastily. "Where the hell is Marie Bineaux?"

"Saks Fifth Avenue. Tryin' on a dress."

"What, in some dressing room cubicle?"

"Sure, I mean, what do you expect? Out in the open?"

"Trying on a dress my ass," Gerard's voice growled. "She's not buying a goddamn dress, Deputy Henry, she's having some quality time with her boyfriend—our fugitive! He's in there with her now—get in there now, now, *now*!"

Within seconds Deputies Henry and Jackson were charging into the changing area, guns drawn, frightening women who were on their way in and out of dressing stalls, prowling the mirrored dressing area. Henry stopped at the door marked "EMPLOYEES ONLY" and, nodding to Jackson to be on the alert, yanked it open.

The electrical closet was empty.

When the saleswoman rushed up asking for an explanation, the deputies demanded she lead them to the Bineaux woman's stall, which she did. The door was locked. Henry pounded hard on it.

The door opened and Marie Bineaux in her jeans but no top, holding her blouse over her bare breasts, looked at them, offended and alarmed.

"What . . . ?" she gasped.

Deputy Henry swallowed. "Sorry, ma'am. We were, uh, looking for a shoplifter."

"Do I look like I'm concealing anything?"

"Uh, no, ma'am."

"I have a backpack here—you may look inside that, if

you like . . . but I'd prefer you let me put on my clothes, first.''

''That won't be necessary, ma'am.''

''Oh, I'm afraid it is,'' she said, as she shut the cubicle door. ''I catch cold without them.''

Henry couldn't help admiring the lovely young woman, and that little touch of French accent made her voice so sexy. . . . He had never been so charmingly humiliated.

Exchanging bewildered shrugs and embarrassed grins, the two deputies made their way out of Ladies' Fashions, making apologies as they went, until Henry could find a quiet corner to call the bad news in to Gerard.

Twenty-one

A manhunter close to his prey experiences a unique brand of frustration. Deputy Marshal Sam Gerard said, "Shit!" and slammed his cell phone to the kitchen table in Mark Sheridan's apartment.

"Easy," Royce said, fingers blazing at the laptop keyboard. "Let's not crash our man's hard drive."

"Sorry," Gerard said, embarrassed. "I think Henry and that New York deputy, what is it, Jackson? I think they blew nabbing our man, at Saks Fifth Avenue. I hope they can manage not to lose Marie Bineaux. . . . Anything?"

"Well," Royce said, eyes on the laptop screen, "all the surveillance was run from this. He encrypted his commands—he's good. I'm better."

"Prove it."

"He's recorded everything on those VCRs. We need to fast-forward through those tapes and see what we come up with . . . the latest one's loaded in now."

"Okay," Gerard said, liking the sound of that.

Royce shifted to a VCR remote control, and said, "This

one was in progress . . . we'll do fast-rewind. . . ."

Nothing was on the latest tape. Renfro loaded in another, and before long something in the stream of images caught Royce's eye. He backed the tape up and found where Sheridan had freeze-framed an image.

"He had several decks going," Royce said, "so whenever he played one back, it superseded the others and recorded the playback . . ."

The freeze frame they were looking at, on the thirty-five-inch TV, was of a now-familiar face. An Asian face.

"Our ubiquitous cultural attaché—Xian Chen," Royce said. "Seems our primary target is searching for our secondary target."

Gerard frowned at Chen's frozen image. "When was that recorded?"

"Yesterday . . . afternoon. See the digital readout on screen?"

Gerard's cell phone trilled and he answered it.

"Sam!" It was Cooper's voice; she was on the roof of their hotel, keeping watch on the front of the gothic brownstone. "I spotted Chen! He just exited the consulate, out the back alley, I think. He's got a briefcase, a big momma."

Royce, who had not heard Cooper's words, was saying to Gerard, "Take a look."

"Sam, look at this!" An eager Renfro was pointing at the TV like a kid showing Dad a toy commercial; on one of the split screens Chen could be seen jaywalking across the street, having exited the alley.

"On our way, Coop," Gerard said. "Switch to walkie-talkie."

"Roger that."

Gerard said to Biggs, "Get Cooper off that roof and find yourselves a vehicle from NYPD. Mr. Royce, Cosmo—come along. . . ."

On the way down to the lobby, to their waiting double-parked Suburban, Gerard alerted Newman about Chen by cell phone.

"I see him," Newman's voice came back. Gerard had positioned him on West 41st across from the consulate. "In foot pursuit."

"Switch to walkie-talkie."

"Roger."

They climbed into the Suburban, Renfro taking the wheel, Gerard in the rider's seat, Royce climbing in back, and soon the NYPD were a memory as the three headed to catch up with Newman and Chen.

As Renfro drove quickly down 42nd Street, buildings blurring by, horns honking, taxi drivers and pedestrians cursing at them, Newman's voice crackled over the walkie-talkie: "He's going down into the subway at Forty-second and Lexington. . . ."

"You heard the man," Gerard said to Renfro.

But soon Newman's voice was back again: "Shit! Chen doubled back, he went down one stairwell and came up the other. . . . Now he's flaggin' a cab."

The Suburban was stopped at a light at 52nd and Madison Avenue. Traffic wouldn't allow them to run it.

They had just crossed through the intersection when Newman's voice returned: "He got in a taxi heading west on Fifty-first! Sam, where the hell are you? We'll lose him! Hurry!"

And the last word had barely escaped Newman's lips when the Suburban pulled up, Royce opened the door for him and the young deputy leapt in back, ponytail swinging.

"Follow that cab," Newman said.

Renfro said, "Very funny," but did so, turning left on Seventh Avenue, heading south, taking his fellow Chicagoans (and New Yorker Royce) and himself on a tour of mid- and lower Manhattan, moving slowly through busy unyielding traffic. The garment district, with its hive of office buildings and factories and clothes-rack-trundling workers, gave way gradually to the funkier Village which blended into SoHo, before the stainless steel towers of the World Trade Center cast their chilly spell.

"Look where we wind up," Gerard said. "Kinda confirms this is all about money, doesn't it?"

Chen's cab had finally stopped and the Asian, in one of his trademark dark suits, his massive briefcase in hand, was stepping out in the midst of noontime traffic, in the dark ravine between towering skyscrapers behind whose respectable facades—turned dingy and dull by time, weather and Manhattan—many a questionable enterprise dwelled.

"Wall Street," Gerard whispered. "Double-park, Cosmo."

Gerard slammed the "U.S. MARSHALS SERVICE" placard in the window and they got out of the Suburban, which blocked two parked cars.

"Noah, we'll cross the street and tail 'im from the other side," Gerard said. "Cosmo, you and the diplomat get behind Chen. . . . Stay back and do your best to blend in."

Only Royce truly fit in with the herd of businesspeople on the lunchtime street, the sea of bobbing heads making it hard to keep track of the small Asian, but also serving to keep the deputies unseen.

Gerard, however, was letting Newman fix his sights on Chen; the warrants squad leader was more concerned with spotting his fugitive, who he was convinced would be somewhere in this crowd. Why Sheridan had kept the Chinese spy under surveillance was a mystery, but Gerard's best guess was that the fugitive planned to kill Chen, though any motivation for that, other than revenge, remained clouded.

Chen was pausing on the corner at the busy intersection of Wall and Nassau Streets, swallowed in the crowd waiting for the light to change. Across the street, Gerard and Newman paused, watching. And Gerard spotted something, someone, on the opposite corner from Chen.

A black guy about Sheridan's height and build, carrying a big black briefcase identical to Chen's, stood waiting to cross. The man who might be Gerard's fugitive certainly didn't blend in with the Wall Street throng, or seem a likely person to be carrying a briefcase: he wore jeans and a T-shirt with a sport jacket, and, oddly, sported a green wool-knit hat, a sailor's watch cap the weather didn't justify.

Into his walkie-talkie, Gerard said, "Across the intersection—green cap, black briefcase! Could be our man!"

Renfro and Royce, clogged within the sidewalk crowd, strained to see around Chen to pinpoint Gerard's suspect. Before they could, the walk signal was illuminated, and then a rush of humanity from either corner was moving toward the other side.

"We're slow," Gerard said, and a nasty thought passed through his mind: if Sheridan snuffed Chen before they could stop him, how great a loss to the world would that be?

As Gerard and Newman watched from across the street, Renfro and Royce moved up closer behind Chen, getting in position to intercept the man in the cap, to grab him. . . .

In the crosswalk, the man in the cap briefly collided with Chen, little more than their shoulders brushing.

But Gerard saw the exchange go down.

"They switched briefcases," Gerard said into his walkie-talkie. "Stay back."

Renfro's voice came over the walkie-talkie: "What's up?"

"Our man would kill him, not exchange briefcases with him. . . . You guys keep tailing Chen. We'll take Green Cap."

Renfro and Royce were in the crosswalk now, keeping after Chen, while Gerard and Newman were doubling back to follow the man in the cap, who was stepping to the curb to hail a taxi. They did not see the fugitive, apparently just another impeccably dressed Wall Street businessman, brush by the man in the cap, injecting the big black briefcase with his Medi-Jector, planting his radioactive bug.

And the fugitive had moved on by the time Gerard was spotting the man in the cap getting into the back of a cab, which quickly found a notch in the traffic and filled it.

"Damn!" Gerard said, and he and Newman pirouetted desperately about at the edge of traffic, looking for a free cab, having no luck, Gerard finally moving into the street and holding out his badge in front of the next car, a dark blue Cadillac Seville, which skidded to a stop at the man-hunter's feet.

The driver's-side window slid down and a startled, well-dressed businessman in his fifties behind the wheel asked, "What's wrong?"

"If you'll step from the car, please, sir."

The confused driver opened his door and Gerard helped him out—actually, yanked him out. Newman braced the man, keeping him from falling; then the young deputy ran around to get in on the rider's side.

"Your government thanks you, sir," Gerard said. "This commandeered vehicle will be returned waxed and detailed."

The cab was in sight and another slow chase began. Ten uneventful minutes of keeping the cab's yellow ass in view came and went, with Gerard checking in with his people from time to time—back on cell phones.

"Biggs, Cooper," Gerard said. "Proceeding north on Third Avenue."

"We find you," Biggs's voice said.

"You have wheels?"

"We're in an unmarked NYPD sedan."

"Good." Gerard filled Biggs in quickly on what had been happening.

Renfro, with Royce in the Suburban tailing Chen in a cab, reported in: "Think he's headed back to the Chinese Consulate, Boss."

"Makes sense."

"Where are you?"

"We seem to be getting onto a bridge."

"Queensboro," Newman clarified. "Hey, look—it's the opening of *Taxi*!"

And it was, as they moved across a clanging cantilevered steelwork span nothing like the suspension bridges otherwise linking Manhattan to the boroughs. The river traffic— small tankers, cement barges, garbage scows and pleasure boats—seemed to be moving faster than they were.

As the commandeered Seville, tailing the man in the cap's cab at a discreet distance, entered Queens, a green Ford sedan bearing Biggs and Cooper fell in behind them. A bleak industrial landscape welcomed them.

The cell phone rang; it was Renfro.

"Cab dropped the Ginsu king at the consulate," Renfro reported.

"Stake him out."

"Where are you now?"

They had been following the cab down streets cutting through the factories and warehouses along the river, but something unexpected was looming.

"Green Cap's cab is pulling into a cemetery," Gerard said.

Surprise etched Renfro's voice: "What?"

"He's entering the main gate right now."

Gerard pulled up outside the cobblestone-fenced cemetery; the wrought-iron archway over the entry said, "Queens Hill Cemetery."

"Biggs," Gerard said, back on walkie-talkie. "Camp out, outside the gate someplace, and wait."

"Roger that, Sam," Biggs's voice returned.

Biggs tooled the green Ford sedan underneath a nearby railway bridge, while Gerard and Newman in the Seville followed the incline through the cobblestone pillars of the front gate and into the cemetery.

"There," Newman said, pointing.

The cab had pulled up in front of a small stone chapel. Gerard stopped, put the Caddy in park, watched as the man in the cap got out of the cab, big black briefcase in hand, moved toward an 1890s neo-Egyptian-style stonework mausoleum marked "Crane" and went around the side toward a ramp and steps that led down into an underground crypt.

"Let's pay our respects," Gerard said, and he and the younger agent left the Seville and, keeping low, moved among the sometimes ornate gravestones of the venerable cemetery. Gerard paused behind a stone topped with a crying angel with one busted wing; the manhunter plucked a small pair of binoculars from his pocket and focused on the man in the cap.

"That isn't Sheridan," he said softly.

The man who wasn't Sheridan was heading down the short flight of steps to the doorway of the crypt.

"Guess who's gonna have a key to the front door," Gerard whispered to Newman.

And the man in the cap withdrew a key from a hiding place in the stonework and unlocked the massive wooden door. Then he—and his briefcase—went inside.

Moments later, the man in the cap—who wasn't the fugitive—returned from the crypt, empty-handed.

"Left the briefcase behind," Gerard noted.

Newman, even without binoculars, could see that much. "What the hell is this about, Boss?"

"I don't know," Gerard said, lowering the binocs, "but I bet you our fugitive does."

And the man in the cap got back in his cab and rolled out of the cemetery.

In a few moments, Gerard's walkie-talkie came alive with Biggs's excited voice: "Sam, he's leaving."

"It's always nice when you can leave a place like this alive," Gerard said.

"What do we do?"

"We stay," he said. "We wait."

Twenty-two

A fugitive plans, and a fugitive improvises. Mark Sheridan, still in the dignified suit and tie he'd worn on Wall Street, though at the moment crouching between sacks of fertilizer in a maintenance shed at Queens Hill Cemetery, had paid cash (with credit card I.D.) to rent two automobiles. In one of them, a blue Lexus, he had followed Chen's briefcase here from the financial district, and when he'd seen the cab turn up the cemetery path, had gone on ahead, parking around the far side and—with one eye on his Watchman and the directional arrow flashing there—scaled the six-foot cobblestone wall. He had made his way to this shed and now he was studying a blinking arrow that signaled the briefcase was no longer in motion.

He checked his watch; then he referred to a card with phone numbers on it and dialed one on his cell phone. After four rings, Marie's voice said: ''Yes?''

''You know what to do,'' the fugitive said. ''Go!''

At the Tudor Hotel, where Deputy Henry was in the security control room, keeping tabs on Marie Bineaux who had gone swimming in the hotel health club, the deputy was gesturing frantically to a surveillance monitor.

"Get me on that line!" he said.

On this particular monitor, Marie Bineaux—who had exited the ladies' locker room after her swim—had just answered a pool-area pay phone.

"Sorry," the fiftyish cow-eyed chief of security said, straightening his tie; his blue jacket bore a Tudor House crest. "That's not a house phone, Deputy Henry."

The Bineaux woman was hanging up, heading back toward the locker room.

Henry, aware that Gerard would tear him a new asshole should he lose the woman, dashed from the security booth on the hotel's first floor, and, finding no elevator immediately available, vaulted up two flights of stairs to the third floor and the health club facility.

In the ladies' locker room, three young women, in various stages of undress, were not pleased to see Henry, but his outstretched hand displaying the USMS badge stifled screams.

Marie Bineaux was not there. Nor was she in the shower area. Or in the restroom—however, a window there had been opened, and a breeze blew in, inviting Henry for a look. A fire escape ladder yawned beyond, dropped to the street, though the Bineaux woman was not in sight.

At Queens Hill Cemetery, where he paced behind a large monument on which perched frowning stone gargoyles, Gerard took the news with his usual grace.

"Fuck!" he said, almost hurling the cell phone.

Newman, crouched behind a smaller gravestone nearby, keeping an eye on the elaborate "Crane" mausoleum, lowered the binoculars and his expression asked, *What?*

"Now Henry lost Marie Bineaux. What in the hell's wrong with him? I'm going to tear him a gaping new asshole. . . ."

The cell phone trilled and Gerard said, "What now?"

"I love you, too, Sam," Renfro said. "Look, a black Lincoln just pulled outa the Chinese Consulate garage."

"Chen in it?"

"Who knows with those tinted limo windows? Want me to follow it?"

"No, get your ass out to this cemetery. Let the NYPD keep tabs on Chen and the consulate."

"Roger that, Sam."

Gerard paced behind the monument, wearing a groove in the grass. Minutes turned into half an hour, with no fugitive in sight, nothing happening. It was as quiet as a graveyard. In fact, the only minor fuss was in keeping with that: groundskeepers making final preparations for a burial toward the other side of the cemetery.

"Sam," Cooper's voice crackled from the walkie-talkie, "we got some movement."

Gerard's pacing halted. "What?"

"Long line of cars with their lights on, heading inside. Think it's what they call a funeral procession."

"If I bust a gut laughing, promise you won't bury me here."

Pacing again, Gerard noted the stream of limousines and other cars moving in at their stately pace, their burning lights like sorrowful eyes in the overcast afternoon.

"Jesus! Sam—you won't believe this. . . ."

Cooper again.

"What, Coop?"

"The last car—I think it's one of those State Department guys, driving."

Gerard held his hand out, "Gimme," and Newman placed the binoculars there. The manhunter quickly scanned the procession of cars until the final one came into view. "Christ, Coop's right—it's Frank Barrows."

"Who?"

Gerard was smiling though he wasn't quite sure why. "Lamb's trusted right hand in the Diplomatic Security Service."

At a fork in the blacktop roads that wove through the cemetery, that final car, a dark-blue Buick, peeled off from the procession, taking an artery that headed it toward the Crane mausoleum.

"Biggs, Coop," Gerard spat into the walkie-talkie. "Drive your butts in here. I want you at the rear of that chapel near the mausoleum." He switched to cell phone. "Cosmo, where the fuck are you, touring the Statue of Liberty? I need you and Royce here five minutes ago."

Renfro's voice had to work its way over traffic noise and honking. "I'm caught on the goddamn Queensboro. But we are movin'."

"I know you don't have a siren, but put on your damn emergency lights. Move it!"

"Roger that."

The Buick drew up near the mausoleum and Barrows parked, getting out; the slender, pale, blandly handsome diplomat, crisply businesslike in dark gray, moved around the side and disappeared down the crypt steps. The binoculars and his high angle allowed Gerard to watch Barrows mimic the actions of the previous visitor, taking the key from its hiding place and unlocking the door and closing himself within the crypt.

"Newman, get inside that chapel," Gerard said. "Find yourself a view that shows there's no back door outa that mausoleum."

"I don't think there's much call for back doors in crypts, Boss," Newman said, but he was moving, staying low, bobbing and weaving amidst the gravestones.

With the binoculars, Gerard slowly scanned the area. The cars had drawn around the grave site and mourners, many in traditional black, were gathering for the graveside service, with folding chairs arrayed in a small open tent for family and close friends, its canvas flapping in the breeze. Gerard was just about to move his binoculars off the crowd when someone separated from it, a blur of black, black suit . . . black man.

Sheridan.

"Biggs, Coop, Newman," Gerard said into his walkie-talkie. "I have a visual on our fugitive. He was among the mourners. Suit, tie, mustache. He has broken off from them. Not running, he looks like somebody out here to visit Aunt Martha's tombstone. But he's moving toward the mausoleum."

The deputies were closing in, Coop behind the wheel with Biggs at her side in their green Ford, Newman poised within the dreary, pewless chapel, keeping an eye on the mausoleum.

Down within the crypt, where the only light came from small high windows with wrought-iron latticework that threw weirdly decorative lacy shadows, Frank Barrows was prying the already loosened cement panel off a vault that was empty but for a big black briefcase. He set the slablike cement panel down on the stone floor, grunting a little, coughing from the powdery dust his action had stirred up in the stale, musty air. Then he rose and withdrew the briefcase, smiling, turning, and looked into the glaring accusing eyes of Mark Sheridan.

The fugitive threw a right cross into the traitor's jaw that knocked Barrows off his feet, sending him tumbling to the stone floor, sprawled against the wall of vaults; but the disloyal diplomat did not let loose of his precious briefcase.

Sheridan was looming over him, emptying a manila envelope over Barrows, documents raining down upon the fallen turncoat—State Department internal documents, policy papers, wire reports, pages stamped "CLASSIFIED" and "EYES ONLY" and "TOP SECRET."

"Look familiar?" the fugitive asked.

Barrows was holding up his palms in a gesture of surrender and pleading. "Why should they? I swear to God, Sheridan—"

"This isn't a good place to take that name lightly." And from under his black coat, from his waistband, the fugitive withdrew the deadly, bulky .45 Colt automatic, and trained it upon Barrows.

"For Christ's sake, Sheridan," Barrows whimpered, raising quivering hands, "don't kill me. . . ."

"Everything you say sounds like a prayer, Barrows."

"What do you want?" The traitor was trembling, his eyes glistening with tears. "I'll do anything you want. . . ."

Sheridan sighed. "I don't think I'll kill you today, Barrows. After all, you're the guy who's going to make me righteous again. Open that briefcase and gather up those documents and stow 'em inside."

Barrows, nodding again and again, said, "All right, I will, I will," and he snapped open the briefcase.

Within were bricks of paper, sheets cut in the shape of currency, even banded to hold their shape; but blank, and white.

Barrows's eyebrows rose to his hairline. "Jesus. . . ." He emptied the briefcase onto the stone floor; nothing but blank bricks—no real money at all. "What the hell . . . Sheridan, what the hell is going on?"

"I'm as surprised as you are," the fugitive admitted, truthfully, not liking this. Had Chen been onto him? Was he again the butt of another of the Chinese agent's scams?

Barrows was picking up the blank bundles, examining them with eyes so wide with disbelief a breakdown might be close at hand; some of the blank "money" came loose from its paper bands and slipped through the traitor's fingers.

Sheridan gestured with the .45. "Put the documents in the briefcase—now."

Barrows, shaking, followed the fugitive's command, shoving the top secret documents into the now-otherwise-empty briefcase.

"On your feet," Sheridan said.

Barrows swallowed, and rose, his suit dirty and mussed, his dignity entirely gone, and the fugitive gestured with the .45 toward the doorway. Barrows stumbled forward, briefcase in hand, and Sheridan got behind him, pushing.

"Move it," the fugitive said.

They made their way up the ramp and into the rather cool, overcast afternoon, the morning's sun a distant memory.

Barrows glanced back. "Where . . . where are we going?"

"To the cops. You're going to help me get my life back, you son of a bitch."

Oddly, Barrows looked over his shoulder, nodding. "That may be the smartest thing to do."

Sheridan prodded him again with the nose of the .45 and then they walked around in front of the mausoleum, unaware that Deputy Marshal Newman, watching from the chapel, had heard that last revealing exchange. The fugitive looked toward the funeral in progress, across the cemetery; he raised an arm.

And from among the limos and cars parked near the graveside, a black Lincoln Town Car pulled out—the other car the fugitive had rented—and made its way, quickly but not speeding, down the blacktop artery leading to the Crane mausoleum.

From his watch point, through his binoculars, Gerard saw the car, and recognized the driver. He whispered into his walkie-talkie: "Marie Bineaux is driving that black Lincoln! Moving toward our subjects!"

Sheridan smiled at Marie, whose fearful expression over the wheel, framed in the windshield, did not surprise him—she had never been part of anything like this before—and as she was about to pull up, the fugitive nudged Barrows toward the approaching vehicle.

"Sheridan!"

The fugitive whirled; it was a voice he had heard only a few times, but it was chillingly familiar: that deputy marshal, Gerard, was moving slowly toward him, floating like a specter through the gravestones, a nine-millimeter in hand and pointed his way.

"We need to talk," Sheridan yelled.

"Drop the gun and we'll talk!" the blank-faced deputy marshal yelled. "Do it *now*!"

And the fugitive would have done that very thing, but before "now" could arrive, a rifle shot exploded the afternoon and Barrows's skull, in a blossoming burst of brain and bone and blood.

The fugitive dove for cover, behind a gravestone, and the manhunter hit the grass; Barrows, the husk of him anyway, flopped to the blacktop in the path of the black Town Car, behind the wheel of which a wide-eyed Marie Bineaux was screaming, panicking, hitting the gas pedal, accelerating, swerving around a fresh corpse that had as yet no grave, while mourners at the nearby funeral service scattered, yelping, shouting, shrieking, seeking cover.

The fugitive, dismayed to see Marie taking off without him, caught a glimpse of the shooter, on the roof of the mausoleum, using a parapet-like ledge to hide behind and steady his high-power rifle. No surprise who it was.

"It's Chen!" Gerard's voice carried to the fugitive as the manhunter informed his team in his walkie-talkie. "Chen's the shooter, from the roof of the mausoleum!"

Marie had slowed now, looking back for her lover but still moving, and the fugitive had no choice; sitting duck though he might be, he did what fugitives do: he ran from behind the gravestone, dodging rifle fire and the corpse of Barrows, dashing toward the Town Car.

Help came from unexpected quarters as Gerard aimed the gun not at the fugitive but at Chen, forcing the Chinese assassin to seek cover, which gave Sheridan the unencumbered moments he needed to catch up with the Town Car. Gerard kept firing up at Chen, moving as he did, edging toward his fleeing fugitive.

Other deputies, guns ready, were moving in—Newman exiting from the chapel and coming around to the crypt side of the mausoleum, Cooper at the wheel as she and Biggs in their green Ford left the blacktop and charged over a grassy slope, thankfully free of headstones.

The fugitive caught up with Marie, who braked for him, and Sheridan got in on her side, as she scooted over, and hit the gas, peeling away, streaking toward the entrance. Bullets from the mausoleum rooftop, courtesy of Chen, kissed the trunk of the Town Car, four times, leaving puckers in the metal; but no window shattered, no fuel tank exploded.

His target out of view, Chen turned his high-power rifle onto the green Ford coming down over the hill; bullets spiderwebbed the windshield but missed Biggs and Cooper. Biggs opened the door of the slow-moving vehicle and rolled out onto the grass, Glock in hand, firing toward the mausoleum roof.

Gerard was running after the Town Car, nine-millimeter in one hand, walkie-talkie in the other, shouting into it, "Newman! Get the Seville! Renfro, where the fuck are you?"

Renfro's voice crackled back: "Block away, maybe."

"Well, he's coming your way—Sheridan's driving a black Lincoln, heading for the gates . . . block the bastard in!"

"Roger, Boss!"

Behind the Town Car's wheel, the fugitive saw the gates approaching; but then he saw something else approaching, a big van, a Suburban, its emergency lights flashing, speeding like a son of a bitch, skidding to a halt—in front of the goddamn gates!

Marie screamed as Sheridan threw his body over her and the Town Car broadsided the Suburban in a body-jolting, gears-grinding, metal-tearing crash. The Town Car, an older model, had no air bags, but those within the Suburban deployed, trapping the deputies.

"You okay, baby?" Sheridan asked Marie, touching her shoulder.

Badly shaken but apparently not seriously hurt, she dazedly replied, "I . . . I think so. . . ."

"Come on, we gotta go," he said, and he pulled her bodily from his side of the wrecked car, snatching her backpack from the seat.

They could make it over the side wall—here, near the gates, the walls were higher, but a few yards away, the cobblestone barricade dropped to six feet. The car he'd rented, damn it, the Lexus, was way the hell on the other side of the cemetery, doing them no good at all, and sirens were screaming, meaning the cemetery would be surrounded by cops in seconds—but if they got over the wall, they could scurry into the maze of factories and warehouses nearby, and maybe have a chance.

He ran with her, almost dragging her, and she stumbled.

"Ow!" She was down on one knee, a hand massaging her left ankle. "It's twisted, Mark . . . go . . . go on without me!"

"No! Come on. . . ."

He put his arm around her waist and she limped along, and soon they had reached the far corner of the cemetery wall. The fugitive leapt up and caught the lip and pulled himself up there; he reached a hand down for her.

"You can do it, baby," he told her. He looked up from her and there Gerard was, cresting a hill, spotting them, running toward them in a full sprint, obviously hurting— the guy wasn't young and, after all, he'd recently taken two .45 shots in the Kevlar—but nothing seemed to stop that bastard.

And Sheridan was having trouble hoisting Marie up. "Marie, come on, baby!"

"I can't . . . Mark, I can't. Let me go!"

"No, we can *still* make it!"

"Sheridan!" Gerard had stopped running, planted himself, handgun in double-grip, in range. "Hold it right there."

"Mark," the dangling Marie whispered, "you've got to let me go!"

He didn't, but she did—she pulled from his grasp, falling away, rolling away, from the wall; now the fugitive was a clear target for Gerard, and as shots chipped away at the wall near his feet, Sheridan had no choice but to dive for the other side.

He hit hard, rolling down an incline, backpack in hand, scrambling across the street, weaving through skidding, honking traffic, finding himself at train tracks, stepping and dancing over them, until he reached a chain-link fence topped with barbed wire. Beyond beckoned the older buildings of a primarily industrial district. He scaled the fence, suit coat tearing on the barbed wire but his flesh escaping any scratch, and dropped to his feet, running down an embankment toward the mouth of the nearest street.

Back in the cemetery, Deputy Marshal Biggs had climbed up onto the roof of the mausoleum, behind the Asian sniper.

"Drop it or I drop you," Biggs said.

Suddenly docile, Chen set the scoped rifle down, turned and flashed the deputy an arrogant smile.

"May I remind you of my diplomatic immunity?" he asked with mock politeness.

"Once, you can," Biggs said. "The second time I'll shove this gun up your ass and shoot."

The fugitive, pulling off his tie as he ran, ripping off the spirit-gummed mustache and flinging it away, ducked into the first alleyway he came to, abandoned his suit coat, yanked off the white shirt to reveal a black T-shirt, and from the backpack withdrew a .45 and a lightweight jacket, a blue windbreaker with a well-filled money belt sewn in and his passports and other "bug out" items in the pockets.

Slipping into the jacket, .45 in his waistband, his appearance at least somewhat changed, Mark Sheridan gingerly stepped out onto the street, where he hoped to blend in with the various factory workers and deliverymen populating the area.

Still a fugitive.

Twenty-three

Gerard, wheezing with pain, clutching his ribs with his free hand, had nearly made it to the cobblestone wall just as Newman pulled up, in the commandeered Seville, drawing right alongside the wall, not far from where Marie Bineaux lay in a whimpering, weeping pile.

Newman hopped out just as Gerard clambered up on the back of the Cadillac, to climb up on the wall.

"Sam, Biggs bagged Chen!"

"Good—put bracelets on the young lady, Noah." Gerard was up on the wall now, standing atop it like a general surveying a battlefield. "I'm going after Sheridan."

"Can you see him, Sam?"

"No, damn it." Gerard talked into the walkie-talkie: "Renfro, Royce—are you all right?"

Royce's voice came back: "Shaken up, but breathing. I think Cosmo took the hit a little worse."

"Sheridan's gone over the wall," Gerard said. "I think he may've gone across the train tracks and over the fence.

Have Cosmo link up with Newman, and meet me on the other side of that fence.''

"Done."

Gerard lowered himself down the other side of the wall, somewhat gingerly, grunting in pain. Then he ran down the incline and, badge held high, jogged across the street as cars skidded to accommodate him. He had to take it slow over the train tracks.

"I see him!" Royce said from the walkie-talkie. "In pursuit!"

The fugitive was walking down a street, warehouses and factories all around; when the deputy's voice called out, "Halt!" Sheridan ran down an alley, and found himself facing a dead end. When he turned he saw, at the mouth of the alley, that diplomatic security agent, the one he'd taken hostage in the swamp. . . .

Sheridan threw a shot at him, high, but enough to make the agent duck away; the fugitive looked frantically around. A door right next to him was marked "LORELI RETIRE-MENT HOME—SERVICE ONLY''; he tried it—locked.

"Give it up, Sheridan!" the diplomatic agent called out.

The fugitive aimed his .45 at the door, at the handle and lock, and—standing at an angle—blasted away. Wood chips and metal fragments flew, cordite scorched the air. Now it was unlocked; he shouldered through.

In the cemetery, Cosmo Renfro—forehead bleeding, hairpiece askew, walking woozily, as if drunk—had found his way to Newman, the parked Seville, and the seated-on-the-grass, leaning-against-the-wall, dazed-looking Marie Bineaux.

"Where's the rest of me?" Renfro asked.

"You up to watching the lady?" Newman asked. "I wanna give the Big Dog some backup."

"What are you waitin' for?"

Renfro stood leaning against the wall near where Marie

Bineaux sat, as Newman climbed up on the Seville's tail and onto, and over, the wall.

Gerard had made it over the chain-link fence, not without snagging his jeans, however, and his ribs were burning and throbbing and occasionally throwing a sharp jabbing pain through him. He was moving, but not quickly. But he had seen Royce pursuing the fugitive, ducking into an alley down the street, up ahead, and he said into his walkie-talkie, "Johnny, I'm right behind you!", even if that wasn't quite true.

Royce was in the alley, easing the busted Loreli service door open, cautiously peering in, when an out-of-breath Gerard lumbered up.

"He's inside," Royce said.

Into his walkie-talkie, Gerard said, "We're in the back of the Loreli Retirement Home! Cover the front—call for police backup. I want this sucker *sealed*!"

Inside, the fugitive found himself in a lounge area of the Loreli Retirement Home, having stumbled through a supply room and a foul-smelling kitchen and now into this nest of forgotten souls. A TV blared a soap opera, young pretty actors performing for withered relics seated in furniture Goodwill would throw out. Even in his feverish frame of mind, Sheridan couldn't help thinking this was the sort of rest home you might expect to find in an industrial neighborhood—an ancient building in shocking disrepair, a paint-peeling open invitation to *60 Minutes,* draped in the scent of death and disinfectant. Sunken-cheeked, vacant-eyed octogenarians—forgotten by society, including their families—watched with varying degrees of shock or disinterest as the gun-wielding black intruder moved into the lobby.

The front desk was unattended, unless someone had seen him and his gun coming, and ducked down; a few more white-haired residents were seated here and there, in cushioned metal chairs possibly appropriated from the lobby of an abortionist who retired in 1937. The elderly bystanders viewed Sheridan with the same interest they might have given a nurse going by with a bedpan to empty.

Had Chen or Gerard shot him at that cemetery? Was he dead, and entering some Hieronymus Bosch–inspired circle of hell?

Then the front doors of the place, double glass doors, called out to him, and Sheridan raced toward them, the daylight filtering through promising freedom. He was almost to them when a figure bolted into view, and came to a running stop, the young deputy, the ponytailed one.

And the young deputy saw him, too, through those glass doors, and raised his revolver.

But Sheridan shot first, letting go with four rounds, patterning them around so that they would miss the deputy but shatter the glass, and send the boy ducking for cover, which they did, giving the fugitive time to find another escape route.

He turned, and the agent from the alley was racing at him, gun raised to fire; Sheridan cut to the right, where the lobby jogged around the front desk, and dashed to the doorway labeled "FIRE EXIT."

As Royce came flying into the lobby, Gerard on his heels, they almost ran into Newman, coming in through the broken doors, glass shards crunching beneath their shoes.

A nurse popped her head up and pointed to the "FIRE EXIT" door; Royce charged toward it, .45 in hand.

Gerard was sucking in air, fighting the pain.

"Sam," Newman began, "I heard Barrows and Sheridan talking—"

"Save it," Gerard said. "Stay here and guard the exit till the cops show!"

"Let me come with you!"

"No!" Gerard was trotting toward the "FIRE EXIT" door. "Stay here, son. . . . Do your job. . . ."

Royce was already a flight up as Gerard clambered after him; the sound of their footsteps, and the fugitive's, echoed hollowly in the stairwell, an awkward frenzied tap dance, and Gerard, *damn it*, he couldn't keep up, his chest, his ribs, killing him. . . .

Above Gerard, Royce had caught sight of the fugitive and fired off several rounds from his .45; but they did not find their targets, apparently, merely chewing and spitting out plaster and wood as echoing footsteps continued above, taunting them.

In the lobby, a distraught Newman, hearing muffled gunshots from the stairwell, fought the urge to break Gerard's order and join in; he paced and anxiously looked out through the shattered-glass doors at the street, waiting for the NYPD.

At the top floor, the eighth, the fugitive, exhausted, had reached the landing; he opened the door and almost fell into the hallway. He could hear that diplomatic agent reaching the landing behind him. He considered filling that doorway with a pattern of shots that would kill the son of a bitch . . . but just couldn't cross that line. . . .

On the landing, an apprehensive Royce was on the opposite side of that door, wondering the opposite side of that same question, as Gerard staggered up the stairs and joined him. Royce edged cautiously toward the door, eased it open a ways, gun poised. Gerard shoved it open, fanning his nine-millimeter at an empty hallway, or actually the juncture of two hallways, which they stepped out into.

Gerard turned off his walkie-talkie and Royce nodded, doing the same; now the only noise was the loud voices from TVs turned to varying channels, fighting each other, as if arguing. With a nod, Gerard indicated he'd take the hallway at the left, and Royce took the right.

Downstairs, the NYPD had arrived in full force, and Newman met them on the street, holding up his USMS badge.

"Seal and evacuate the building," he said. "You got a building filled with geezers, so it won't go fast and it won't go easy."

Then Newman rushed inside and headed to the stairwell, saying into his walkie-talkie, "Sam, NYPD's here—I'm coming up!"

But Gerard, on the eighth floor, didn't hear, his walkie-talkie switched off; checking rooms occupied by bedridden residents, their hollowed, haunted eyes looking through him, Gerard found no sign of his fugitive. A men's room was empty, though out the window he noted the NYPD deploying around the building. Good.

It didn't occur to Gerard that Noah Newman might be charging up the fire stairwell to provide backup; but he was.

Royce had been checking rooms, too, with an identical lack of success, and then he stepped into a room where an elderly gentleman sat by an open window, just a skeleton sheathed in skin wearing wispy white hair on his scalp and an oxygen mask on his face. Royce, too, had experienced the empty eyes of the invalids on this floor; but this old boy's eyes were alive. They bore in hard on Royce . . . and then they looked upward.

So did Royce, and a drop of blood hit his face.

And then the fugitive dropped down on the agent, from the space above the door where he'd wedged himself between open pipes and the paint-peeling ceiling. Sheridan took Royce down onto the hardwood floor and raised a fist in hopes of slamming the son of a bitch into unconsciousness.

But Royce was nearly as well versed in the killing arts as Sheridan, and judo-flipped him; both men scrambled to their feet, and neither had lost the .45s in their fists, mirror images of death. Sheridan couldn't bring himself to shoot the man and with a bellow of anger hurled himself at Royce, tackling the agent, neither of them losing their guns, but tumbling through, crashing and splintering through, a louvered doorway into the adjoining, empty bedroom.

Deputy Noah Newman had reached the landing. Pushing through onto the eighth floor, he noticed something neither Royce nor his mentor had picked up on: small, subtle drops of blood, a tiny sporadic red trail from a wound. Newman followed that trail to the corridor at right, and the sound of a struggle, of things being knocked over, told him his detective's instincts had been correct, as did the faces of the elderly residents craning their necks outside their rooms in alarm.

Newman followed the sound to the room where an aged shrunken gent in an oxygen mask was cowering in his chair. A tremulous, gnarled finger pointed toward where the sound was drawing the deputy, anyway. He moved through the busted-to-shit louvered doorway, gun in hand.

At first he didn't know what to think; then it came to him, and Newman said, "Drop it," but the other man reacted more quickly, and Deputy Noah Newman took two .45 shots to the chest, dropping in a shocked and bloody pile, revolver tumbling from his fingers.

Gerard, still working his corridor, had not heard the scuffle, but the gunshots alerted him, and he raced toward them, and when he came to the room where the old man in the oxygen mask was gesturing frantically, he rushed through the one room and into the next, almost stumbling over a fallen, bloody Noah Newman.

"Christ!" he said.

Across the room, a disheveled, panting Royce was at the window, wildly firing up, his .45 fragmenting the afternoon;

he was in the process of scrambling out onto the fire escape to pursue their fugitive.

"Help Newman!" Gerard demanded, and Royce looked back at the manhunter, who was ripping a sheet from the nearby bed. Royce came over, from the window, as Gerard used the sheet to hold against Newman's chest wounds; the young deputy was awake, eyes wide, not quite glazed, and he was gasping for breath.

Gerard got out his walkie-talkie, turned it back on, identified himself and said, "We're on the eighth floor of the Loreli Retirement Home, Room 814. Officer down! We need an ambulance, Deputy Newman has been shot."

Forty-five in hand, Royce dropped to his knees by the wide-eyed Newman.

"What the hell happened?" Gerard demanded.

Royce's brown eyes were like a pitiful puppy dog's. "Sheridan and I, we were struggling, both had guns. Newman ran in and the bastard . . . ," Royce choked on the words, his eyes filling with tears, ". . . shot him. Then he, I dunno, cuffed me with the gun and I was dazed, but I got a shot off as he climbed the window . . . only I fucking missed. . . ."

Newman was trying to talk.

"Don't," Gerard said. "It'll be okay, son. You'll be fine. I promise."

Newman struggled to speak, but he was choking, coughing blood.

"Did you copy?" Gerard snarled into the walkie-talkie. "Eighth floor, Loreli Retirement Home, officer down, ambulance needed ASAP!"

A young NYPD cop came rushing in, gun drawn, eyes wild.

"Get your EMS people up here *right now,*" Gerard demanded. He looked at Royce, indicating the bloody sheet bunched over Newman's wounds. "Hold down on this."

Royce nodded gravely and took over, as Gerard rose and strode to the window and crawled onto the fire escape, broken ribs be damned. Nine-millimeter in hand, he paused on the 'scape landing to use the walkie-talkie: "Sheridan's on the roof. I'm on him."

He put the walkie-talkie away and climbed the fire escape in a blinding rage that canceled out the pain.

A fugitive often faces unpleasant options. Mark Sheridan was on the graveled rooftop of a building cluttered with roofing construction equipment, a job half-finished or abandoned; like a rat in its maze, he wound through the stuff, and sought the rim of the building, peering down to find an escape route and instead seeing cops moving in and around the building, surrounding the place. Finally he worked his way to the farthest side, and peered over, to see if any option other than giving up remained open to him. . . .

"*Sheridan!*"

That voice again, but touched with something new: fury. Gerard's young deputy had been shot and the marshal would not allow that to go unavenged. A fugitive gets to know his hunter, even though they spend so very little time together; and Mark Sheridan knew his shit was in the fire.

But he didn't turn.

"Turn around," Gerard demanded. His footsteps echoed across the rooftop, as the manhunter wound his way through the construction equipment.

"You're going to have to shoot me, Marshal."

"Don't tempt me."

"I didn't shoot your boy."

"Step back from the edge and face me, you son of a bitch!"

The fugitive kept his back to the lawman. "Go ahead and shoot. It's one of my better options at this point."

"Step back and turn around. . . ."

"Can't do it, Marshal. Keep in mind, I didn't shoot your man. Also . . . I can't let you catch me."

And the fugitive dove from the rooftop.

Shocked, Gerard rushed forward, never expecting a suicide jump from this man, suddenly realizing Sheridan had grasped a cable attached to a roof hoist, a cable now going taut where the hoist was secured to the roof.

And at the edge of the building, Gerard looked out and down in amazement, so frozen by the audacity of it he didn't raise his gun at first, the fugitive swinging on the cable in a magnificent arc, a human pendulum, letting go and dropping onto the green roof of an elevated train station below.

Sheridan landed hard, but was up and scrambling on the tiled roof and Gerard raised the nine-millimeter to shoot as a rumbling filled the air and the fugitive, the luckiest unlucky bastard on the face of earth, sprinted down the rooftop and leapt onto another roof, that of a departing train.

Running the building rooftop, like a sweetheart alongside a beloved's train as it leaves the station, Gerard watched in defeat and disbelief as the train gained speed and roared away, its stowaway grabbing onto the aluminum roof, holding on for dear life as, once again, Mark Sheridan got away.

Twenty-four

At the end of the day, a manhunter is only a man, as human and susceptible to injury, physical and emotional, as any man he hunts. A single-minded hunter of men like Samuel Philip Gerard may present to the world, particularly to his team, his family of coworkers, a hard-bitten facade; but all facades eventually crack, and Sam Gerard, in the back of an EMS ambulance screaming its way to an emergency room, was not a hunter, but a man, and a tormented one.

Clutching the hand of Deputy Marshal Noah Newman, who was strapped into a gurney and hooked up to I.V.s as the faces of paramedics hovered like concerned angels, Gerard did not allow his helplessness, his hopelessness, to show. He smiled tightly down at Newman, whose eyes were pools of fear; the young deputy, despite the sucking chest wounds, was trying to talk.

"Shoosh," Gerard said gently, a father calming a child woken from a nightmare. "Talk later. Rest now."

The fear in Newman's eyes was tearing Gerard's guts out.

"Don't you worry, Noah," Gerard said. He squeezed the hand. "You're gonna be fine. You think I'm gonna let somethin' bad happen to one of my kids?"

The boy smiled up faintly at Gerard, but the smile froze into a grotesque mask of pain and Newman began to choke; a paramedic moved in as Gerard screamed at the driver to move the goddamn thing, his voice strangely shrill, a second siren.

When they arrived at NYU Med Center, the paramedics and the hospital's emergency staffers did their jobs, hustling the still body out of the ambulance and inside the ER, but Gerard did not join the race. As he stumbled from the rear of the ambulance, his clothing, his hands, streaked with his young deputy's blood, Gerard knew there was no need for hurry. The race was over. As the rocketing ambulance had emerged from the Queens-Midtown Tunnel, Deputy Noah Newman had looked up at him, with fear and pain and some terrible unspoken regret, and the hand Gerard had been holding had gone limp, and the fear had gone from the eyes, and so had everything else.

Gerard did not go inside. He walked away, and as soon as he found enough darkness to wrap himself within, he collapsed to his knees and wept like a child for the child he'd lost.

A fugitive is no less human than the men who hunt him; he bleeds, he cries, he hurts in all the ways a man can hurt, though he lives a life of heightened realities that at once deepen certain emotions, while numbing others. Physical pain must be borne up under; and emotional pain is a luxury that can be indulged only in rare quiet moments. A life on the run is at once wanton and controlled, a balancing act where the first fall is the last.

Mark Sheridan sat in a blue Toyota that he had stolen from a subway stop in Queens; around him was a landscape of industrial desolation not unlike the one he'd fled to from the cemetery. But this was New Jersey, and he was reluctantly embarking on a backup plan, actually a solitary variation on it that he would not have chosen had any other option been available.

He had stopped at a service station and cleaned himself up, washed himself up, as best he could; his face had gotten nicked, his clothes torn here and there, from his breakneck dive onto that train. He had hurt his ankle, much as Marie had running from the cemetery; he'd wrapped it in an Ace bandage—funny thing, his elbow hadn't been hurting him at all. Now he sat in the stolen car and studied not his face, but Marie's, on the forged passport photo that she would not now need.

He, too, wept; bitterly, hand covering his face. For the first time this fugitive felt true guilt; he had viewed himself as wronged, by his coworkers, by his government, an innocent man on the run, justified in doing things he would never normally do, but had to do, for survival's sake.

But now he truly was guilty. He had ruined the life of the woman he loved. He would flee, and they would punish her for it. Aiding and abetting. She could do a lot of time, harboring, helping, a murderer.

The public nature of the shooting at the cemetery meant major media coverage, which meant Uncle Sam would not be able to cover up the embarrassment of traitorous state department employees. With Mark Sheridan gone, Marie Bineaux would be a scapegoat.

He would have turned himself in, if that would have lessened Marie's woes; but he was convinced it would not. Besides, if Gerard didn't kill him, over that deputy, then a state department traitor would. He had about as much chance to live to trial as Lee Harvey Oswald had. His best shot at ever helping Marie, or himself, was to flee, perhaps to disappear again, for a time, and then emerge to go after

Chen, possibly in China, where the snake would no doubt be deported. Or perhaps that state department traitor, when time had lulled the evil motherfucker into complacency.

Someday, in some way he had not yet figured out, Sheridan would clear his name, and win freedom for Marie.

But until then, he must remain a fugitive.

He rubbed his face dry with the windbreaker sleeve, and checked his watch. From a pocket he withdrew a foil-wrapped tablet and swallowed it dry. He stuck the empty wrapper in a windbreaker pocket, and used a handkerchief to wipe the steering wheel clean of prints.

Then he slid out of the car—not noticing Fate, with its huge hand, removing the tiny foil wrapper from his pocket and depositing it onto the front seat—shut the car door, wiped its handle clean and hobbled into the night.

Twenty-five

The fugitive's instincts were correct about the media circus the murder of Frank Barrows would attract. Outside the U.S. Mission to the United Nations, a Hollywood premiere might have been unfolding, the night dancing with the lights, and bobbing with the Minicams, of news crews. CNN reporter Andrea Zinga was speaking into a microphone as Marshal Catherine Walsh pushed through.

"Many details are still unclear," the CNN reporter was saying, "but we can now confirm that State Department and Diplomatic Security Service Special Agent Frank Barrows was shot and killed today at Queens Hill Cemetery during a stakeout to capture fugitive Mark Sheridan . . ."

Inside the glass tombstone of the mission, within a conference room converted to a task force staging area, Bertram Lamb and other senior Diplomatic Security officials were gathered grimly around watching the CNN broadcast-in-progress on a TV that had been carted in. The screen was filled with images of the aftermath of the cemetery

211

shoot-out, including Barrows's corpse limp and bloody on the grass, just a tasteful glimpse.

"Sheridan is the prime suspect in two murders at the United Nations parking garage six months ago," the reporter said, her voice playing over Sheridan's military photograph. "Though unconfirmed by the Diplomatic Security Service, sources at the scene report that Barrows may be implicated with Sheridan in the selling of top secret documents to the Chinese government."

"Frank Barrows," Lamb was whispering, even paler than usual, shaking his head. "My God. He was my daughter's goddamn godfather, for God's sake."

The CNN reporter was saying, over Newman's USMS file photo, "Deputy United States Marshal Noah M. Newman was also shot and killed as Sheridan eluded police in a spectacular escape, the fugitive leaping onto the roof of a moving subway. Law enforcement officials emphasize that Sheridan is armed and dangerous."

The report concluded with a request for anyone with information to call either the NYPD or the State Department Task Force, and two 800 numbers were given as Lamb clicked off the TV with a remote.

Deputies Renfro, Biggs and Cooper were gathered around the conference table discussing tactics with NYPD personnel, some of whom were seated, though none of the deputies allowed themselves that luxury. They had, however, taken time to freshen up and change clothes; his luggage still M.I.A., Renfro, wearing one of Biggs's oversize shirts tucked into the jeans he'd worn on the plane, was decorated with the occasional bandage, his forehead bearing the largest one. The atmosphere in the room was bustling but somber, urgent yet professional.

Gerard stood along one wall, where the window side of two-way glass looked into a booth where Agent Royce and the Korean NYPD plainclothes cop, Kim, were questioning

Chen, who sat in his familiar black suit at the small table with his hands folded and his expression faintly, though arrogantly, smug.

Royce sighed and exited the room as Detective Kim continued questioning the assassin. A weary Royce almost stumbled up to Gerard; he alone had not changed his clothes, and his suit still showed the rumples and dried-to-black blood speckles of the struggle with Sheridan. Even Gerard had gone back to the International to shower and put on a fresh shirt, tie, jacket and jeans.

Royce's smirk had no humor in it. "Chen has only two words for us: 'Diplomatic immunity.'"

Gerard, studying Chen through the glass, said nothing.

"He's right, too," Royce said. "All we can do is deport the bastard."

Again, Gerard said nothing, moving along to the next two-way glassed booth and gazing in where a man sat, alone, free from the hassle of interrogation: the black courier from the financial district, the man in the green knit cap who had left a briefcase of money-cut blank paper in that Queens Hill Cemetery crypt. His clothing was the same as this afternoon, minus the cap, and he was sitting with one leg crossed, smoking a cigarette, as calm as a vacationer on a lakefront porch.

"Antonio Kimber," Royce said, tagging along. "One of our kites. Says he received instructions by phone to make the exchange. Phone records bear him out—he was paged from Barrows's office number this morning."

A third booth was where Marie Bineaux had been interrogated by an NYPD plainclothes policewoman and Deputy Holt. They were leading the young woman out, hands cuffed behind her; Holt shook her head at Gerard, indicating the questioning had gone nowhere.

"Won't talk without a lawyer present," Holt said.

But the Bineaux woman got suddenly talkative as she

recognized Royce from the unpleasant interview at her Bucktown apartment back home.

Straining as Holt held onto her, Marie Bineaux—strangely beautiful with her hair in disarray and no makeup and defiantly glittering eyes—almost snarled at Royce: "He didn't lie and he didn't cheat and he didn't use me! I let *him* go!"

The policewoman and Holt hauled her off, and Gerard wandered into the empty interrogation booth. Royce, unable to read the man's mood, backed away, returning to the futile Chen questioning.

Finally making her way into the task force staging room, Catherine Walsh, typically businesslike in her gray suit, had left her crisp confidence behind, replacing it with an understated but obvious distress. She sought out her deputies at the conference table.

"Where's Sam?" she asked Renfro.

Renfro nodded toward the interrogation booth where Gerard was standing, hands wedged in his jeans pockets, staring.

"Not doing well?" she asked.

For once Renfro didn't have a fast answer; but his glum expression said volumes.

Soon Catherine entered the cubicle, saying softly, "Sam?"

He kept his back to her, didn't acknowledge her presence.

She went to him, touched his arm, said, "Sam, I'm so very sorry."

Gerard turned to her. The sorrow in his blank face was immeasurable.

"Oh Sam," she said, squeezing his arm. "He was a fine young man. We're all going to miss him terribly."

Something around Gerard's eyes moved; but he said nothing. The eyes were red, she noted.

"Surely . . . oh Sam, surely you're not blaming yourself for this, in any way. . . ."

His silence said yes.

"This wasn't your fault. I know you loved that boy, but Sam, blaming yourself, it doesn't make any sense, it won't do any good."

A tiny smile flickered. "Thanks for trying, Catherine."

He walked past her, out of the booth; she followed but knew there was nothing more she could do or say. She was on her way to talk to Bertram Lamb, to help coordinate this nightmare, when Deputy Henry, in the company of Detective Stans, approached Gerard. She didn't hear the news Henry had brought.

"We found a ditched car," Henry told Gerard, the words tumbling out of the bright-eyed deputy's mouth, "a car that had been reported stolen from near the subway stop at Sixty-Fifth and Queens."

Gerard came alive. "Where was it found?"

The chunky plainclothes cop said, "Jersey side of the Holland Tunnel."

Gerard moved to a map of the city that had been pinned to the conference room wall. "Show me."

Stans pointed to the map, almost without looking.

"This was in the front seat," Henry said, holding up a glassine evidence bag within which was a plastic bubble wrapper with foil backing—a pill casing, obviously torn from a perforated sheet of medication, probably an over-the-counter variety.

Gerard took the evidence bag from Henry. "Anything link this to our fugitive?"

"Oh, yeah," Henry said, grinning. "Somebody finally got sloppy, besides me—we got half a latent, you believe it? Sheridan's right index."

Gerard granted the deputy a faint smile of absolution for his recent fuckups. "Well done, Henry."

Henry let out a breath, basking for a moment in the redemptive glow, as Gerard studied the evidence within the bag; on the back of the foil was a tiny red identification dot.

Gerard turned to the chunky NYPD detective. "Where's the nearest drugstore?"

Stans said, "I'll drive you."

Within minutes, Gerard was inside Kaufman Pharmacy on Lexington Avenue, thrusting the evidence packet under the nose of a young male pharmacist with wire-frame glasses and thinning brown hair.

"Can you identify this?" Gerard said, indicating the red dot on the back of the foil.

"It could be one of any number of nonprescription remedies. . . ."

"Okay."

And Gerard moved to the shelves, searching for flat, bubble-wrapped medications, and began ripping open packets as he found them.

"Hey, hey!" the pharmacist called, coming from behind his station. "What the hell . . . ?"

Gerard lifted his USMS badge in its leather case, returned it to his pocket and kept looking; it took almost three minutes but then he found one containing a foil sheet with the signature red dots on each square.

He read the box: "Tetralezine. For motion sickness. Take first dose one hour before departure."

Snatching his cell phone from his pocket, Gerard dialed Renfro, who said, "Where the hell did you run off to?"

"Put Detective Kim on the line."

Renfro did, and Gerard told the Korean detective, "He's taking a boat out, fucking immediately. What docks are closest to where that car was left?"

"Bayonne, but no passenger boats sail out of there.

That's strictly a cargo terminal, freighters and container ships."

"Don't some of those freighters have passenger berths?"

"I can sure find out fast enough."

Hopping in the unmarked car waiting at the curb, Gerard instructed Stans to hit the siren and in less than four minutes, the manhunter was striding into the conference-room-cum-task-force-staging-area.

Renfro fell in step with Gerard, telling him, "Lester Shipping has a freighter, the *Atlas Avianca,* loading grain at Bayonne. Leaves tonight with three passengers. Didn't have any names for us, said immigration didn't require it; it's a Canada run."

Gerard was in the middle of the room, near the conference table; the NYPD personnel, the diplomatic agents and in particular his deputies were gathered around, looking up with expectant expressions. Now was the time for the big pep talk.

"I don't have any speech to make," he said irritably. "Just stay here and do your jobs. We've got a lead and I'm running it down. Get back to work."

And paying no attention to the stunned expressions he was leaving in his wake, Gerard walked away, moving toward Royce, as Renfro again fell in step with him.

"You want me to get Bayonne PD in position over at the docks, Boss?"

"No."

"Whadaya mean, no?"

"Which part of it don't you understand? Sheridan spots any cops, he might wriggle away. He's done it before . . . Royce!"

The rumpled agent brightened. "Yes?"

"Can you get me a helicopter, five minutes ago, at the Fifty-ninth Street pad?"

Royce nodded, moving away as he dialed his cell phone.

Renfro and Gerard were alone at one side of the big room.

"Sam . . ." Renfro swallowed, as if needing to taste his words before risking speaking them. "You don't really mean you're going over there . . ."

"Alone."

Gerard began to move away, and Renfro grabbed his arm.

"At least let me go with you, Sam."

"No."

"I know how you feel about Sheridan . . . I know what you want to do."

"Do you?"

Renfro's upper lip pulled back over his teeth in something that wasn't quite a smile. "You want to kill his ass, right? You think I don't? But something's wrong here, Sam, don't let your grief blind you. Fucking Sheridan didn't kill Barrows, you know. . . ."

The fugitive's words—*I didn't shoot your boy*—ran involuntarily through Gerard's mind.

Renfro was shaking his head. "Hey, I feel the same as you, we all do, but it ain't worth it, Boss."

Gerard pulled his arm away and began to walk toward the conference room exit; Royce, across the room, was nodding that the helicopter was set.

"Goddamn it, Sam," Renfro said, and stepped in Gerard's path, blocking him. "Listen to me. Hell, man, you're as close to a best friend as I ever had . . . I don't have enough friends to lose another. One's enough in one goddamn day. Please. Don't do this."

"We're not friends, Cosmo," Gerard said, and he gave Renfro as cold a look as he could summon. "None of this is personal. We just work together."

Renfro didn't quite know what to make of that. Then he shrugged. "Fine. Okay. Go fuck yourself and your career and everything it ever stood for. Shit on every goddamn fuckin' thing—rules, regs, code. Only don't kid yourself into thinking this is about settling a score. This isn't about Noah Newman—it's about Sam Gerard, who never loses, who never gets beat, who always gets his man, even if the poor bastard is innocent, like Richard fucking Kimble. 'Cause this is about you, Sam, isn't it? It's always about you."

"Finished?"

"Yeah. I guess I had my say."

"Good. Now get the hell out of my way."

Renfro reeled as if he'd been slapped, and perhaps he had; then he stepped out of Gerard's path as the manhunter stepped into the hallway.

Gerard was barely out of the conference room when Catherine Walsh called out to him.

"Sam!"

He didn't stop, footsteps echoing on marble.

"You're *not* going without backup. That's a direct order."

He kept moving. Footsteps resonating.

Now she was calling out, dignity be damned, her voice echoing over his footsteps. "You've sacrificed everything for your career—including *us*. . . . Are you going to throw that away, too?"

Now he stopped. He turned.

"I'm just checking out a lead," he said. "No backup. No police. You owe me that much, Catherine."

An empty expanse of hallway stretched between them.

"We're both making a mistake," she said, barely loud enough for him to hear.

But he heard, and she slipped back inside the conference room, and he went to catch his copter.

And his fugitive.

Twenty-six

With the Queensboro Bridge looming behind them, an unpleasant reminder of the afternoon's tragic events, a government sedan pulled in at the 59th Street heliport, stopping near a waiting helicopter, its blades already churning the night air.

Gerard stepped from the sedan, coat and tie flapping in the copter wind, and he noted another government sedan parked nearby. Someone had beaten him here—another attempt to talk him back into his senses? .

Fat fucking lot of good it would do them.

He strode to the helicopter and someone within opened the door for him; not the pilot.

"Get in," Royce yelled, working his voice above the whirring blades. "Let's go!"

Gerard yelled back at him; he would have yelled chopper noise or not. "What the hell are you doing here? How'd you get here before me?"

"You were wasting time talking to Cosmo and Catherine. Time's flying; so should we."

"Get your ass out of there!"

"No. I'm coming with you."

"Like hell!"

"You lost one friend, one colleague . . . I lost two. Consider yourself trumped. . . ." The eyes in the young face seemed old, suddenly, and cold. "Look—I know what you want to do, and I won't stop you."

That caught Gerard by surprise.

"There's no time to argue!" Royce yelled. "Get in!"

Gerard did, and soon the copter was ascending with the cantilevered steelwork span of the bridge receding behind them as they rose over the narrow island of Manhattan, its skyline glimmering below like out-of-place stars. The copter skimmed the sky and followed the Hudson to the docks of Bayonne, New Jersey, gliding over a shipping canal in a bleakly industrial landscape where plants plumed smoke, tanks sprouted like steel mushrooms, and aircraft-hangar-like sheds stretched to the shoreline.

Only one berth on the dock seemed busy, at the moment, ablaze with floodlights as brown beads that were soybeans traveled on conveyer belts from a nearby storage bin, feeding a chute that poured the beans into the yawning binlike container holds of a long, rather narrow ship, its wedding cake of smokestack-bridge-cabins piled fore, with the lower cargo bins endlessly stretching aft.

"Bet that's our boat," Gerard said. He told the government pilot to find a place on the dock to set down, but not too near the ship; he didn't want to announce their arrival to a possible passenger.

Soon Gerard and Royce were climbing the steep gangway up into the *Atlas Avianca;* the night was cool and breezy and their clothing fluttered. A thirtyish, in-need-of-a-shave officer in whites—maybe that was off-whites—met them as they stepped on deck. He introduced himself as First Officer Bunn and, as they flashed their badges and credentials, he let them know a supervisor from Lester Shipping had called ahead.

"You want cabin number three," the First Officer said. "It was booked for a man and wife, but only one of 'em showed. Black guy."

Gerard showed him a photo of Sheridan. "This black guy?"

"That's him. Gonna be trouble?"

"Where is he?" Royce asked.

"A-deck. I'll point you."

The *Atlas Avianca* was a timeworn whitewashed metal ship; by no means the Love Boat. As they descended a companionway to A-deck, hatchway doors were on only one side of a narrow hall and Gerard led the way, as they looked in vain for numbers on the hatchways and found nothing.

"Cabin three," Royce whispered. "Must be the third door."

"Counting from which end?" Gerard asked.

At that moment the hatchway between them swung open, separating Gerard and Royce, a sudden steel barrier thrown up between them.

And Royce found himself face-to-face with the fugitive.

Sheridan, in fresh clothes, a clean blue T-shirt and jeans, bandages here and there, notably on his forehead, had just been stepping out to get some air, and to keep a watch on the docks, to see if anyone was coming looking for him.

On the other side of the steel barrier, Gerard had yanked his nine-millimeter from its holster, but he was trapped in the shallow hall, helpless, listening to the sounds of a violent scuffle on the other side of that hatchway. He shoved his shoulder into it, but the two men struggling on the other side kept it wedged in place.

The young agent went clawing under his coat for his gun, but Sheridan headbutted him, hard, right in the face, and as the agent reeled back, dazed, the fugitive hammered double fists into the side of the man's neck, which dropped him to the floor.

Sheridan ran down the corridor, and Gerard's weight finally slammed the hatchway door shut, and he knelt over the fallen Royce, face bloody, nose streaming red.

"Get him," Royce moaned, barely conscious.

Gerard looked up and the fugitive was dashing up the companionway they'd just come down. He barreled after his man, leaving Royce to fend for himself.

When the manhunter flung open the hatchway onto the narrow, low-railinged observation deck, bursting into the cool night air, he looked to right and left, no Sheridan. He was about to look above him, where indeed Sheridan had gone, having scurried up a metal ladder to the deck above, when the fugitive leapt down on him, from behind.

But Gerard was able to spin out of the fugitive's desperate diving grasp, and turned on him; Sheridan was barely on his feet after the jump, trying to catch his balance, and like a football lineman Gerard held up his arm in a horizontal bar and slammed right into the bastard, plowed into him hard, knocking the man back into the low railing, the momentum carrying Sheridan over, carrying both of them tumbling over, for a three-story drop into an open cargo container.

Mountains of soybeans broke their fall, puffs of dust rising from the dried brown pellets, as Gerard landed in a belly flop, the impact sending the nine-millimeter flying from his fingers. The fugitive had landed on his back, saw the gun go sailing, and backstroked through the beans after the weapon, but the soybeans sucked it down, like quicksand.

The world shifting under him crazily, his ribs aching, burning, but pain and rage spurring him on, Gerard swam toward the fugitive, pawing at him, finally leaping onto him, pummeling him, the fugitive lashing back return blows, even as the sea of beans tried to swallow both of them. The vicious blows of both men soon had them bleeding, from the eyes, from the mouth, and the dustlike particles clung to that red wetness, and stung like hell, both men coughing, squinting in the dust storm, as they wrestled and punched and attempted to kill each other even while they fought the soybean undertow.

More beans were cascading down upon them, raining on them, hard brown rain, as the chute from the conveyer belt continued its work. Finally a deckhand heard the scuffling and seconds later a klaxon began to screech, and the crew stopped work, the downpour of soybeans ceased, as crewmen lined the edge of the hold to witness the bizarre struggle below.

They fought and clawed and battled each other and the unstable "ground" beneath them, scaling a slope of beans as they brawled. Then Sheridan was on his back, at the peak of the slope, on a mound of beans that had some mass, and he used this new stability to jam a knee into Gerard's ribs, knowing that was where it would do the most good. Gerard sucked in dusty air, gasping in blinding pain, thrown onto his back by the pain, the brown beads oozing up around him.

Sheridan leapt at Gerard, but was thrown off, not by Gerard, but by a gunshot from above; the report of a weapon echoed and rang through the metallic compartment as the fugitive, wounded, tumbled down the soybean slope.

Gerard looked up and saw Royce, his face streaked with blood, wearing that familiar smirk, aiming down with a nine-millimeter. The agent fired another round at the fugitive, who was clutching his bleeding shoulder, trying to get to his feet, which couldn't find purchase in the capricious beans.

The shot missed and clanged into a metal wall and ricocheted and zinged while both Gerard and Sheridan ducked and prayed.

When it was safe, Gerard yelled up, ''Royce!'' and frowned at the agent.

Royce's smirk disappeared and he lowered his weapon.

The manhunter staggered to his feet and somehow made his way around the soybean dune, where the fugitive was getting up, and Gerard knocked him down with a hard right hand. The hill of beans separated them from the view of any spectators; the manhunter looked down at the helpless fugitive, thought about everything he wanted to do to the son of a bitch who killed Noah, felt everything that he had stored up within him gathering for release. . . .

But all he had to do, to get even with Sheridan, was stand by and watch; because the fugitive, wounded, battered, was coughing and choking and sinking into the instability, beans circling up around him in a brown whirlpool.

Sheridan looked at Gerard, and even as the beans sucked Sheridan down, the fugitive did not plead for help from the man who had hunted him; he just gazed at him hard, and Gerard heard the words again, without them having to be spoken: *I didn't shoot your boy.*

Sighing, Gerard reached out.

Sheridan grasped the offered hand.

An avalanche of hard brown beans pounded down on them, Gerard able to stumble back, protecting his face, but the fugitive—already sucked under to his waist—was swallowed by the soybean shitstorm.

Then Gerard was getting pulled under, and pounded, and shielding his face, Gerard looked up and could see Royce gloating down, triumph touching the patented smirk as he stood next to the crewman at the controls who, at Royce's direction, had unleashed the grain chute.

Then Royce's eyes caught Gerard's; the manhunter didn't say a word—he just glared up at the younger man, who withered under Gerard's searching stare and tugged the sleeve of the crewman, who then stopped the flow of soybeans.

Gerard swam through beans to where only flailing arms and Sheridan's pain-clenched face could still be seen; then the face went under and only hands grasping for air remained. He was near the drowning man when he looked up again and saw Royce's glowing expression, enjoying Sheridan's demise even as distant sirens drew ever nearer. A gleam from the floodlights reflected off Royce's shiny nine-millimeter, tight in his hand.

Heartless motherfucker, Gerard thought, and grabbed both black hands extending from the sea of beans and yanked Sheridan up, till his face emerged, spitting and gasping and coughing.

As Gerard continued digging him out, Sheridan managed to ask, "Why . . . why didn't you let me die?"

"They pay me to bring you in," he said. "That's what I'm going to do."

"You know," Sheridan panted, his face smudged with soybean dust, "I think this time . . . I'll let you."

The men traded the faintest smiles; something oddly like respect passed between them.

Royce was climbing down a metal ladder; Bayonne police were gathering above.

"Cuff our prisoner, Agent Royce," Gerard said.

"My pleasure," Royce said, walking awkwardly through the shifting beans. Then he sneered at Sheridan. "You're lucky to be alive."

Sheridan said, breathing hard, "Bet you didn't think my chances . . . were worth a hill of beans."

Royce said nothing, holstering his shining nine-millimeter and getting out the cuffs.

Gerard yelled up, "We're going to need an ambulance. We have a wounded man!"

His voice echoed within the metal chamber.

Gerard turned to look at Sheridan, who had passed out, leaving questions unanswered, the manhunter's feet still shifting uncomfortably beneath him.

Twenty-seven

The night finally kept the overcast afternoon's promise of rain; as relentless as Sam Gerard himself, it pounded the squat, forties-vintage faded-redbrick buildings comprising Hudson County General Hospital, and streaked the windows of a private room where a fugitive lay, hooked up to life support and dangling pouches, eyes closed, the running stopped.

As expected, the circus of the media had descended upon the hospital, and NYPD and State Department and USMS personnel, Gerard's warrants squad included, had for a time crowded the small facility; but with a weakened, wounded Sheridan in custody, there was little to see or do. In a matter of hours, everyone had cleared out, except a few Bayonne cops and one representative of the Justice Department—Deputy Marshal Samuel Gerard—and one from the State Department—Diplomatic Security Service Special Agent John Royce.

At one end of a long, dimly lighted corridor, a coveralled, not terribly industrious janitor mopped the floor and then scooted his bucket away in a grating fingernails-on-blackboard manner. And at the other end, in a small waiting area near the doorway to Sheridan's room, where a single bored cop stood watch, sat Gerard and Royce, plopped in orange-Naugahyde-covered chairs on either side of a small blond end table scattered with issues of *People* magazine. To their backs were windows dark with night and rattling with rain and thunder.

Both men wore their same rumpled clothing from the struggles of the afternoon and evening, having pounded the soybean dust from themselves as much as possible, though an unlikely field-hand scent lingered on the lawmen. Despite the endless day they'd put in, Royce had been adamant about standing guard on this "slippery son of a bitch," insisting he had too much invested in the fugitive to let him out of his sight. Gerard had allowed that, but—after a confab with Catherine and his warrants squad—took the night watch with Royce himself.

Tired as they were, neither man was sleepy, and Royce was using the time to catalogue, and tag, the smattering of belongings from the fugitive's cabin on the *Atlas Avianca*. It wasn't much of a job—some clothing, fake passports, several handguns, bricks of hundred-dollar bills from the lining of a windbreaker, which had already been tagged.

A doctor, a round-faced thirtyish Asian, stepped from Sheridan's room.

"Is he conscious yet?" Royce asked.

"No," the doctor said quietly, and adjusted his wire-frame glasses, as he walked closer to the two men. "Maybe by morning. He lost a lot of blood; we've given him two transfusions already."

"Don't make a big effort on our account," Royce said, and returned to his work, writing items down on a sheet on a clipboard, transferring them to an evidence carton at his feet.

The doctor was eyeing Gerard. "Frankly, Deputy . . . you look exhausted."

"I got treatment when I got here," Gerard said.

"But you didn't get sleep. I'm going to prescribe some, right now—catch an hour or two. You'll find an open bed in ward seven."

Gerard yawned and stretched, which only made his ribs ache worse. "Hell, maybe you're right. Thanks, Doc."

The doctor smiled a little, nodded, went off down the hall, skirting the janitor, who hadn't made much progress in the last five minutes.

"Hope the doc isn't a friend of Chen's," Gerard said.

Royce smirked. "Not every Asian is the yellow peril, Sam."

"You don't mind if I'm paranoid?"

"Be my guest."

Gerard got up, stepped into the fugitive's room and came quickly back. "Naw, he's all right. Breathing, anyway."

"You almost sound disappointed." Royce was tagging a heavy .45 Colt, checking the chamber for a bullet; he removed the clip and tagged the weapon, saying, "Must be the gun that shot Noah."

"Let me see." Gerard took the gun, examined it briefly, noted the filed-off place on the barrel where the serial number had been, handed it back. "So you finally took my advice."

"How's that?"

"That was a nine-millimeter Glock you were taking potshots with, back on the boat."

"Just like yours." He smirked again. "You're my role model, after all."

"Mind if I have a look at it?"

"Sure," Royce said, and withdrew the shiny automatic from his shoulder holster and handed it butt-first to the deputy marshal.

Gerard took it, ejecting the ammo clip, which he rested on the seat beside him, slipping it under his leg so the clip wouldn't fall to the tile floor. Then he checked the slide, ejected the bullet in the chamber, and looked the weapon over.

"Nice piece," Gerard said. "Even after it's been fired a couple times, still's got that 'new car' smell. This didn't come from Coop; isn't part of our armament stockpile."

"No, it's mine. Picked it up in Chicago, just hadn't made the switch yet. You know how it is . . . you get used to a weapon."

Yawning, Gerard replaced the clip in the Glock and stood up, leaning in to slip the gun back into Royce's underarm holster, as the young agent said, "You know that doc was right—you really do look like you could use some rest. . . . You're not as young as me, you know."

"Don't get too cocky. . . . I'm fine. Could use a cup of coffee, though." Gerard stretched and rose, saying, "Be right back," and drifted down the hall, nodding to the bored-looking uniformed cop outside the fugitive's door.

Then Gerard paused to glance back. "You want a cup?"

"Sure—black, two sugars."

Gerard walked on, then paused again. "Coffee shop's closed at this hour . . ."

"Some detective," Royce said with the familiar smirk. "Try the first floor nurses' station."

Gerard smiled wearily, soon disappearing down the stairwell at the corridor's end.

Now Royce was alone in the gloomy hallway with only the cop at the fugitive's door for company. He slipped off his suitcoat, rose, yawned, walked over and held out the evidence-bagged .45 to the cop.

"Mind securing this for me?"

The cop threw a hitchhiker's thumb at the hospital room door. "What about him?"

"He's not goin' anywhere. I got him."

When he had the hallway to himself, Royce pushed the unguarded door open, slipping a small handkerchief-wrapped object from his pocket, stepping silently into the darkened room. The only light was from the moon, its beams diluted by the storm.

Lightning strobed the room white and revealed the unconscious fugitive in bed, ribboned with unhooked wires and tubes, tied off with soft restraints, gentle blue plastic ropes for a dangerous patient made docile by injury.

In Royce's hand, the handkerchief keeping it free of fingerprints, was a small disposable scalpel he'd lifted, earlier. Taking no chances, he clamped his hand down over the slumbering fugitive's mouth, and began slicing through the restraints.

"What a colossal pain in the ass you've been, Sheridan," the agent said. "But at least you're finally cooperating . . . 'shot trying to escape,' that'll be helpful."

Carefully, now that the fugitive's arm restraints were snipped, Royce backed away from Sheridan and withdrew the Glock, keeping him covered—wouldn't do for the wound, the powder burns, to be too closely placed—as the fugitive, sitting up in bed, glared at him, the whites of accusing eyes wide in the black face.

Royce tossed the scalpel in Sheridan's lap, the handkerchief staying behind in the agent's palm. "Cut yourself the rest of the way free. Go on."

"I thought maybe you were just another flunky," Sheridan said, complying, sawing his ropes. "But you're *the* one, aren't you? The motherfucker behind it all."

Lightning strobed the room again, highlighting Royce's expression of crazed arrogance.

"You're the flunky, Mark. Couldn't have done it without you, though—a delivery boy to take the fall, if the shit hit the fan."

Sheridan cut at the soft ropes across his midsection. "You're covered in it, you son of a bitch."

Royce shook his head, his expression amused and evil. "I don't think so. With you dead, things are looking suddenly . . . tidy."

"You set up the plane . . . You called Chen to hit me at the cemetery."

"Yes, but you know what they say about when you want something done right . . ."

And Royce's arm raised into position as he aimed the gun. "Now drop the scalpel, and get out of bed."

"You're a fucking traitor."

"Matter of perspective, Mark. I'm an American through and through. The purest capitalist you ever met. I'm what you've been fighting to preserve, all along."

Sheridan, doing his captor's bidding, cutting through the restraints, suddenly lurched at Royce, who stepped back and laughed softly as the well-oiled killing machine that was Mark Sheridan fell to the hospital-room floor in a spasm of pain, dangling by an uncut rope clutching his right ankle.

Royce leveled the Glock, waiting for the fugitive to raise his head to get a clean shot at him, when some fool turned on the lights.

Gerard.

"What are you up to, Johnny?" the manhunter said easily.

Like a sophisticated computer morphing technique, Royce transformed himself, stunned traitor suddenly a composed law enforcement officer.

"Thank God you're here, Sam," Royce said, glibly. "Son of a bitch was trying to escape. But I stopped him, and he admitted it, he admitted killing Newman."

"Why?" Gerard asked innocently. "Was there any question?"

233

"No, I just . . ."

"Well, better shoot him, then, 'fore that cop gets back and screws up our story. . . . Since you're settling a score, maybe you want to kill the bastard with your old weapon."

And Gerard held up the evidence-bagged .45 with the filed-off serial numbers on the barrel.

"That's not my gun," Royce said, shaking his head. "That's *Sheridan's* gun."

The fugitive, that one last restraint tying his leg to the bed, began to carve away at that soft rope; but he was weak, reduced to the sidelines, a spectator in this confrontation.

"I don't think so," Gerard said. "I think you just filed off the serial number and planted it with Sheridan's shit in his cabin. You see, I think this is the same gun Sheridan took off you in the swamp and used to put two bullets in my chest, or anyway my Kevlar. Then you retrieved that gun, Johnny, remember?" With his free hand, Gerard touched his ribs and smiled half a smile. "Believe me, I remember."

Gerard reached a hand in his sportjacket pocket and came back with two small objects, which he jiggled in his closed hand, like dice. Then he opened his palm and the two disfigured slugs were there, his souvenirs from the swamp.

"We won't need any of your state-of-the-art high-tech gear to match these up to the bullets that killed Newman, will we, Royce?"

"Sam, listen to me, what happened to Noah, that was a tragedy, but it's got you off balance . . . you're not thinking straight, you're disturbed."

"Naw," he said. "Just stupid. Letting myself get suckered by a punk like you."

The mask dropped; Royce's face shifted like wax and then congealed into the blank amorality below the boyish surface.

"Just tell me one thing, Royce," Gerard said, and his

tone was not unkind. "You worked with us. How could you do it? Why did you do it?"

"Shoot Noah? No choice. He came fumble-assin' into that room when I was about to put two rounds in Sheridan's head."

"And Noah got those rounds, instead," Gerard said quietly, "and Sheridan got away."

"No malice in it," Royce said. "Just like I don't take any pleasure in this, Sam . . ."

And Royce fired the Glock point blank at Gerard.

Or anyway pulled the trigger; because the Glock only clicked, hammer falling on an empty chamber. His face contorting, Royce fired again and again, and the weapon clicked like a cigarette lighter out of fluid.

Gerard was holding out a nine millimeter ammo clip. "Looking for this, Johnny?"

Royce frowned. "What the hell . . . ?"

"I must've accidentally switched clips on you. That one, in your Glock? Must be my empty one."

"Well," Royce said, smirk curdling. He heaved a sigh, as if his entire body was surrendering. "You gonna shoot me, or slap the cuffs on me?"

"I'm thinking that over."

Royce stretched, put his hands on his hips, scratching his side, saying, "Well, either way, Deputy . . . I'd say this is about over."

The dangling fugitive saw it before Gerard, saw Royce's hand slip behind him and a .38, tucked in a holster at the small of his back, was getting yanked out to bring around . . .

"Gun!" Sheridan yelled, lunging awkwardly for Royce, jabbing Royce's gun arm with the tiny scalpel, just as the traitor fired, punching a .38 slug into the wall over the head of Gerard, who was diving for cover.

Scalpel sticking out of his arm, Royce winced with pain

and rage and screamed, "God damn," as he turned the weapon on the fugitive, about to drop the hammer, interrupted by a shot from another weapon, the report resounding in the small room like another thunderclap.

Deputy Marshall Sam Gerard lowered the gun he'd just fired—John Royce's .45.

And Mark Sheridan, having scooped up Royce's .38, watched as Royce tumbled and stumbled against the side wall; he'd been hit between the shoulder and the neck, some major artery getting in the way of the big bullet's path, apparently, because a geyser of blood was arcing out to paint the floor red. Royce pressed a hand to his shoulder and throat, and the blood sprayed and oozed through his fingers, shooting crimson streamers, running in scarlet trails.

Then the wounded agent's legs went out from under him and he slid down the wall and slumped to the floor, in a pool of his own gathering blood. Lightning flashed through the room, thunder shaking the nearby window where rain trailed down the glass like tears. Still clutching his wound, Royce looked up at Gerard and that familiar half-smile formed.

"See? You . . . you are my role model. I finally did get that . . . back-up piece."

Gerard trudged silently over, standing in Royce's blood. "Don't you think it's about time you wiped that smirk off your face, son?"

Royce's eyes widened, his mouth dropped open and his hand went limp over the still gushing wound, which no longer made any difference. John Royce was as dead as his venal dreams.

A fugitive often faces unpleasant options. Right now Mark Sheridan, who had a .38 in his hand, was facing Sam Gerard, who had a .45 in his hand.

"Like the man said—what happens now?" the fugitive asked.

The sounds of quickly approaching footsteps down the long corridor could clearly be heard.

"Your call, Mark," Gerard said casually, stepping away from the corpse. "Mind if I call you 'Mark'? Can't keep up with your goddamn last names."

"I cooperated."

"You cooperated, and I believe you're innocent."

"But you'd still come after me, wouldn't you?"

"It's what they pay me for."

"You know something, Gerard?" The .38 was still in Sheridan's hand. "I think you'd come after me even if you were dead."

"Maybe not. I'd be off salary. You don't really want to start running again, do you?"

"What I really want to do," Sheridan said, "is get some rest."

The two men just looked at each other; then they both laughed a little, and the fugitive handed the .38 over to the manhunter, and stumbled past the corpse to collapse in bed, as the echoing footsteps grew louder and faces filled the doorway.

Twenty-eight

A fugitive exonerated, an innocent man accused of a crime, knows well that "THE TRUE ADMINISTRATION OF JUSTICE IS THE FIRMEST PILLAR OF GOOD GOVERNMENT," a sentiment carved in stone near the Corinthian colonnades of adjoining courthouses in New York City's Foley Square.

Mark Sheridan, in a dark-blue suit with a red-and-white-striped tie, stepped into sunshine from a van that had drawn up in front of the gold-leaf-crowned thirty-two-story U.S. Courthouse. A phalanx of New York USMS deputies moved him up the steps through clamorous media as, off to one side, CNN's newest correspondent, Stacia Vela, faced a Minicam.

"The Justice Department confirmed today that they have granted full immunity to Mark Sheridan," Stacia said into her microphone, "in exchange for his cooperation in the investigation of a secrets-selling ring within the State Department, masterminded by the late John Royce, a special agent of the Diplomatic Security Service...."

At the top of the steps, Sam Gerard and his warrants squad stood with the woman they were returning from custody, Marie Bineaux, freshly coifed and well scrubbed and picture-pretty in a demure black-and-white dress. Marie pushed forward as she saw Mark coming up, and Sheridan flew to her arms as the deputies formed a human ring around them, to give them a moment's privacy in the midst of chaos. The lovers embraced, and kissed.

"From now on," Sheridan whispered into Marie's ear, "the only running I'm doing is straight into your arms."

The former fugitive caught Gerard's eye, as the manhunter and his deputies protected the couple from the press of the press, and the tiniest look passed between hunted and hunter, a silent expression of thanks and respect on both their parts.

"Quieter life for you, now," Gerard said to Sheridan, who was still holding his lover close to him. The manhunter was referring to the witness protection program the couple would be disappearing into.

"But not you," Sheridan said, with a little smile.

Gerard smiled, too, a little, and looked away.

By the next evening, the so-called fugitive squad—honored by the presence of Marshal Catherine Walsh—was back in Chicago, gathered around a big table at Emitt's Bar. The cop haunt was otherwise lightly populated, but Gerard and his team were not alone, the big-screen TV blaring another report on the case they'd just closed. The screen was filled with the bright-eyed, smiling visage of John Royce, his government photo I.D., just an All-American boy.

"Turn that off!" Deputy Marshal Samuel Gerard ordered the bartender.

As Royce's image winked away, Cosmo Renfro—hairpiece perfect, beautifully attired in an Armani jacket, his luggage having finally caught up with him—said, "I'll say this about Royce. . . . Once a prick, always a prick.''

"Here here," Biggs said, and swigged down the last gulp from his glass of beer. They were already on the second pitcher.

Gerard and Catherine Walsh were seated together down at the end of the table; while Cooper, Biggs and Renfro were busy trading good-natured insults, Gerard leaned close to the woman he still loved.

"Marshal," he said. "Do I owe you an apology?"

"Don't you know?"

"I think I owe you an apology."

"Would that be a personal apology, or professional?"

"With me it kinda tends to overlap. Let's call it both."

She sipped her beer, smiled prettily at him. "Apology accepted."

"I'd like to make it up to you." He allowed the old intimacy into his voice.

Her reply, however, was cool. "Not right now."

His hurt expression made her laugh.

"In a couple hours, maybe," she said. "Right now I'd rather make you suffer. . . . How *do* you figure a guy like Royce, Sam? He was a golden boy, had it made. . . ."

"I have no fucking idea," he said, sipping his Diet Coke. He still hated puzzles.

Cooper said, "Hey, Sam! Let's introduce the guest of honor, already!"

Catherine, thinking they meant her, began to protest mildly, but Gerard had risen and moved to a wall where a number of framed photos of Chicago law enforcement officers hung in a sort of hall of honor. One of the framed photos was shrouded with a black cloth.

"Your attention please," Gerard said.

Everyone in the bar looked his way, not just his team. Every cop in the place. They knew this ceremony. They all knew it too well.

Gerard whisked away the cloth and revealed a smiling portrait of their late friend.

"I give you Deputy Noah Woodrow Newman," Gerard said, raising his Diet Coke glass. "Friend, colleague . . . United States marshal."

"To Newman," Renfro said, raising his glass.

The other remaining warrants squad members raised their glasses, as did Marshal Catherine Walsh, and they drank to their late friend.

Then, one by one, they each told a story of the dumbest thing they could remember the ponytailed knucklehead doing, their tears blurring into laughter, their laughter into tears.

MAX ALLAN COLLINS has earned an unprecedented eight Private Eye Writers of America "Shamus" nominations for his "Nathan Heller" historical thrillers, winning twice (*True Detective,* 1983, and *Stolen Away,* 1991).

A Mystery Writers of America "Edgar" nominee in both fiction and nonfiction categories, Collins has been hailed as "the Renaissance man of mystery fiction." His credits include four suspense-novel series, film criticism, short fiction, songwriting, trading-card sets and movie/TV tie-in novels, including such bestsellers as *In the Line of Fire, Waterworld,* the *NYPD Blue* novels and *Air Force One.*

He scripted the internationally syndicated comic strip *Dick Tracy* from 1977 to 1993, is co-creator of the comic-book features *Ms. Tree* and *Mickey Spillane's Mike Danger,* and has written the *Batman* comic book and newspaper strip. An epic graphic novel about Capone-era crime, *Road to Perdition,* is forthcoming from Paradox Press/DC Comics.

Working as an independent filmmaker in his native Iowa, he wrote, directed and executive-produced the 1996 suspense film *Mommy,* starring Patty McCormack; he performed the same duties for a sequel, *Mommy's Day,* released in 1997. The recipient of two Iowa Motion Picture Awards for screenwriting, he also wrote *The Expert,* a 1995 HBO World Premiere film.

Collins lives in Muscatine, Iowa, with his wife, writer Barbara Collins, and their teenage son, Nathan.